Blind to Danger

David Lindsley

www.davidlindsley.info

Blind to Danger

For Jo.

Acknowledgements

Although I was born in India and lived there for over a decade and although I have since spent much time in the fascinating country on business and pleasure, writing this book presented me with several problems. For a start, I was raised in the time of the British Raj, and later visits showed me that mannerisms and forms of speech have evolved quite significantly from those I knew as a boy. Furthermore, my more recent visits were not long enough to make me comfortable with writing about Indian characters. In short I needed help, and I was fortunate to have many contacts who were only too pleased to assist.

Among the many people who gave me valuable assistance in writing this book, I must pick out for special mention my good friends Anup Bhamm and Ravinder Sharma who pointed out some inconsistencies and suggested modifications. I am very grateful to both of them.

I am also grateful to the management of the Novotel in Hyderabad, who provided me with much useful advice and information.

As ever, I am indebted to my wife Jo, who has once again endures the long periods of isolation while I wrote the book, and who used her amazing proofreading and continuity skills to keep me from making too many errors. Any that are left are mine alone.

Chapter 1

The ringing of the phone drilled into her sleep. Her mind fuddled, she propped herself up on one elbow and rubbed at her face and gritty eyes. She blinked at what she saw and tried to re-focus and convinced herself that she'd made a mistake. But against the blackness of the room the green display stubbornly continued to read "02:12". At that point half of her became worried: telephone calls at such times were rarely anything but bad news. The other half of her was resentful and angry at this insensitive attack on her much-needed sleep. She patted her hand across the bedside table to find the phone, picked it up and looked at the display. The caller's name was unidentified and the number meant nothing to her. She mumbled something incomprehensible into the mouthpiece.

Suddenly the last traces of sleep were driven away and her attention snapped to the instantly recognised voice of her father. 'Alexis?' He asked from far-distant Houston.

Again a division into halves: one relieved to hear his voice, the other concerned – something had to have gone wrong.

'Dad! It's 2 a.m. here in London. Has something happened?'

'No. Everythin's fine kid, really fine.'

'But where are you? This …' she looked at the phone's display again to see if she'd made a mistake, 'this isn't your number.'

1

His answer sounded evasive. 'It's another cell. I'll explain later.'

'So why ...'

'I'm sorry kid, I know it night-time over there in London, but I need your help and I need it fast. And I need to warn you about somethin'.'

Confusion blurred her thoughts again. 'Help? Warn me?'

'Yes. Look, I want you to visit someone – a guy – as soon as you can and give him some information. Get him to call me.'

It was a terse set of instructions with no accompanying explanation. 'I'll try Dad,' she said, 'but who is he and what's going on?'

There was a momentary silence before he spoke. 'It's too much to tell right now, but it's important, honey – real important. The guy's name's Foster, Dan Foster. D'you think you can call on him tomorrow? The place he's in isn't far from London, I'm told.'

She was wide awake now and asked, 'Do you mean actually visit him? Not just a phone call?'

'That's right.'

She thought for a moment. As a freelance graphic designer and having made good progress on a project for her most demanding client, she could afford the time. 'As it happens,' she said, 'I'm ahead of schedule on the job I'm doing right now, so I guess I could. What's his address?'

As she listened to his voice on the phone she found herself breathing deeply and slowly. Somehow his tension had

2

managed to seep through the telephone link and into her from across the miles, and when she asked him again what was going on his answer had seemed hesitant, as though he was holding back. But she had told him that she could help and she would.

'All I know is that he lives on a houseboat,' he said. Then, cutting across her exclamation of surprise, he continued, 'Yes, that's right honey, a damn houseboat. It's called *Lake Goddess* and it's at a town called Kingston upon Thames ..'

She smiled. He pronounced the name of the river as starting with a soft "Th" and rhyming with "Games". She had been away from the States long enough to know the difference.

'That's all?' she asked.

''Fraid so. Think that's enough to find him?'

'Don't know. I can ask around, I guess. But what about a phone number?'

'Sorry kid. Can't help.'

She smiled to herself. This was turning into a tall order: find someone, here's his name but there's no address, no telephone number. 'OK. So I call on him. What do I say?'

He laughed. 'I'll email you the information.'

Then he went on to remind her of the need to be careful; to make sure that she wasn't being trailed. If she saw the slightest sign of anybody acting suspiciously she was to abandon the visit, return home and call her father when she got in. And she wasn't to use the number she normally called him on; she was to use this one instead.

It was bizarre; the first time in her life that she had heard her father ask for anyone else's help. It unsettled her. Up to that moment she had known him only as a strong, supremely self-confident man, steadfast even after his wife – her mother – had suddenly died five years earlier. Somehow, that loss had seemed to spur him forward in his business dealings at the same time as it had brought the two of them together for support in their shared grief. They had become very close, and with one brief exception, there were no divisions between them.

And that one exception was firmly in the past now.

But now the small fragments of information he had given her were all that he offered. It was very strange, but nevertheless she agreed to give it a try.

She sensed the relief in his voice as he ended the call.

The next morning, as her commuter train screeched, rumbled and clattered it way out of London's Waterloo terminus she reviewed the plan she had made after receiving that call. She had already followed her father's advice about security; looking behind her as she walked from her flat to the station. Now she planned to leave the train at Clapham Junction and board the next Kingston-bound one at the very last moment. It had vaguely amused her to act like a fugitive in some sort of adventure movie, but her father's tone had been serious and she had no doubt in her mind that he had been worried about her mission.

At Clapham she switched trains as she'd planned. She leaped aboard the Kingston train just as the automatic doors started to close, an action that earned her an annoyed shriek from the guard's whistle.

As the train approached Kingston she suddenly realized that she didn't know the area at all – had never visited the town, in spite of it being close to her home and in spite of its fame as a shopping centre. But as she walked out of the station she spotted a sign that helpfully pointed the way to Kingston Bridge. She threaded her way along the crowded streets and through a busy shopping mall, looking at it all with interest and vowing to make a return visit when this mission for her father was behind her.

Soon she found herself on the bridge and stopped to look out over the balustraded parapet with its cascades of bizzie-lizzies hanging from its lamp-standards. She shaded her eyes against the brightness of the sky to study the line of houseboats moored along the bank to her right. The craft formed a beguiling sight in the morning sunshine, their hanging flower-baskets catching the light in a blaze of colour that was reflected in the mirror-still water of the Thames. The first touches of autumn were approaching and although the clear blue sky promised a fine day ahead she shivered as if a sudden icy draught had brushed against her. She turned and looked back the way she had come, but no suspicious-looking people were visible on the approach road. She allowed herself a slight sigh of relief.

As she returned her attention to the line of boats she realized that finding her target might be easier than it had sounded the night before. There were only a few vessels tied up alongside the towpath, and they all seemed to be houseboats. Apart from a solitary dog-walker strolling along the path, there was no sign of movement around the craft. She squared her shoulders and continued her way along the bridge, settling her rucksack on her shoulder as she went.

A few minutes later she was walking along a small wooden jetty against which the boats were moored. She scanned their names carefully and then spotted the name *Lake Goddess* carved into a polished mahogany sign at the bow of a long black-hulled narrowboat nearby.

She hesitated, unsure of whether and where to knock. Then she heard footsteps on the boards and a voice from behind asked, 'Can I help?'

She turned to see a tall, well-built man coming along the jetty towards her. He was bearded and deeply tanned. She guessed he was in his late fifties; his hair was flecked with white and his beard was turning silver.

'I'm looking for Dan Foster,' she said. He appraised her carefully. She was young, still girlish in some ways; tall and slim, she had light brown hair that was tied back in a ponytail. Her skin had an almost luminous, fragile softness, giving her the sort of beauty that women envied and men found irresistible. Her full lips and hazel eyes were accentuated with the lightest touch of carefully-applied makeup.

'That's me,' the man said. 'I'm Foster. And you are …?'

'Oh, Alexis …' she paused. 'Alexis Klein.'

His head tilted slightly and his blue-grey eyes looked a question at her.

'Oh, I'm sorry,' she said. 'This will seem very odd to you. In fact it's pretty strange to me too. You see, my father rang me last night and asked me to call on you. He's in Texas. I would've phoned you, but he didn't have your number.'

He gave a small grin and nodded towards the boat. 'Let's go aboard; you can tell me there.'

A few moments later she was looking round the saloon while he busied himself in the adjoining galley, making coffee for them both.

She liked what she saw. The cabin was a cosy, comfortable haven, the highly polished mahogany bulkheads framing large windows that looked across the river to the pubs and cafes lining the opposite bank. She stooped to examine a glass-fronted case below one of the windows. It was filled with novels, literary reference works and a spattering of scientific and engineering textbooks. Nearby, a separate case housed a bound set of books. She looked closely: it was *Groves' Dictionary of Music*. A deep-buttoned leather armchair in the centre of the cabin was matched by a swivelling captain's chair at a small but tidy computer desk. She sat down on one of the chairs that surrounded the square table in the centre of the saloon and studied a silver-framed photograph on the bookcase; it showed two young men sitting alongside each other on a wooden bench. They were smiling and both bore a strong similarity to Foster. She put the picture down and looked around for a photograph of a woman, a wife perhaps, but there was none.

'All right Alexis,' Foster asked when he put two steaming mugs of coffee on the table and sat opposite her. 'What's this all about?'

'Really, I don't actually know very much at all,' she answered. 'My dad's a lawyer in Houston. From what he told me last night he's gotten himself involved with a case in India ...'

A slight frown crossed Foster's face. 'India?'

'That's right. There's a lawyer out there who's in some kind of trouble and he's asked dad to help him out.'

'Easy on! How come a lawyer in India even knows about your father, a lawyer in America, let alone thinks he can help?'

'My Dad's quite well known,' she answered, and her shoulders squared slightly with pride. 'He's headed up a lot of high-profile cases against big American corporations.'

Foster frowned at her for a moment, then he clapped his hand to his forehead as sudden realization came to him. 'Hang on,' he said. 'Of course! Your father – is he Scott Klein?'

'Yes he is.'

Foster leaned back in his chair and contemplated her seriously. 'You weren't kidding when you said he's taken on some big corporations – he's been a wasp in the pants of Global Consolidated Resources for one. Given them a lot of grief.'

'That's right,' she acknowledged. Then she pulled her rucksack from where she'd put it, hefted it onto her lap and took an email printout out of it. 'And they're involved here,' she said as she handed it to him. 'Dad sent me this last night.'

Foster took a pair of spectacles from the shelf beside him, put them on and started to read the message. Eventually he put the paper down, took off his glasses and looked hard at her. 'Well!' he breathed. 'This is one hell of a thing you've brought me.'

'Yes,' she said. 'There was some kind of accident at a GCR power plant in India – five people died and many more injured. It was pretty bad.'

'So I see. And the company was fined twenty thousand Rupees ..'

He detected anger in her tone as she commented, 'That's right. I looked that up on Google this morning. It works out at four hundred and forty Dollars US. That's less than a hundred bucks per corpse; a hundred bucks to replace the breadwinner of a family. That's not enough; not nearly enough. Something's wrong.'

'I agree. But it seems that this Indian lawyer,' he put on his glasses again and looked down at the message to check the name, 'This Kalpak Desai; he was acting for GCR. Then, for some reason, before the Inquest had even started he got fired – or decided to quit, I can't make out which. Then GCR came after him. He's in deep doo-doo now: bankrupt.'

'But it wasn't because of that case,' she said. 'Read on.'

He did as she asked and then shook his head. 'Christ!'

'Exactly!' she said. '

'I see why he has a grudge against GCR and thought your father could help. But can we be sure he isn't just some kind of loony?'

She shook her head vigorously. 'Believe me; Dad wouldn't have gotten himself involved unless he was convinced there was something in it. He wouldn't act on just one disaffected guy's word alone. He would've checked everything – over and over again.'

Foster shrugged. 'OK, so what happened when Desai asked your father to get involved?'

She grimaced. 'That's when GCR came down real hard. When Dad had convinced himself that Desai was onto something he flew out to India. But when he got there he was stopped at Immigration and sent back home.'

'What?' Foster exclaimed in shock. 'Is that in this email? I haven't read it all.'

'No, it's not there. He told me that part on the phone last night. He said there was more, but he'd tell you all about it if you agreed to help.'

Foster looked at her. 'I don't see how I'm going to get involved in this, or what I could do.'

'Dad said you looked into things like this,' she said, 'as an engineer, a consultant. He says you specialize in power stations.'

'I do.' He frowned quizzically at her and asked, 'How long have you been in England?'

'Just under a year,' she replied. 'Why do you ask?'

'Because if you'd been here eighteen months ago you'd have seen my ugly mug in every newspaper and on TV.'

'Oh?'

'Yes. I uncovered a conspiracy: some rogue guy in the States who was working in collusion with your Defense Department had run a scheme to trigger off power cuts; blacking out entire countries. It was intended to be used against an enemy in the event of war but it misfired and brought down the British power system by accident.'

'Oh, I do remember it,' she said. 'It was big news in the States too. High-profile guys in the government were fired.'

'Some here too.'

'A lot of people were killed in the Underground system, weren't they?'

He clenched his teeth and looked out of the window for several moments. 'Yes,' he said quietly, still looking out at the river outside. 'My fiancée among them.'

'God!' she exclaimed, then added, 'Oh God! I'm so sorry. I didn't mean to tread on your feelings …'

His voice was dull when he responded. 'It's done now. Over.' He shook his head as if trying to shake away memories. 'They'd planted a sort of virus in the computer systems controlling power stations. "The Darkfall Switch" they called it; like nightfall. Some geeks picked up the name from a role-playing game and thought it funny to name the virus after it, because it brought darkness to the target when it was deployed.'

'And London?' she queried. 'The Underground? It was the target?'

'No it wasn't. As I said, it misfired. What happened here was what they call "collateral damage".'

'Oh Christ! And your fiancée ….'

'She was travelling on the Underground when it happened. Everything blacked out, trains stopped, escalators stalled; somebody panicked and lots of people were trampled to death.'

'God!' she said, then pulled herself up short, 'Oh I'm sorry. I keep saying that, don't I?'

He ignored the question. 'But that's in the past,' he said. 'What you've brought me here is something that I *could* get involved in, but …'

'But what?' she asked.

'Well to put not too fine a point on it, it's finance – filthy lucre. I get paid to find answers; it's how I earn my money. Here, your father's sniffing around something that may never pay off. Yes, it involves power stations and I'm a power-station engineer so it's interesting to me. But it'll cost a lot of money to get to the bottom of what happened, especially as it's in India. And in the end it may turn out to be something routine – a simple accident. Or not. It may turn out that this guy Desai is really onto something; in that case your father takes GCR to court and even then he may or may not win. So – well, it may pay off or it might not. Perhaps your father can afford to take that risk: I can't. If it was here in England it could be another thing, but India?'

'You'll need to talk with dad about that.'

'How do I contact him?'

'I've written his number on that email. You can get him there at, say, four o'clock London time.'

Foster looked at the message and then up at her. 'That second number – yours?'

'Yes. I want you to keep me in touch with what's going on.'

Foster tilted his head and the laughter-lines at the corners of his eyes deepened, displaying wry humour. Realizing that she had sounded as though she was issuing orders, she coloured with embarrassment. She decided to end the conversation and stood up to leave. Foster scrambled to his feet to show her to the door and took her elbow as he guided her along the narrow jetty.

She could sense him watching as she walked along the towpath and was proud of her slender waist and trim ankles. It puzzled her; *he's old enough to be my grandfather*, she thought, *my father at least*. She looked back as she reached the towpath but he had disappeared within the boat.

Back in the saloon Foster went over to the computer, sat down and tapped at the keyboard. A few minutes later he knew a little more about the case in India and, more importantly, a lot more about Scott Klein.

Klein had been a small-time lawyer in Houston before he had been called on to act for a community that was taking Global Consolidated Resources to court over an industrial accident that had caused widespread pollution and environmental damage. He lost the case, but the loss had triggered something: it had seemed to incense him. Battling GCR became a personal vendetta, and after that initial defeat he had seemed to take them on at each and every opportunity. Some cases he won, others he lost, but the battle-list was endless – and the number of his successes was growing faster than the list of losses.

Foster's search of the Internet yielded no indication that Klein had been involved in the law case in India that had led to Desai's downfall. His brief research had shown that the case revolved around a power station at a small town called Varikhani, in central India. Foster smiled as he looked at the list of companies that had supplied equipment to the plant, then he looked at the clock on his display and after a moment's thought reached for his phone. It would be late in Kyoto at this time, but he knew that his friend Saburo Mizutani, Chief Executive Officer of Takimoto Heavy Industries, would still be at work.

The Varikhani plant had been built by a major multi-national consortium. The boilers that burned local coal had been supplied by Takimoto Heavy Industries, known as THI, who had also supplied the turbines that were driven by that steam to rotate the massive electrical generators.

'Konbanwa, Mizutani-san,' Foster said when he was connected. He was rewarded with a hearty laugh.

'Konbanwa, Foster-san! Genki desu ka?'

'Okage-sama de,' Foster thanked him, then continued in English, 'And you, my friend?'

'I too am fine, Foster-san. It is good to hear your voice after so much time.'

'I understand that business is good for Takimoto.'

'Yes indeed,' Mizutani replied. 'We have small problems sometime, but business is good. Yes, very good.'

Foster knew that the normal *modus operandi* in Japanese commercial transactions was for an extended exchange of such pleasantries to take place before any serious business started, but he also understood Mizutani well enough to know that he would not be offended by a little Western haste. Yet he also knew the virtue of approaching transactions in a certain polite and well-constructed way. 'I need some help, Saburo,' he said, 'in connection with Varikhani.'

There was an extended silence before Mizutani replied, 'Ah! That was not good project for us.'

'Even less good for the men who died.'

'Indeed so,' Mizutani replied. 'But…. before we talk, Foster-san, I need to know: is this official? Are you involved?'

'Not yet. But I may be. Scott Klein wants me to help him.'

'Klein!' Mizutani exclaimed, the shock detectable even at this distance. But his mastery of pronouncing Western names was unshaken; there was none of the usual Japanese confusion of Ls and Rs. 'He is big enemy of GCR…. and they are our clients, very good clients.'

'Yes, so I understand,' Foster said, noting the sudden wariness in Mizutani's tone. 'And you know that I wouldn't want to put you into any kind of a difficult situation; but I *would* like to hear your side of the story before I agree to get involved – that is, *if* I get involved.'

'Thank you,' Mizutani replied. 'Then I will tell you.'

Five minutes later Foster hung up the telephone and sank back in his chair. Mizutani had told him that his own staff had investigated the explosion at the Indian power station, and come to the conclusion that some unknown cause had been responsible. Every piece of equipment in THI's extent of supply had been carefully examined – taken apart if necessary – and then re-examined. In the end the company had been exonerated. However – in Mizutani's words – 'there was evidence of carelessness or neglect at the site; perhaps even sabotage'. In spite of Foster's questions over this point, he had learned very little else. But from Mizutani's words Foster guessed that the faults had been on the part of the plant owner, not its builder.

And Mizutani would not – could not – cast any slur on a client, not even a distant one.

What Foster had learned, however, was that THI had attended the Coroner's Inquest in India, and he could see why they had been satisfied: because the verdict was that the explosion had been the result of an equipment malfunction; failure of a gas valve – which had not been supplied by them. No blame was attached to the main contractor.

Then he returned to the computer screen and Googled Global Consolidated Resources. What he discovered expanded on what he already knew: that it was a multi-billion Dollar international conglomerate whose scope of supply ran from drilling for oil and gas on-shore and off-shore, mining coal, and through all the processes culminating in the operation of power stations that used those fuels to generate electricity. They operated these plants on the "build/own/operate/transfer" or BOOT principle – having the plant built by specialist contractors, and then operating it for a while before handing it over to the main electricity company or power authority in the host country.

During the operating period they sold the electricity and kept the profits to repay their investment. At Varikhani their contract had been with India's National Thermal Power Corporation, or NTPC, and it was for a duration of five years. After that time had elapsed the plant would be handed over to the Indians and GCR would move on to new pastures.

This type of operation freed the local power authority from making the huge up-front financial investment needed for such a massive project. It also protected them from any teething troubles, because by the time the contract ended the plant would have been thoroughly shaken-down and proven. Another gain for the authority was the value of "knowledge transfer": the plant builder would train their engineers in its operation and maintenance. GCR financed all of this on the basis of future revenues earned from the sale of electricity while they ran the plant.

The "Global" part of the company's name was no over-statement: their interests ranged from Alaska, through several Western and Southern states of the US, then into most of Central and South America, across much of Africa and the Middle East and into Europe, Russia and the Baltic, down into India, China, Australia and New Zealand, not to mention remote islands in almost every ocean of the planet.

The company was indeed global in nature as well as name.

At four o'clock as agreed, Foster called the number Alexis Klein had given him. It was a direct line, and her father answered immediately.

'Scott,' Foster said. 'I'm Dan Foster. Your daughter asked me to ring you.'

'Oh Dan, thanks for calling. It's a pleasure to speak with someone I've heard so much about.'

'Good things, I hope.'

'Absolutely! But anyway, did you read the email I sent to Alexis?'

'Yes I did. It's an interesting story all right. I see that the Indian guy, Kalpak Desai, lost everything. He was up against GCR – and they make dangerous enemies. You of all people know that they play hard-ball.'

Klein gave a bitter laugh. 'I sure do.'

'But he backed out of the case before the Coroner's Inquiry had even started. Why?'

'Because the evidence had been tampered with.'

'What!' Foster's amazement sounded in his response. 'How?'

'Desai says his case file was opened and a report taken out and replaced with another one. He discovered the switch only moments before the Inquiry opened. He immediately told the coroner and asked to be allowed to withdraw from the case.'

'You believe him?'

'Sure do,' Klein said. 'But I don't just take these things on trust. Oh no, I checked it all out. The court records show that he did allege interference with his file and that he did withdraw from the case.'

'Desai sounds like a remarkably honest man.'

'That's what I concluded.'

'What was in the report? The original one, I mean.'

'He says it was a load of stuff that would have been very damaging to GCR: dangerous cost-cutting, violation of safety rules and deviations from proper procedures, use of untrained and unsupervised people in critical operations, wholesale bribing of officials … It's a truck-load of dynamite. It was written by a member of staff at the power station. Desai knew it wouldn't be in his clients' interests to present it to the court, but he believed they were the facts. Having foreknowledge of those facts would help him build a defence against them. Like a good advocate he would work around them and defend his client. What he didn't want was for someone to suddenly produce a report like that as evidence against his client's interest: evidence that he wasn't aware of in advance.'

'Understandable enough.'

'Yes, but when that file disappeared he became convinced that his client wanted to cover up the truth. He suspected they thought he might not want to go along with the deception, so they'd substituted a fake report.'

'But that's crazy!' Foster exclaimed. 'He'd spot the switch the moment he opened the file.'

'I know. I suppose they thought he'd be discombobulated when he saw it, but wouldn't want to say anything in front of the coroner and just carry on.'

'But it didn't get that far.'

'Exactly! He spotted the switch before he went in to court. I guess he agonised about it, but time would have been pressing. If he went in with the substitute file he was worried that the coroner might spot it as a fake and tear him to shreds. They were playing a dangerous game and, more importantly from his viewpoint, he felt that they didn't trust him to handle it his way. So he decided to quit.'

'How did he know that it was GCR who played the switch?'

'He didn't actually know, but who else would try to hide evidence against them?'

Foster thought about it and realized that it made sense. More significantly now, to somebody like Klein, who had led a legendary crusade against Global Consolidated Resources, such allegations would have been manna from heaven.

Then he asked, 'And what about the second report?'

'Cleaned up. According to it the company came up smelling of roses. The report – the fake one – said that the explosion had been caused by a faulty gas valve. GCR came down on Desai like a ton of bricks when he quit, but when he accused them of tampering with evidence they threatened him. That's when he got really pissed off and set out to contact me. He'd heard about me and my actions against GCR and he emailed me.'

'So what did you do?'

'After checking as much as I could from here I flew to India. As soon as I could. Christ!' he interrupted himself, 'You ever had to get an Indian visa? It's a nightmare.'

Foster laughed. 'I know,' he said. 'But your daughter said you were refused entry.'

'Yup! I'd flown via Dubai, but the Indian Immigration service stopped me as soon as I showed my passport in Hyderabad. Took me off to some kind of cabin and then told me that my entry had been refused. I argued and fought; showed them my visa, but they wouldn't shift. When I asked to see somebody from our Embassy they just put me straight back on the next plane back to the US.'

'Christ!' Foster said. 'They must have some good connections.'

'That's what I thought.'

'So what happened next?'

'As soon as I got back here I called Desai and told him what had happened. Apparently he'd been hanging around the Arrivals area of Hyderabad Airport, waiting for me. When I didn't show up he asked what had happened and was told I'd not boarded the plane in Dubai.'

'What did you tell him to do?'

'I told him to go back to the coroner with a copy of the report – he was to keep the original in a very safe place. He did that and when he handed it over the coroner re-convened the Inquest. That threw everyone into a panic.'

'I bet it did. What was the outcome?'

'The finding was that GCR had displayed a lack of care and they were fined about two million Dollars.'

'Wow!' Foster exclaimed. 'That's a bit different from the original four hundred bucks. Still not enough, in my opinion, but better.'

'Right!' Klein said. 'But the main point is that it would have cleared the way for big compensation claims.'

'Would have?' Foster queried.

'Yup! GCR struck again. They appealed against the verdict … and this time the findings of the Coroner's Inquest were quashed. The scuttlebutt is that they bribed a few people …'

Foster was stunned. 'They don't mess around, do they, these Global people?' he said. 'But what's your involvement now?'

There was a short silence before Klein replied: 'You've gotta understand Dan, that right from the start this looked a good one for me against GCR.'

'I can see why. But look, just what do you want me to do?'

'Answer some questions for a start. For example, there's a lot of the technical stuff I don't understand. There was reference to a gas valve in the substitute report. I'm not an engineer, but I don't see what a gas valve was doing there on a plant that was burning coal.'

Foster grinned. 'Probably the gas they used to light off the coal.'

'Uh-huh! Could that have done it – caused such a big explosion?'

'It's happened elsewhere. But that was long ago; modern operational procedures make it almost impossible. The computer systems control it all; they blast air through the whole furnace before they try to light the burners. It's completely automatic. The whole thing was put together by THI, and they're a very competent and thorough organization.'

'Could the computer be overridden?'

'Not easily.'

'So what does that leave?'

Foster thought for a while before answering: 'Hard to say really. It could be ignition of gas that had collected in the various ducts and chambers – and that ignition happening before the burners were purged...'

'Purged?' Klein interrupted with the question.

'Yes, that's what I mentioned just now: they blast air through the whole thing to make sure all the gas has gone before they try a light-off. The explosion could have been caused by some sort of failure of that process, or it could have been deliberate sabotage. From here I can't tell. But in my opinion both would be very unlikely.'

'But not impossible?'

'No, I guess not.'

'Any other theories?'

'Lots, but I'd be guessing.'

'So how do we find out for sure?'

'Somebody would have to go to the plant and carry out a very thorough investigation. Plants like that are fitted with very sophisticated monitoring and recording systems these days.'

'Like aircraft flight data recorders?'

'Exactly like those. So somebody could look at all the records, question the people who were there at the time; that sort of thing. It'll be more difficult now, because so much time has passed.'

A long silence. Then Klein asked, 'Could that somebody be you?'

Foster smiled to himself. 'Could be. But I need to be paid, and I'm not inexpensive. Then there's travelling costs and subsistence. It would mount up.'

Klein's voice was almost plaintive as he asked, 'You wouldn't do it on a speculative basis?'

'You mean no win, no pay?'

'Yup! But lots of pay if we do win.'

'Not a game I play.'

There was a long silence before Klein spoke. 'Sounds like it's a non-starter then.' He sounded crestfallen.

'It does,' Foster agreed. Then a thought came to him and he added, 'But look …. there is one thing I could try. I could call in a favour. Leave it with me for a day or so – I'll come back to you if it pans out.'

A few minutes later, when he rang Alexis Klein to report on his conversation with her father she asked him what his idea was.

'A pal of mine once asked me to do a job. At the time I was too busy … but I could do it now and combine it with a little trip to India.'

'That's great, Dan!' she said, and there was real pleasure in her voice. Foster warned her that his contact was in Japan so, because of the time zones involved, it would be the next morning before he would be able to start the ball rolling.

'OK,' she said, 'shall I call round tomorrow to see how you've got on?'

He smiled. She'd really got the bug. 'Fine. Around midday OK for you?'

A power-station boiler is an enormous thing, and it earns masses of money for its owners while it runs. Larger than a big office block, it burns fuel to produce steam, which is then superheated to over five hundred degrees Celsius. The steam is fed at a high pressure to a turbine which spins at a few thousand revolutions per minute. This, in turn, rotates a generator producing electricity at several thousand volts and thousands of kilowatts. The costs of building and operating this type of plant are mind-blowing and if even only a minor improvement can be effected in the efficiency of the process, the payback over a period of time is huge.

One way of achieving such improvements is to optimise the way the boiler works. It's like tuning an orchestra: when all the players are in tune they make beautiful music. But tuning the computer control system of a power plant is a hugely complicated matter, since it involves hundreds of parameters – flows, pressures and temperatures – each of which interacts with the others, sometimes in unexpected ways.

A few years earlier, Saburo Mizutani had asked Foster to look into optimization of boilers, carrying out a series of investigations into how to control them more effectively, to see if efficiency gains could be won and if they could, how big a payback would result.

At the time, Foster had declined the invitation, but now …

Mizutani was surprised when Foster called him the next day.

'Two calls in two days!' he exclaimed. 'I am indeed honoured, Foster-san!'

Foster broached his request warily and there was a long, contemplative pause before the CEO replied. 'Of course, Foster-san. We would like you to carry out the optimization on one of our boilers. But it would be …. difficult, yes difficult, for it to be at Varikhani. GCR is important client and if your work there shows that they were,' he paused, plainly searching for words. '…. that they were negligent, and if you found this out while acting as our agent, then it would not be good for our future business with them.'

'No. But remember that the Inquest is closed. The lawyers have given their verdict: you're clean. So, as far as anyone is concerned, the case is over and done with. Besides, there would be no reason for them to suppose that I doing anything other than optimising the boilers.'

Foster could sense Mizutani working out all the possibilities in his chess-player's brain before the answer came. 'That is so.'

'But if I find evidence that they *are* negligent and if I think that any more damage or injury could occur it would be best for me to report the fact to you, before anything else went wrong. After all, if there was another incident GCR could even try and turn the blame for it onto your design or quality of manufacture. Surely it is better for them to clean up their act before anything like that happens.'

'Perhaps. But …' Mizutani said in a final attempt to deflect Foster away from Varikhani, 'it would be better, I think, for you to work on another plant. It would be more safe for us all.'

'I respectfully disagree,' Foster said, carefully maintaining the necessary degree of politeness. 'Varikhani would be ideal – a new plant, with new systems. Where else could we find that?' He was gambling that THI would not be able to offer another ready-made test-bed – and the gamble paid off.

After a long, pregnant pause Mizutani conceded defeat. 'Very well, Foster-san. But you must be careful. Do not be seen interfering in the case of the earlier explosion.'

'Of course. I shall work on the optimization and report back to you. Anything else I find would also be reported to you, but without anybody else knowing.'

'That is good. But first we will need clearance from our client.'

'Naturally. So we're rolling, are we?'

'Foster-san!' Mizutani laughed. 'We have no contract, and this project could be very lengthy ...'

But Foster had already been thinking about the financing of this, and had an answer ready. 'Tell you what, Saburo,' he said. 'I'll do a deal with you: if you pay my air fares, hotels and meals, I'll do the study on a simple day-rate basis. How'd that be?'

And that's how, with little more discussion, they finally came to agree terms.

Before the conversation ended, Foster gave Mizutani a list of the electronic equipment he would need, and the Japanese man told him that he knew that much of it was already available on site – in the hands of the instrumentation staff there. The rest would be obtained and shipped to India immediately.

When Alexis Klein called round at noon the next day as arranged he told her what had happened. She was delighted.

'Have you told dad yet?' she asked.

'No. I thought you'd like to do that.'

'Yes thanks. That'd be great!'

She rang her father's number and told Klein the good news. And then, before Foster could intervene she added. 'Dad, I want to go along too.'

Foster reeled back. He could hear her father's exclamation of surprise and protest, and then she continued: 'No Dad, it's OK – really OK. I told you – I'm ahead of the game on my project and a couple of weeks away wouldn't be a problem. I was thinking of taking a vacation anyway. And it's India, dad. You know how much I've always wanted to go there.'

She listened to the response before handing the phone to Foster. 'He wants to speak with you.'

Foster took the phone and said, 'Scott, I didn't know she was going to say that. I don't think it's a good idea. In fact it's a terrible idea.'

'I'm not crazy about it either, Dan. But I know Alexis; once something' gotten into her head she won't let go.'

'But think of the practicalities, Scott! It'll be hard enough for me to get a visa of my own in a short time – you know how tough that is. Getting one for her could take weeks and I don't want to wait that long; every day that passes will make it harder to find out what happened. Evidence could be lost or covered up – not necessarily deliberately, but simply because things have moved on.'

'I know, I know. Look, Dan, just talk it out with her. If she's set her mind on it and you can't persuade her to change it,

I'll go along with it. Not that anything I say could stop her anyway.' A long silence followed before he continued, and Foster could sense the concern in his tone as he spoke: 'But Dan, remember – she's my daughter. I don't want her getting hurt …. Not in any way.'

As he cut the call, Foster looked angrily at the girl. 'I don't know what you're doing …' he started.

'Doing?' she interrupted coolly. 'What I'm doing is going to see a place that's always interested me. That's all.'

'But don't you see? If you come along and GCR find out your name they'll put two and two together. There'll be no hope of my working on site without them knowing what I'm up to. Everybody in the business knows your father's name, and how he hates the company. In fact I'm surprised he didn't see that risk too.'

'I won't be on site. I'll be doing the tourist thing.'

Foster stared at her. 'So you come to India and stay away from where I am?'

She thought for a moment. 'OK, a correction then: I don't want to just do the tourist things, like seeing the Taj. I guess you'll be out in the *real* India, and it would be great to see that.'

'Power stations are rarely near tourist attractions,' Foster agreed. 'You'd certainly be well off the beaten track. But unless you stay well away it's likely they'll cotton on to what I'm doing.'

'So you're suggesting I trail round India on my own?'

Foster shook his head in frustration. He was beginning to get annoyed with her. 'No. I told your father that if you talked me into this I'd look after you. But your name – Klein – can't you see the problem?'

She coloured slightly and then looked down. When she spoke her voice was subdued. 'It's not a problem. You see, the name on my passport isn't Klein; it's Marshall.'

Foster was taken aback, and she explained: 'I came to England to get away from an unhappy marriage … and a messy divorce.

'I'd been an idiot. Dad told me I was making a mistake, but I just thought he was being over-protective. It took me just a year to see that he'd been right all along. It's never easy to see that.'

'Oh,' Foster said, cooling down. 'I'm sorry …'

'Don't be. I made a big mistake and I paid for it. Now I'm away from all of that.' She looked up and sighed before finishing: 'And I'd rather not talk about it, if you don't mind. Point is, I didn't get a new passport. When I go anywhere I'm still Mrs Marshall. I'll change that one day, but for now it suits me … us. Doesn't it?'

Foster leaned back in his chair and sighed. He could see that she was determined.

Finally he said, 'OK, I'll see what can be done – about the visa and … about your accommodation.'

She smiled. 'What do you mean: accommodation?'

He smiled. 'Big power stations aren't built in cities any more,' he explained patiently, 'they're usually well out in

31

the sticks; miles from anywhere; well away from tourist areas and hotels. The usual thing is for the company that's employing me to provide me with a guest-house or an apartment – somewhere close to the site. My clients this time have agreed to give me one to live in for the duration of the job. I'll see if they can provide two. It doesn't really matter; people will talk. Engineers have an earthy view of things. They'll put two and two together and make six … or sixty-six.'

'I don't care,' she said. 'They can think what they like. Anyway, I'll pay.'

'I told your dad I'd look after you, Alexis. And that means looking after your reputation as well. And as for you paying, it won't be too easy. These company houses are usually rent-free to people working on the site. But I'll find out.'

'Well thank you, kind sir!'

'Now, I've got some things to do. Make yourself at home while I get on. Then I'll take you to lunch.'

'My treat!' she said. 'You're helping my Dad, remember?'

Half an hour later they were sitting in Foster's favourite pub, drinking "warm English beer" as she called it, and eating Moules marinière. Foster explained that he'd pulled a few strings to get them quick visas – or at least a promise of them. His previous work with Her Majesty's Government, and the contacts he'd made then, promised to ease the passage of the visa applications. He'd also emailed Saburo Mizutani to ask if he could bring a friend; and if he could arrange separate accommodation for her.

He could imagine the huge grin that would have burst on the Japanese man's face when he read the message. They had shared many riotous moments in Tokyo's Ginza night-club area in the past. They had joked about what Foster referred to as Mizutani's richly lecherous imagination; the epithet had been hard enough for Foster to say on that Asahi beer-soaked evening, but the men had agreed that it was even harder for Japanese people to pronounce it.

'I have learned,' Mizutani had giggled over his ice-cold beer one night. 'But my friends say …. "Lichly recherous"!'

The two men had collapsed in hysterical laughter while the shyly smiling Geishas accompanying them had looked at each other and tried to understand what was happening.

With these memories in his mind, Foster warned Alexis that matters might take some time to resolve. 'All we can do now is sit back and wait,' he said.

She took a sip of her beer and looked at him. Her eyes were shining. 'Gee Dan! I'm so excited. All my life I've wanted to see India: the Taj Mahal, the Himalayas, everything.'

Foster laughed. 'There's almost a thousand miles between those two, and "everything" covers a hell of a lot of territory. India's vast.'

'Never mind, I'll see what I can.' Suddenly the laughter went from her eyes. 'I've told you about my marriage,' she said quietly. 'What about you?'

'Not a lot to say. Marriage broke up. Then I met Fiona ...'

'The one in the Underground disaster?'

'Yup.' He hesitated; even after all this time the memory still hurt. 'After that I went to ground for a while – a long while. Then I met someone. She was on the rebound, wanted to show the world that she was on top of things.'

'She not around now?'

'No. I came back one night and she'd cleared out. We'd had a great time together but ... Well, she left a note. Said things were getting serious and she didn't want that. When I thought about it, I saw she was probably right.'

'Nobody since?'

'Not really.'

They finished their lunch in silence.

Chapter 2

The tumult in the Arrivals Hall of Hyderabad's Rajiv Gandhi International Terminal was deafening, with a closely-packed, noisy and excitedly agitated crowd swirling around in a confused and colourful melee. Through the big windows of the terminal, Foster could see that dawn was breaking. It had been afternoon when they left Heathrow and although British Airways' business-class service had been faultless they had slept only fitfully. At one point Alexis's head had dropped onto his shoulder and he had smiled down at her in a fatherly way as her light brown hair cascaded over his chest.

Searching the seething mass of meeters-and-greeters packing the arrivals hall, Foster spotted a small man jumping up and down at the edge of the throng, holding a placard high above his head. On it, written in huge black marker-pen lettering was: "Dr Dan Foster" followed by the THI logo.

Foster waved to the man who saw the gesture and gave a broad grin before bravely beginning to force his way through the crush towards them, a porter hard on his heels. Their progress reminded Foster of a tug towing a barge through heaving seas. 'Dr Foster,' the Indian shouted above the noise as soon as he was within earshot. 'I am Aadesh. I am pleased to greet you sir. I am your driver. Come! Come with me.' He grabbed their hand baggage and commanded the porter to take charge of the trolley with their larger cases. Their small group wheeled round and began to forge its slow progress out of the terminal with the porter using the trolley as a battering-ram to clear away unwary obstacles. '*Juldi!*' Aadesh cried, urging the porter to go faster – for no reason that Foster could imagine, unless it was merely to give the impression of efficiency.

The air-conditioned terminal had been cold, the odour of the crowd detectable but not rank. Outside, the day was already beginning to warm up under a pale pink sky and Foster smiled as he breathed in the unique, characteristic smell of India in the Monsoon season: a blend of spices, dust and damp earth. There were clear signs of heavy overnight rain all around; concrete roofs and canvas awnings alike were beginning to steam.

'Wait here, sir!' Aadesh commanded as they reached the road. He scurried off, clutching at his rolled umbrella, skipping over puddles and dodging cars that tooted their horns without rancour as he zigzagged across their path. The two Westerners waited at the kerbside, their porter keeping one foot on the trolley as he wound and unwound a bright orange cloth round his forehead. Then a black Honda CR-V appeared, swerving heedlessly across the hooting traffic and stopping beside them. Aadesh jumped out and opened the rear door so that the porter could load in the baggage. He thrust a 50-Rupee banknote into the man's hand and waved him away angrily as the porter began to wail and plead for more.

Aadesh opened the doors for them , and when they were all seated he leaned across the back of his seat and grinned. 'These miscreants,' he said, shaking his head, 'they always ask for more money. Especially if we have Western guests. But 50 rupees is absolute fortune to them sir, absolute fortune!'

Then he started up and they lurched off through the traffic, braving the squeals of brakes and the tooting of many horns.

'Is it always like this?' Alexis said against the background of noise. 'It's chaotic!'

'It's India,' Foster replied. 'Everything's different here, even traffic rules. You should see them at roundabouts or level-crossings: you'd swear there'd be horrific accidents all the time but there rarely are. It all works itself out in its own way, with lots of horn-tooting.'

'Those horns!' she exclaimed, her voice scarcely audible above the constant cacophony around them.

'Quite something, isn't it?' Foster agreed. 'But there's no aggression in them though; they're just telling people that they're there.'

'Looks like they've had some heavy rain last night,' she said as the car splashed through puddles, drenching unwary pedestrians in waves of rainwater.

Foster laughed. 'It's still the Monsoon season. They'll get several inches of rain this month.'

'The Monsoon has finished early sir,' Aadesh elaborated, concentrating on the crowds surrounding them. 'They say that last night's rain may be last we have this year.'

Alexis settled back in her seat and looked out of the window in wonder, drinking in the sights and sounds of this exotic land. They headed towards the city and drove past cream-coloured towers and domes abutting modern slab-sided apartment blocks. But just in case anybody forgot that this was India, the blocks' windows were not simple rectangles of glass; they were bordered with elaborately curved Oriental frames.

As they approached the city centre the road became increasingly crowded and progress slowed as they negotiated their way past jostling cars, buses, rickshaws, bicycles, suicide-bent pedestrians, unconcerned ambling cows and inquisitive trotting pariah dogs. But somehow they emerged unscathed from the confusion and then the countryside on each side of the road opened up to scrubland with green fields, trees and residential compounds surrounded by low, white-painted concrete walls glaring in the growing daylight. After they left the main highway, the road became little more than a ragged-edged, puddle-strewn strip of asphalt lined by luxuriant bushes and trees.

Everywhere around them was green – lush, verdant green.

After they'd travelled for about an hour, Alexis asked Foster, 'How far is it?' But before he could answer the driver looked over his shoulder and said, 'It is about hundred miles, madam. It will take us four or five hours in this accursed traffic.'

As he spoke, Alexis's eyebrows rose and her eyes bulged as she stared past the driver and through the windscreen. While talking to her his attention had been completely diverted from the road ahead and a small, brightly-coloured and garlanded motor-tricycle was about to lurch across their path. Alexis closed her eyes as they closed on each other but Aadesh turned his attention back to the road in front just in time, and with a flick of the steering wheel a collision was narrowly averted.

Foster put his hand over his eyes theatrically and then looked at her, shook his head and winked. 'You'll get used to it,' he said helpfully.

When they arrived at their destination they stepped out of the car, stretched their cramped legs and looked around. They had parked in front of a large complex of buildings, all identical single-storey concrete boxes, all painted white. All were roofed with corrugated-iron sheets. The complex was shaded by tall Sal trees growing between the bungalows.

Aadesh took them to a side-by-side pair of these buildings, each surrounded by a low whitewashed wall beside which luxuriant bougainvillea shrubs grew, ablaze with delicate purple-red flowers.

'They are apartments sir, madam,' Aadesh explained. 'Company is providing one for each of you. Major-domo will come later. He is also company provision too. He will look after you, sir and madam; bring food, cook and serve to exactly your requirements. He will also arrange for apartments to be cleaned and for dhobi-wallah to do laundry.'

Foster couldn't work out who the "company" might be – THI? Global? – but it scarcely mattered; the point was that they were to be housed and looked after.

The driver took Alexis's bags to one of bungalows, fumbled for a key, opened the door and let her in. Then he took Foster to his and repeated the exercise. He promised to call back at 8 the next morning. He would take Foster to the power station and then return to take Alexis sight-seeing.

'This is most excellently beautiful and historic area, sir,' he said. 'There is much to see. I will look after madam, sir; I will be most careful escort and guide.'

Before unpacking, Foster used his mobile to call Desai. In one of the many emails that had been exchanged between himself and Klein, the American had listed the lawyer's telephone number, another mobile.

'I am pleased to hear from you Dr Foster,' Desai said. His voice was cultured, his English good, even if the intonation was typically sing-song. 'Mr Klein said you were coming here. I presume you have reached Varikhani?'

'I have indeed, Mr Desai,' Foster answered. 'I'm in the company apartment. When can we meet, and where?'

'We must be careful, Dr Foster. GCR must not suspect that we are in contact. Mr Miller, their Project Manager at Varikhani is a dedicated company man. He is also very clever and dangerous. But our caution must extend to everybody at Varikhani – tongues will wag if we are seen together.'

'I'm sure,' Foster agreed. 'Where are you at present?'

'In Hyderabad. It is far from Varikhani, so there is less chance of somebody from there seeing us.' Desai said. 'But company people do visit city centre from time to time, so there is some risk if we meet here actually. May I suggest you make a tourist visit to one of our national monuments at this weekend? It would be a natural thing for a visitor to be doing.'

The timing was not an issue: they had arrived on the Thursday, and Foster had agreed with Mizutani that after he had made a brief visit to site to introduce himself, he'd take a few days rest to get over the jet-lag before he started work, so this plan suited him well.'

'Yes, fine. What do you suggest?'

Desai had evidently been giving much thought to the problem, because his answer came quickly: 'There is an 13th Century fort at Golconda, Dr Foster. It is near here – Hyderabad – so you will need much time to reach it. Also, there is steep climb when you arrive. Therefore I suggest you make a weekend excursion; stay overnight at Novotel hotel. I am sure that the company will make all reservations for you if you request.'

Foster groaned inwardly. The long drive back to Hyderabad would be even more gruelling at the weekend, because the roads would be packed. But he agreed, and said he'd contact Desai when all the arrangements had been made.

After their long flight from London, both of them were exhausted. By then the day's heat had already started to build up and the air-conditioning of the bungalows was beckoning, so they agreed to have a few hours' sleep and meet for supper in Foster's place that evening.

Aadesh's promised "Major-domo" turned out to be a tall, broad-shouldered man with a stiff military bearing and a brilliant broad smile under a carefully trimmed moustache. He was wearing a crisp pale blue uniform with brass buttons, and Foster felt a subconscious impulse to straighten up and stand to attention in his rather military presence. He introduced himself as "Mahaan Shah" and repeated what Aadesh had listed as his duties. The three of them agreed that it would be best for the two Westerners to eat alternately at each other's bungalow over the coming days. They would start at Foster's that evening and begin the next day with breakfast at Alexis' place.

41

'I understand you are staying for two weeks, sir,' Shah said when they were seated at the dinner table.

'Probably,' Foster responded. 'May be more, may be less. Depends on how I get on. Oh, and we won't be staying here this weekend. Mrs Marshall and I would like to leave for Hyderabad on Friday afternoon. We need to be back in time for dinner on Sunday.'

Shah nodded his understanding and withdrew, reappearing several minutes later with plates of delicious lamb curry and rice with chapattis and poppadums. He laid these in front of the two guests and then brought ice-cold bottled water and broke the seals for them.

'Don't drink the tap water here,' Foster warned his guest. 'Always use bottled – and make sure the seal's intact first; I doubt we have any crooks round here but it's not unknown for people to fill used bottles with tap water and sell them on.'

'The result being?'

'Severe Delhi-belly! Stay clear of ice cubes and salads too. The dreaded stomach troubles may get you anyway, but with care and a bit of luck you can escape.'

While they ate, Alexis told Foster that after unpacking and showering she had taken a short stroll round the apartment complex. 'There are huge black clouds on the horizon, so I thought I'd take a look around before the rain came back,' she said. 'There's an amazing sight out there; there are columns of white smoke in the distance – it looks like a thick bank of cloud. Completely covers the horizon from one side to the other. And I've never seen so many pylons and overhead

42

cables in one place. I could scarcely see the sky. It was a nightmare mesh of metal, like I was in a cage.'

Foster laughed. 'Those columns are actually banks of condensation coming up from the cooling towers....'

'Are those the big white hourglass-shaped things I saw?' Alexis interrupted.

'Yes. You're in the middle of a huge power-generating area here. There's a lot of coal around this area; they burn it in power plants like Varikhani and send the electricity that they generate round the country through those cables that you saw.'

'Coal?' she exclaimed. 'I thought that coal was a no-no these days.'

'It's got a bad press,' Foster admitted. 'But even in the UK, if we were to shut down all the coal burning power plants, the country would come to a standstill almost immediately. It's the same here; worse, in fact because the growth in demand always outstrips India's power-generating capacity. As it is, they have daily blackouts in many cities.'

'But aren't coal mines dirty and dangerous?'

'I suppose you could think that, but everybody tries to minimise the risk and the dirt. Long gone are the days of pit ponies and child labour. Anyway, the coal hereabouts isn't mined: it's open-cast; they scoop it off the top of the earth and feed it directly to the power stations around here.'

She pondered this while forking through the rice on her plate. 'I'd like to see a power station,' she said finally. 'I've never thought about them before. Will you take me along? I don't know anything about them.'

'Most people don't. They just take it for granted that the lights will come on when they click a switch. They forget that for that to happen, someone, somewhere has to be working, 24/7 every day of every year. As for seeing the plant, I'll see what I can do. It may take a day or two to fix things.'

'That's fine. I'm looking forward to being escorted around the district by Aadesh tomorrow.'

Foster grinned. 'He says he wants to show you what he called "the excellently beautiful and historic area"!'

'Sounds cool!'

Foster laughed. 'Oh, I doubt it'll be cool,' he said, and then became serious. 'But look, there's something I need to warn you about first.' He looked round to see if Mahaan Shah was in earshot. Deciding it was safe he whispered, 'How do you plan to let your father know how you're doing?'

'I've emailed him from my Blackberry already,' she replied. 'And he's replied.'

'That's OK. But, this is important: make very sure that you delete all messages between the two of you as soon as you've finished with them. We don't want anybody else reading them. And I suggest you delete your dad's name from your phone's contact directory. Fill in his address by hand each time; I know it'll be a nuisance, but it's safer.'

Foster's sleep was broken by a deafening drumming above his head; it was as if a platoon of muffle-booted Irish dancers was performing a jig on the roof of the bungalow. He lay there for a while, thinking about the informal weather forecast that Aadesh had made on their arrival in India: it had been no more accurate than a Met Office forecast back home. Dawn had just broken and the low sun was barely visible between the horizon and the blanket of cloud overhead. A dull reddish light filtered through his window and he climbed out of bed to look out. The rain was falling in solid sheets from heavy black clouds and the road outside the bungalow compound had turned into a roaring torrent of muddy water. The overloaded gullies and drains gurgled under the onslaught. He watched for a while before turning away to shower and dress. In spite of the rain it was already warm, so he put on shorts and a T-shirt. Then he went to the outside door, opened an umbrella that was stowed beside it and sprinted, squelching through the puddles, to Alexis' bungalow for breakfast. He knocked at her door, shaking the umbrella outside the porch.

She opened the door and smiled a welcome. She was wearing a crisp white blouse and white jeans, and Foster thought she looked gorgeous.

'Good morning!' he said, 'No Shah?'

'He's in the kitchen. Hope you like a full English breakfast! I made an executive decision for you.'

'A good choice,' he smiled.

She led him to the small dining room where Shah had laid the table with earthenware bowls at each place, each containing a half-grapefruit with the segments carefully separated. A silver and glass sugar shaker stood in the centre of the table.

'Is the Monsoon always like this?' she asked as they took their seats, her voice raised to be heard over the rain's thunderous roar.

'Yep. Actually, we've been lucky. It can rain like this for days on end during the season.'

But as they ate their breakfasts the noise gradually diminished and by the time they had finished the rain had passed and the sun broke through the clouds.

Foster returned to his bungalow, stepping carefully across the deep puddles that remained on the pathways. He hadn't been inside there for very long before there was a loud tap on the door.

'Dan Foster?' the man outside asked when Foster opened the door. He was brawny and red-headed and his accent was heavily Scottish. Foster nodded and they shook hands.

'I'm Peter McBride,' the newcomer said, 'GCR's Commissioning Manager for the Varikhani Project.'

'Pleased to meet you, Peter,' Foster said. 'I believe you're the one who'll be showing me round and making introductions.'

'I am indeed. Are you ready to go now?'

As they drove to the power station McBride explained that he was at Varikhani on secondment from his normal base near Edinburgh. He told Foster that he had taken great interest in the optimisation work that he'd been told was about to start. Aware of Foster's reputation, he understood why Takimoto Heavy Industries had hired him to help improve their products' performance, and he was eager to help out.

As their Land Rover drew up in front of the glaring white power-station building the two occupants emerged into the warm, damp morning air. The car park was glistening under the bright sun and although much of the surface water had burnt off in the heat torrents of water were still gurgling away through the drains.

They walked towards the enormous blank cliff-face of the building looming over them and Foster smiled in anticipation. He loved these things: from the tall chimneys reaching skyward in the distance; through the deep, all-pervading hum of the massive transformers nearby; to the dry crackle of the corona discharge coming from the insulators dangling from the high-voltage pylons over their heads. But no sense is as evocative as smell and as they entered the big glass swing-doors the unmistakable tang of steam, wet coal and hot oil brought back many memories to Foster: the sheer exhilaration of being part of a team working together on such an enormous enterprise, the tense anticipation as something new was being brought to life for the first time – and the anger and fear when something went disastrously wrong.

After they had signed in at the reception desk, their first stop was at the main control room: a vast space, like the command deck of Starship Enterprise, clinically clean with huge computer screens lining the walls. In the centre of this room men sat quietly at a semi-circular control desk, intently watching their displays and occasionally making adjustments via trackballs. The room was heavily air-conditioned, to the point where the men at the console wore quilted waistcoats emblazoned with the GCR logo. Looking over the desk was a gaunt man with thinning fair hair who turned to examine the newcomers as they entered.

'Hello, Sam,' McBride said to him, 'This is Dan Foster, the specialist that THI's brought in to optimise their boilers.'

'Sam Miller,' the man introduced himself as they shook hands. His accent was Texan, his voice the deep rasping growl of an inveterate smoker. He examined Foster carefully through steely blue eyes. 'I'm GCR's Project Director for Varikhani. I hear you're gonna be doin' some testin'.'

It was clearly a question rather than a statement and Foster replied in the affirmative.

'Well Foster, let's get this absolutely clear from the start,' Miller drawled. 'I'll get these guys to help you as much as you like. One thing we're not short of here is bodies – clever, computer-savvy bodies – yeah, we got plenty of those all right.' The statement was made in a sneering, derogatory tone. He stared hard at Foster before continuing, 'But you gotta understand that our first priority here is output – mega-fuckin' watt hours. Any test you do that bites into those hours is a chunk out of our income, and we stand or fall on covering our costs – so that just won't be happening. Your client is a supplier to us; he does what we say and that goes for you. Right?'

Foster bridled at the man's aggressive arrogance. Of course he was aware of the financial realities of power station operations: he'd lived with them all his life. But if he was to achieve his objectives he would *have* to "bite into those hours". If the turbine-generators worked flat-out day and night the boilers that fed them with steam scarcely needed much in the way of sophisticated computer control systems, let alone any to be optimised. In reality conditions were always changing, and his work would enable them to operate efficiently when the throughput changed – a very different matter indeed. It was like a car going flat-out along a highway: it could be fine-tuned to work well at that speed, but getting it to perform efficiently when the driver's foot was taken off the accelerator was something else. To show that he

48

was succeeding Foster would have to ask the operators to reduce the plant output from time to time. Yes, that would reduce the revenue while it went on, but the observations he made then, and the changes he introduced as a result, would pay off in the longer term. Both men knew the facts; both wanted their own way.

Foster decided to postpone the inevitable conflict. Right now he needed to see how everything was working under the existing régime. He explained as much to Miller, who growled acceptance and stalked off.

McBride looked at Foster and winked. 'Be careful, Dan,' he said quietly. 'There are some people whose bark is worse than their bite; I'm afraid Sam's the opposite. We've all been at the receiving end of his wrath.'

Foster grinned. 'Thanks,' he said. 'I'll be careful.'

McBride looked carefully at him and said, 'Want to look round?'

Ten minutes later they were in hard hats and white overalls, their eyes protected by safety glasses, their feet in steel-capped boots. The black ear-defenders clapped to the sides of their helmets looked like Mickey-Mouse ears. Thus kitted out, they set off to tour the plant.

They started at the turbine hall where the four massive horizontal steel cylinders of the steam turbines drove giant generators, each producing over a million horse-power.

Slender curls of white steam drifted from glands up to the glazed roof high above. The roar of the machinery was continuous and tremendous and the two men lowered their ear-defenders to shut it out. In these conditions conversation was all but impossible, but eventually McBride tapped at Foster's arm and shouted something as he waved to a door set into the wall behind the turbines.

It was still noisy when they went through the door, but the quality of the noise here was entirely different: here it was a deep all-pervading rumble. Unlike the turbines in the hall behind them, the four boilers here were in the open air; they stretched upward and extended sideways as far as the eye could see – a mass of grey-painted steel and heavily-lagged pipes. The day's tropical heat was building up already but it was as nothing compared with the radiant energy that blasted at the men from the huge labyrinthine construction. They could feel the savage heat blasting their backs as they waited for the lift to take them to the top of the boiler complex. The lift was little more than a steel-mesh cage but once they were inside it some of the noise became muffled and they swung their ear-defenders up to allow a degree of conversation.

'How long will you be here?' Foster shouted.

'Another few weeks,' McBride answered. 'Long enough. I've been here for fourteen months now.'

'Your family here with you?'

McBride nodded. 'Aye.'

'How do they like it?' Foster asked. 'The family.'

'The company looks after us very well and my wife and the bairns quite enjoy it. There's even a company school for the ex-pat kids. But we're all looking forward to going home again.'

'I can understand that,' Foster said as the cage came to a shuddering stop.

They had alighted at the top level and they stepped out onto a steel checker-plate platform. Through the steel mesh under their feet they could see the dizzying drop to the floor two hundred feet below them. Above and beyond, two slender chimneys reared another four hundred feet into the sky; they were crowned with powerful flashing strobe lamps that were visible even in this daylight and they were painted with broad horizontal red-and-white bands, the intention being to make them very visible to any aircraft foolish enough to fly low in this security-restricted area. A barely-visible plume of light yellow-brown smoke rose from the chimneys into the hot pale-blue haze of the atmosphere high over their heads. Beyond the chimneys, a row of gigantic cooling towers formed a dramatic background, with clouds of white condensate pouring from their dazzling white concrete throats and billowing into the sky.

If it had been uncomfortably warm at ground level, up here it was sheer hell. The morning sun was already bathing them in heat and the hot metal around and below them added to it mercilessly.

The two men walked round the top level of one of the boilers and Foster made a mental note of things he spotted. On their circuit they had to clamber gingerly over the long steel cylinders of soot-blower assemblies. These would from time to time drive into the furnace to blast high-pressure steam into the combustion chamber to clean the boiler's tube-walls, because ash clinging to them reduced the transfer of heat from the furnace to the steam.

Neither of the men had any desire to stay here longer than necessary but at Foster's suggestion, instead of taking the hoist back down, they began to clamber down the steel stairways. They stopped off at each level and at some they circled the boiler again, Foster making mental notes at each stop.

Half an hour later they were sipping iced tea in McBride's air-conditioned office. Even though they had passed along several passageways and through many doors, the roar of the machinery was still audible here and the floor was gently vibrating. A circle of wavelets formed on the surface of the tea when they put the mugs down.

'I hope you got the general picture,' McBride said.

Foster looked at him in silence for a while before he responded, 'Yes thanks; that was fine. Now that I've seen the layout I'd like to go back to my apartment and make plans for the work I've got to do over the next few days. OK?'

'OK, I'll run you back.'

As they stood to leave Foster said, 'I'd appreciate it if you could set up a meeting on Monday with everybody who'll be involved. Will that be possible?'

McBride said he would try to set up the meeting, but before they broke up Foster asked, 'Tell me: how long has this place been operating?' The incident he was going to try and investigate in his secondary, under-cover guise, had happened eighteen months ago.

McBride thought for a moment and then said, 'The first unit was commissioned about two years ago – a few months before I arrived. The last unit came on load about a month ago.'

The four boiler-turbine units would have been commissioned one after another; coming 'on load' meant that they were producing power.

'Why do you ask?' McBride continued.

'It's just that some of the things I saw looked … well, they looked like they were in serious need of attention.'

McBride clenched his teeth as Foster went on to describe some of the oddities that he'd noticed, like loose cables snaking across the floor, leaky valves hissing, connections taped-up with gaffer tape and so on. Such slovenliness might be expected on an ageing, carelessly maintained plant: on a brand-new one like this everything should have been in pristine condition.

'They'll get tidied up,' the Scot said, and then ruefully added in an undertone, 'or perhaps not. Everything was built in a big rush and even though we've got through that phase of the job, the pressure's always on us to keep the plant running at maximum throughput for as long as possible. Sometimes, to put a lash-up right we'd need to shut down … and the Assassin wouldn't tolerate that.'

'The Assassin?' Foster queried.

McBride gave a sheepish grin. 'Och! Aye, it's a sort of extended rhyming slang: Miller the Killer. And an assassin's a killer.'

53

'Ah! I see.'

'He's got a reputation for firing people, or getting them fired, if they say or do anything that doesnae line up with his thoughts. Nobody questions our Sam, or goes against him.'

'I've met the type,' Foster said, then asked, 'Has he been here, at Varikhani, from the beginning?'

'Aye. All of this is his wee baby,' McBride waved his arms around to indicate their surroundings. 'He negotiated the original bid, pushed it through the evaluation phase; now he sits in on every project meeting – he's everywhere. As a matter of fact he was chairing the meeting when THI said they wanted you to come aboard. You should ha' seen him! He fought tooth and nail to stop you coming.'

'Oh? And who overruled him? After all, if he's in overall command, surely he has the power to veto visits?'

'Would have thought so, wouldn't you. But somehow – and I don't know exactly why or how – he was overruled. Nobody here did it, that's for sure. The rumour is that it seems to have been somebody from Houston.'

'Global's head office?'

'Aye!' McBride nodded. 'That's right. The very top. And if you asked me, I'd guess that THI made them an offer they couldn't refuse.'

Foster grinned. *Good man, Saburo! I owe you one.*

'Either way,' McBride continued, 'it stuck in Sam's throat. He went ape for a few days; went round bollocking everybody for every little thing. Everybody tried to keep out of his way.' He smiled as a memory came to him. 'The poor *chaprassi* who had to bring him his mail, he had no chance. I saw him once, shaking and being physically sick with fear because he had to go into Sam's office with an email printout. Somebody had jokingly said it was something that would "make Sam's day", and the poor wee bugger heard. Sam has life-or-death power over those sods' lives; if they cross him they get thrown off the job – and the chance of them getting another job hereabouts after then is zero. They'd be reduced to begging in the streets, and they all have families to support. The *chaprassi* was only the messenger, but he'd get blamed for the message all right.'

'But why was Miller so worked up?' Foster asked. 'Surely he knows that, OK, what I'm doing here will help THI in the future, but it promises to help Miller as well. If the efficiency of all Global's world-wide power plants increases by even a fraction of a percentage point it will save the company millions of dollars each year. And Miller can say it was down to him letting me work here.'

McBride pondered the point, then said, 'Maybe. But that's tomorrow and while you're here our Sam feels vulnerable. Aye, exposed even.'

'Exposed to what?' Foster asked, looking quizzically at him.

But McBride shrugged and ended the conversation by suggesting they broke up for the day.

As they drove back to the residential area, Foster commented on McBride's courage in driving on the Indian roads, through Indian traffic, coping with Indian driving habits. The Scot laughed. 'I only drive on and around the site,' he said. 'And then only when I'm very nearby. Most of the time I use a company driver to go out on the other roads. Everybody does – all the ex-pats at least. It's far safer.' He laughed. 'We get a few people who arrive out here thinking they're the great masters of all they survey. They think the roads are like the ones back home in the States or the UK – Italy at the worst – and then they find out the reality. One day later, two days at the most, they're happy to hand the keys over to the company driver!'

Not much more was said on the journey, but one thought kept returning to nag Foster: *Why was Miller so agitated? Why did he feel exposed? Was he hiding something? If so, what was it?*

Chapter 3

The torrential rains of the Monsoon season had mostly passed but the days were still hot and steamy; the nights were little better. To avoid most of the heat, Foster and Alexis had started their journey from Hyderabad at an early hour of the previous day. Now, as they arrived at Golconda Fort, Foster had waved off the scattering of touts and so-called "tour guides" that crowded round their car as they arrived and their driver Aadesh had finished the job, sending the touts scattering with an annoyed wave of his hands: '*Jao!*' he yelled at them, 'Go!'.

Then, after passing the tidy green, rain-dampened lawns at the base of the historic monument they had entered through massive rusty gates and worked their way through a tall Oriental archway before starting the strenuous climb up through the time-ravaged granite ruins. The fort was a complex jumble of massive stone blocks that encrusted the small hill on which it had been built, like barnacles on a seashore rock.

As they climbed the steep stairways and passages they went from hot sunshine to cool shade. They passed along granite-sided passageways and through magnificent arches, across bridges spanning moats, up to the Durbar Hall. From the top of the hill, Foster and Alexis looked down across a green vista of treetops to the white boxes of houses that stretched to the smoky horizon of the vast Deccan plateau below. Up here it was cool and fresh; distance muffled the incessant cacophony of tooting car horns crowding the roads far below them. The sounds that were left seemed to be absorbed by the bulk of the putty-coloured walls and towers of the fort that encircled them.

They felt the history of ages seep into them.

On the previous day the two Westerners had arrived in Hyderabad and checked into the sprawling luxury of the Novotel. GCR's Indian administrative assistant at Varikhani had made the bookings for them without comment; Foster knew that the staff at the power station had been told about his companion and he was sure that there would have been much curiosity about the relationship between him, grizzled and white-bearded, and his pretty young companion. No doubt when the assistant reported back that they wanted separate rooms the news would quickly spread through the closed community's grapevine and there would be raised eyebrows and knowing winks.

In the evening, after the heat of the day had abated, Alexis had walked through the hotel's gardens with Foster, gasping at the luxury of the swimming pool with its surrounding of emerald lawns, brilliantly-coloured shrubs and tall palm trees. 'I didn't bring a cozzie,' she said smiling at him and when he looked surprised she added, 'You see? I'm learning to speak like a Brit! Once I would have called it a swimsuit. Anyway, I'll see if I can buy one tomorrow.'

They had then taken a light supper in the hotel's Mexican-themed restaurant, and as they left she suggested that they should have a nightcap in the bar. Foster declined the offer, saying he was tired and they would need to be up early the next morning. It was only partly true: in reality he was strangely unsettled by the American girl. He found himself attracted to her, but he definitely didn't want to become involved. After all, she was the daughter of the man who was his client. He felt it would be unwise to sit with her in the seductive comfort of the dimly-lit bar while the alcohol began to take effect and lower his inhibitions.

And perhaps hers. He hadn't been able to work her out. In his own mind she was a young girl towards whom he felt very protective – in a fatherly, or even grandfatherly fashion. He enjoyed being with her, and the curious looks they received from everybody didn't worry him at all. To the few who had asked, he said she was his niece, who for many years had wanted to see India. And apart from being very beautiful she was lively and intelligent; their conversations over these few days had ranged far and wide.

But he had no way of knowing how she felt about him so for the sake of safety he had maintained a cool cordiality towards her.

Now, leaning over the fort's parapet, they watched a large black bird circling lazily on the updraft of cool air that swept up the hill. When she came near him and pointed to it he explained that it was a raptor called a kite. Her movement had brought her upper arm into firm contact with his and she made no effort to move away as they leaned on the stone wall. He felt excited at the contact.

'It's beautiful, Dan,' she said quietly. 'This wonderful old fort with its gardens and passageways. But all that out there,' she waved towards the horizon blending into purple mist, 'it's so vast and mysterious. I feel I could stay here forever.'

Foster turned, perched his sunglasses on top of his head and looked at her quizzically. 'Could you?' he asked. 'Could you really?'

She tilted her head, pouted and thought carefully before answering. 'Yes, I could. I really think I could.'

He turned back to look over the parapet again, and once more her arm leaned against his.

They stayed like that for a while and then their thoughts were interrupted by a voice calling from behind: 'Dr Foster? Dr Dan Foster?'

They turned to see a small wiry Indian standing a few feet away, clutching a scuffed black leather briefcase. Unlike Dan and Alexis, who were in casual clothes, he was wearing a smart brown, well-kept but slightly worn-looking business suit with a neatly knotted striped tie at his neck. This outfit was inappropriate for this place and the sweat that streaked his face marked the exertion of his climb. 'I am Desai,' he said as he mopped at his face with a large off-white handkerchief, 'Kalpak Desai.'

'I'm pleased to meet you Mr Desai,' Foster said as they shook hands. 'This is Alexis Marshall. She's Scott Klein's daughter.'

Desai stared at her in shock. A frown crossed his face and he blurted out, '*Mr Klein's* daughter?'

'Yes,' Alexis answered. 'Marshall's my married name.'

'Ah! I see.' But the frown stayed on his face as he addressed Foster agitatedly: 'Do people at Varikhani know who madam is? Father being Scott Klein? Do Global Consolidated know?'

'No,' Foster reassured him. 'No they don't.'

'That is good,' Desai said, looking only slightly relieved. Then he seemed to make up his mind and confront the inevitable. He waved towards a short flight of stone steps nearby and said, 'There is place here where we can sit and talk. It is totally private. Come.'

'Can I call you Kalpak?' Foster asked as they headed up the steps. 'I'm Dan.'

Desai grinned and rolled his head from side to side in assent. This typically Indian gesture made Foster smile fondly.

They arrived in a small secluded area whose only other occupant was a large pale-grey *langur* monkey. The animal loped away at their approach and leaped onto a high wall on which it sat with its long tail dangling and twitching. It stared at them belligerently for a while, a mixture of curiosity and resentment showing in its black face with its encircling white beard; then it lost interest in them and began to scratch, searching its fur chest carefully for fleas.

They found a stone bench on which they sat; Foster and Desai next to each other, Alexis a short distance away. With the exception of the monkey they were alone up here and Desai lost no time; he opened his briefcase and drew some papers from it. He held them as he talked.

'I have prepared briefing note for you sir,' he said, clearly unwilling to refer to Foster as anything other than "sir", 'but I will tell you what it says.'

He started to recount his story, and the tale he told was horrific.

During the start-up phase of the first power-generating unit at Varikhani, something had gone wrong – suddenly and very seriously wrong. A massive explosion had occurred and three maintenance engineers had been killed instantly. Another two died later in hospital and five more were badly injured. All the injuries had included third or fourth degree burns.

A Coroner's Inquiry had been convened and the small legal firm that Desai worked for had been engaged to defend GCR's interests. Desai, a partner in the practice, was a diligent man and he had made it his business to interview several of the site staff.

One man's statement had been particularly disturbing. Ashok Mahajan, the manager of the control and instrument department was responsible for the many devices that measured pressures, temperatures and flows around the plant and for the valves and dampers that controlled them, plus the complex computer systems that interconnected all of these. When Desai interviewed him, Mahajan had seemed to be very nervous. Desai had sensed that something was amiss, and he patiently picked away at his statements, uncovering more and more inconsistencies until eventually Mahajan blurted out that all these questions had been addressed before, in a report that had been written about the accident by a member of his staff shortly after the incident had occurred. Mahajan had been so startled and disturbed by what the report said that he had not passed it up to his superiors.

Now he was reluctant to hand over the document to Desai, but the lawyer had persevered, reassuring him that its source would not be identified. He explained that it was vital that he saw the report because if any information that had been concealed from him came to light in court, he would have difficulty in countering it.

Eventually Mahajan had given him the report – or rather, a copy of it. Desai had quickly read through it and was staggered by its damning conclusion. It clearly showed that, without any shadow of doubt, inadequate operational procedures – mercilessly and meticulously detailed in the document – had been the cause of the accident.

Now it was Desai's turn to become worried. He saw that his clients would be blamed for the failings and mismanagement that had led to the deaths, so he set about constructing an elaborate defence of their interests. He called for a meeting with Sam Miller and told him what he had discovered. The American became incandescent with rage. 'What fuckin' report?' he shouted. 'Nobody told me there was a report.'

Desai said that he knew nothing about the provenance of the report but, as far as he could find, nobody else had seen it. However, on the off-chance that they had, he would be pre-armed and able to defend GCR to the best of his ability. He outlined how he intended to counter the report's findings – should anyone have obtained a copy of the report and raise them in court – and at that stage Miller had seemed to be satisfied with his approach.

Desai then told Foster what Klein had already said: that when the inquest opened he found that his briefcase had been opened. The report had been extracted and replaced with another one. This second report made no mention of negligence or malpractice, but instead blamed the explosion on the failure of a piece of essentially simple equipment.

Desai had been staggered. He was deeply unhappy with this turn of events. In the light of the second, replacement report, it was most likely that the court would find that the accident had been the result of a single failure in an otherwise well-run operation. The coroner would have considered it as little more than an unfortunate occurrence; any fine levied would have been trivial and little or no compensation would have been payable to the victims' families.

That would be good for GCR, but if the original report were to turn up after all – and it was always possible that other copies had been made – then it would be infinitely worse for his clients, with a charge of perjury very possible.

The original report had been very clear that the disaster had been the result of poor operational procedures, lack of care and flagrant violation of safety rules. If it turned up, and if Desai failed to exonerate his client, blame would have been laid very firmly at GCR's door. With evidence of perjury before him the coroner would have no option but to refer the case to a higher court. After then, legal processes could have been opened – at least in India and possibly even in the United States, GCR's base – with the possibility of corporate manslaughter charges being levelled at the company's senior executives.

The pay-outs to the survivors and to the victims' families would have then been considerably magnified.

The court proceedings had dragged on, covering the minutiae of the legal matters and throughout these Desai had been deeply distracted. He suspected Miller, or more likely one of his stooges, of having removed the evidence. And after a sleepless night he made up his mind. This was a game he was unwilling to play.

The next day he made a statement to the coroner that his case file had been tampered with, and asked permission to withdraw from the defence team. With a sudden flurry of excitement and curiosity, the hearing had been abruptly adjourned while GCR found another advocate.

But before the hearing was re-convened Desai found himself being threatened by a furious Miller, who told him that he would make sure that the lawyer would never again be able to work in any kind of legal capacity, in India or elsewhere.

Within days of that warning, Desai had been fired by his practice and since then Miller's threats had come to terrible fruition. In his increasingly desperate search for a new job of equivalent status to his old one he found that all doors had been closed to him. He was now living on meagre savings while he frantically searched for any kind of employment.

Meanwhile, GCR had brought in a new lawyer who told the coroner that Desai had been confused: that there was no evidence of tampering with any report. He then produced the fake report. This one laid the blame for the accident on a defective valve that had leaked and allowed gas to collect in the boiler, where it had ignited explosively.

'Can you prove any of this?' Foster asked Desai when the Indian had finished speaking.

'Oh yes, sir,' Desai replied. 'Without any shadow of doubt. I have been back to re-interview this man Mahajan and he insists that negligent operational procedures did indeed cause the accident. It was not leaking valve. He reminded me that original report proves it. I told him that copy he gave me had been subsequently stolen, so I have no evidence to offer. He was very concerned about who had stolen report, and where it could now be held. He said that he had been severely reprimanded by Mr Miller for having the report written in the first place, and then for not passing it on.'

'This is all in the report he gave you?'

'Yes sir. Mahajan is very worried man. He knows that if existence of report is disclosed he will be blamed for it. He blames me for its loss. He is afraid that he too will lose job. But in the end I have persuaded him to give me copy of the document. But in return I must not identify him as the person who gave it to me. He has kept original.'

Foster was puzzled. 'If he was so worried about the report, why did he mention it to you in the first place, let alone show it to you?'

'Mahajan is confused, sir,' Desai said. 'He is acting in eccentric manner and does not know what action to take that would be in his best interest. But also I am thinking that if legal proceedings start again he will be able to demonstrate that he is basically honest: that he was ready to take correct path by giving me report.'

'You're saying,' Foster said, 'that if another court case were to be opened he would be able to claim that he had been on the side of the angels ...'

'Angels?' Desai asked.

'Yes. Showing that he was an honest and diligent man.'

It made a sort of convoluted, Indian-type sense but though Foster still wasn't convinced, he needed to make progress. He asked, 'And what did you do when you got hold of the copy?'

Desai's face suddenly showed a mixture of regret and frustration. Tears welled in his eyes. 'Oh sir,' he said. 'Sir, at that time I telephoned Mr Klein.'

'Ah!' Foster breathed. 'I see. That's when he got involved.'

'Yes sir. I had read of his many confrontations with Global Consolidated Resources Company, and I thought that perhaps he could help. They had attacked me; if Mr Klein attacked them I thought that they would perhaps withdraw actions against me. Maybe it was not logical, but I was in need of help. So I turned to him.'

Alexis had been quiet up to this time, but now she interjected, 'That's when Dad tried to come out here, to India ...'

'And got stopped at Immigration,' Foster concluded.

'Yes indeed, sir,' Desai said. 'That is correct. It too was action of the company. They have many friends. But Mr Klein telephoned me when he returned to USA. He advised me to go back to coroner – this time with report.'

'And you did?'

'Yes, sir. The coroner, Jivas Gopal, he carefully studied report and immediately re-convened the Inquest. He is good man, sir; very honest. The new finding was that there was lack of care at site and Global Consolidated Company was fined ten thousand Lakhs.'

'How much is ten thousand Lakhs?' Alexis asked.

'Around two million US dollars, madam,' Desai answered quickly. He had clearly worked out the conversion in advance, and memorised it.

'That's what your father told me,' Foster said. 'But he made the point that it wasn't just the size of the sum – the big deal was that it cleared the way for serious compensation claims against Global.'

'Indeed, sir,' Desai said. 'And coroner also referred matter of perjury to Andhra Pradesh High Court.'

'Over the substitution of the damning report with the whitewashed version?'

'Yes sir. But it does not matter: the case failed …'

Tears appeared in his eyes again and he stopped speaking. The matter was clearly too painful for him to continue.

'I know it failed,' Foster said. 'Scott Klein told me that the company appealed and the findings were quashed. He suspected that some palms had been greased. And then they took you to court, claiming damages for breach of confidence.'

'Yes, sir,' Desai said quietly. 'But by then I had no money. I had lost job. Appeal for legal aid was rejected; I was ordered to pay damages. I could not afford …' He stopped speaking. By now the tears were flowing freely down his cheeks at the painful memory. He concluded, 'I am bankrupt sir. Bankrupt. My house has been taken away, and I am living in my uncle's house with my family. It is a disgrace.'

Foster stared at Desai. He knew now what he had to do, and it would not be easy.

That night he and Alexis sat at the bar of the Novotel. She was sipping at a gin and tonic; he had his favourite single malt, Balvenie Doublewood, in front of him.

'That poor little man,' she said. 'I feel so sorry for him.'

'So do I,' Foster said grimly.

'What are you going to do?' she asked. 'Do you think you can help?'

'I don't know. But I've got to find each and every sign of negligence on Global's part and get irrefutable records of them all.'

'Do you think you can?'

'Sure can! I've already seen several examples and I'm confident that I'll find more if I look round a bit more. Once people get sloppy, and if they're allowed to get away with it, then the rot runs wide and deep. But what I need most of all is to identify the cause of the explosion.'

'This report – do you think that what it says is true?'

'Without actually seeing it I can't be sure, but I am bloody sure of one thing.'

'What's that?'

'No leaking gas valve could have caused that explosion; not in this day and age. Obviously the coroner wouldn't have had enough technical knowledge to question what he was being told. But I do.'

'Why couldn't it have been the cause?'

'Several reasons. Mainly, these valves are always provided in threes – in what's known as a triple-block-and-bleed, or TBB, arrangement ….'

'What's that?' she asked.

'Three valves, two of them one after another in the line to the plant, and a third in-between, venting to the atmosphere. They're interlocked so that it is physically impossible for the gas to go where it isn't wanted. If any gas does manage to seep past the first valve when it's shut, the bleed valve – which is open – vents it to the air, while the second block valve stops any getting past.'

'Any other reasons for your suspicions?'

'Plenty! Even if any gas managed the unheard-of trick of getting past the TBB set it would be vented away when they purged the boiler – blasted air through it – before they started to light the burners.'

Foster had managed to get her allowed onto the site the day before they left for Hyderabad, and so she now knew a little more about power stations. She had told him that she'd found it a noisy and rather frightening environment, but now she did at least have some rudimentary idea of the size and complexity of the plant.

Now she asked, 'The computers that control all this – isn't that all a bit hi-tech for India?'

He laughed. 'In spite of the poor people you've seen begging in the streets, and despite the squalor of the slums, this is a very fast-moving, technically able, wealthy and advanced country. In fact,' he waved towards the big windows, 'although Hyderabad out there was once called "The City of Pearls" today, more often than not, it's known as "High-Tech City".'

She pondered that thought before returning to the subject of the accident, 'That explosion – does that sort of thing happen often?'

He laughed. 'Fortunately not. Most power plants these days are designed, manufactured, commissioned and managed by competent and diligent people; but, like in most industries, there are a few rogues.'

'And that's where accidents happen?'

'Yep! Looked what happened to Challenger.'

'The space shuttle?'

'Yup! Long before the shuttle exploded on launch, NASA knew of the design flaw that led to the disaster. They and their private contractor deemed it to be "an acceptable flight risk".'

'God! And you think something similar could be happening here?'

'Sort of. But that's what I've got to find out.'

'So how dangerous is a power station?'

He thought for a while, and then said, 'Take one example. The steam coming out of the boiling water in your kettle at home is at 100 degrees Celsius. The steam coming out of a power-station boiler is at more than five times that temperature ... and the pressure is several thousand pounds per square inch. If it leaks out you just can't see it. Steam is quite invisible – what you call steam is actually a condensation cloud that forms when it starts to cool – it's reverting to lots of little droplets of water. So where it emerges from a boiler it squirts several feet before the condensation makes it visible; but the bit you can't see is still there and it's still lethal: it's at the pressure and temperature I mentioned. You can't see it and, with all the other noises around, you can't hear it either. If you happened to walk through a steam jet like that you'd be sliced in two, as quickly and cleanly as if you'd been cut by an invisible knife.'

'That's horrible,' she shuddered. 'I'm surprised that anybody should want to work there with such risks around. It must be really frightening.'

'No it isn't. Everybody's very careful, that's all. And virtually everybody loves working there. Besides it's a job that takes you round the world. To isolated islands and places in the middle of nowhere.'

'How come?'

'Everybody needs electricity, so power stations are everywhere. And the people who work on them see places and meet people that are way off the tourist trail. I don't know any other job like that. Anyway, it's the huge machines that fascinate us all.'

'Why?'

He grinned. 'Big boys' toys,' he said. 'And they don't get any bigger than that.'

'I don't think I'll ever understand men,' she said quietly.

'It's not only men. These days, plenty of women work in power stations.'

'I don't understand them either, then.'

After a short silence he asked, 'When you said about not understanding men, it wasn't just them and their big toys was it?'

'No,' she said ruefully. 'I thought I did understand them but then Jim …'

'Your ex?'

'Yes. I thought we understood each other pretty well. Two minds with but a simple thought – that sort of thing.'

'But?'

She was lost in bitter memories, and the answer was a while in coming. 'Then I find he's checked in to a Boston hotel room with another Mrs Marshall, and when I ask around I find it's not the first time. It hurt.'

'I'm sorry,' Foster said quietly as he took a sip of his malt.

She shrugged, looking down at her own drink. 'It happens.' Then she turned to face him. 'What about you?' she asked. 'You told me you'd been married once, before the Underground thing. What happened?'

'Bit similar to your thing. Came home and found wife in bed with another man.'

'Ugh!'

'Yes. Got divorced.'

'Any kids?'

'Yes, two boys. They're grown up now.'

'Are they the two in the photograph on your boat?'

'That's them!'

'Do you see them often?'

'Not often. But we've become closer recently. They don't know about their Mum and the other guy. But I do feel guilty. They grew up without really knowing me, and I didn't really know them either. But we're putting that right now, between the three of us.'

'And then?'

'Then there was Fiona …' he paused before adding, 'and after I got over losing her I met a woman who was a high-flying executive. We had a lot of fun together. And then she went.'

She smiled at him. 'A bit careless with your women, aren't you?'

He shrugged his shoulders and grinned sheepishly. 'You could say that.'

She shrugged as well. 'None of my business anyway.'

They were silent together. After a few minutes, while they each contemplated their drinks and took the occasional sip, she suddenly spoke.

'Do you wonder what people think?'

He looked a question at her. 'About us,' she explained. 'You and me – here together.'

His reply was slow in coming. 'I'm sure the yarn about you being my niece is doubted by all. They probably think I'm a dirty old man and you're a gold-digger.'

She laughed. 'How wrong they'd be, at least the first bit. You haven't even made a pass at me.'

'No,' he said seriously. Then he smiled and added, 'No I haven't. Not because I haven't wanted to. You're a very beautiful woman, Alexis, and this is an enchanting place; but you're less than half my age.'

'And you promised my dad you'd look after me,' she pouted.

'Yes. In fact I did.'

'I'm a big girl now, Dan. That's something my Dad doesn't always seem to understand. And I guess he thought he'd been right when my marriage broke up. He never said anything but I suspected that he didn't really like Jim.'

'A father's natural instinct,' Foster observed. 'To resent a man making a love to his little girl.'

'Perhaps,' she said.

Some time passed, and Foster had just taken a sip of his malt when, quite suddenly, she looked straight at him and quietly said, 'How about we go up to your room?'

Foster almost spluttered, and then he carefully put his glass down on the bar and looked at her. She was smiling, and if he hadn't heard what she'd just said he would have said it was an entirely innocent smile.

Every instinct in his body urged him to accept her invitation but he fought against them. 'I don't think that would be a good idea, Alexis,' he said finally.

'Why not?' she asked. 'This is a wonderful romantic place. And I'd like it ...'

'And what?'

'If I was vain enough I'd say you'd like it too.'

He smiled. 'And I'm sure you'd be right, but...'

'But what? Is it your old-world up-bringing? Well, my generation .... we see things differently.'

'Differently?'

'Yes. We see sex as something to be enjoyed. No hang-ups. As long as both parties are free.'

He took another sip of his drink while he thought before saying, 'And what about the age difference?'

'Oh that,' she said dismissively. 'I've never thought that age should matter.'

'And where do you think this thing would go?'

She frowned at him. 'Go? This is for today, Dan – for tonight. Look at me. We get on well. It'd be fun. Nothing to base any long-term plans on.'

Foster was beginning to feel intoxicated. He'd had a little too much to drink, and her beauty was adding to the magic.

He took a long, deep breath before saying, 'All right then. Let's go.'

The first pink light of dawn was filtering through the pale cream voile curtains when he woke. She was lying beside him on her side, with her back turned to him. For a while he looked at her fine, flawless skin and the curve of her slender neck. He wanted to touch her, to stroke that neck, to run his finger along her shoulder and down her spine, but he resisted, so as not to disturb her sleep. He lay back, looking at the ceiling and re-running the events of the night through his memory. There was a lot to remember.

Eventually she stirred and turned to face him.

'Good morning, sir!' she said sleepily. 'I trust you slept well?'

'I did indeed.'

She snuggled against him. 'That was perfect. You're quite something, you know.'

'So they say,' he said with a cheeky grin.

She punched his chest lightly.

He ran his fingers through her hair and said, 'You know, I promised your father I'd look after you.'

'And you have.'

'Mmm, I'm not sure that this is quite what he meant.'

'Dad knows I go my own way.'

'Yes, he warned me.'

There was a long silence before she spoke again. 'I'll need to get back to my room,' she said. 'But can I shower here first?'

While she showered his mind moved on to thoughts of the work that he had to do at Varikhani, and about his two projects there – one overt, the other covert. But his thoughts were continually interrupted by memories of the night. And of her.

When she emerged from her shower she said 'I've put on yesterday's outfit for the moment. I'll change back in my room.'

'OK,' he said, 'Then we have to get a move on, I'm afraid. Breakfast first and then the long ride back to our bungalows. '

She came over to him and sat down on the bed. 'Are we going to share a bungalow?' she asked.

'I don't think that would be safe,' he said sadly. 'Mahaan Shah will be bound to spot something and we don't want rumours circulating.'

'Why? What does it matter?'

'I've got to be squeaky clean. They know you as a married woman and if they think … Well, it won't look very professional if I'm seen to be having only part of my mind on the job in hand.'

'I suppose so,' she agreed. 'But I want last night to be repeated – again and again.'

'So do I. We'll work out something.'

After breakfast, they found Aadesh waiting for them at reception. He explained that he had stayed the night locally with a cousin. Foster paid the hotel bill and they set off on the long drive back to Varikhani. While they travelled, he told her his plans.

He was going to start the programme of monitoring the plant in preparation for his work. He had asked to borrow a fast event-recorder from the station instrument workshop and would link this in to the pressure, temperature and flow signals that he wanted to monitor as he made his tests. In most cases he would be able to tap into existing instruments, but some measurements weren't available and he would need to have very specialised devices installed. He had specified these to Mizutani at THI and he expected to find them waiting at the plant when he arrived. He would co-opt some of the control and instrumentation staff to carry out the installation, and this would give him the opportunity to question Ashok Mahajan, the departmental manager.

He wanted to get inside any defences that Mahajan – or Miller – might put up.

In this way he would be dealing with his obligations to THI while at the same time discreetly probing into the situation and events surrounding the other matter.

Throughout the course of this explanation, Foster was careful to avoid making any direct reference to the explosion, in case Aadesh overheard. The driver had been hired by the Japanese THI company, so Foster had no fears that he might be a spy planted by GCR, but he knew how rumours circulated in small closed communities and he didn't want anybody to pick up anything that might leak out to Miller's cronies through idle conversation.

'And what are you going to be doing while I'm busy on site?' he asked Alexis.

'Aadesh says there is a lot to show me yet,' she said. 'He reckoned I'll be occupied for at least another day.'

'OK,' Foster said. Then he had a thought and added, 'When you've done at and around Varikhani, why don't you go back down to Hyderabad. You can stay in the Novotel until I've finished my work at the plant. There's a lot more for you to see and do in the city.'

She smiled at him and whispered, 'And it keeps plenty of clear blue water between us?'

'Yes. But I can come down to see you next weekend.'

'That would be nice,' she murmured and squeezed his hand out of the driver's sight. 'I didn't get a chance to try out my new … cozzie.' She smiled at the last word, obviously still amused at her use of colloquial English.

'OK,' Foster said. 'I'll make the arrangements when we get to Varikhani. I'm sure THI will be happy. It clears the cost of your food and accommodation off their books, because I'll pay for the Novotel …'

'Oh no you won't,' she interrupted. 'I'll pay my own way. I'm a modern American girl, Dan Foster; don't you go forgetting it.'

When they reached Varikhani and after they had settled in Foster went over to her bungalow, where the ever-attentive Mahaan Shah later served them dinner.

'There's one big question in my mind,' Foster said as they ate, and when he was sure that Shah couldn't hear his words. 'Why on earth is Global so terrified of this thing? Two million bucks is nothing to them. I'm sure there's something else going on here, something that makes them desperate to push the whole Varikhani incident out of sight.'

'Dad said they would be faced with big compensation claims,' she suggested. 'Could it be that?'

'I doubt it. Big is a relative term. A few thousand dollars can change a man's life completely out here. Five, ten million – it would hardly scratch an outfit the size of Global Consolidated. It'd be covered by their insurance anyway.'

After they had finished eating he rang the Novotel in Hyderabad. She had written down her credit-card details for him and he used these to book a double room for her for the few days of the coming week and the next weekend. When he said she would be on her own at first, but he would be joining her later on the receptionist showed no reaction.

Hotels are used to such things and deal with them with worldly-wise aplomb.

Chapter 4

Peter McBride met Foster at the plant gates and escorted him to the instrument department offices. After they departed, Aadesh drove back to the guest quarters to collect Alexis for the day's sightseeing.

The offices were in a single-storey concrete building set between the two central boiler-turbine units. The two men stepped in to the air-conditioned workshop and made their way along a corridor lined with plain wooden doors leading to various offices: "Instrument Technicians" said one; "Calibration Laboratory" another; a third was marked "Commissioning Team". Each label was in Hindi and English and engraved in white lettering on a shiny black background. A few labels bore the name of the individual occupying the office, again in Hindi and English.

A deep all-pervading hum was audible throughout the building: it came from the machines and transformers and transmitted itself through the steel skeleton of the structure.

'That's my office,' McBride said as they went past a door labelled "Main Contractor Commissioning Manager". He smiled as he added, 'You can tell who's permanent and who's transient; the transients' doors just show their job title, and they don't bother to translate into Hindi.'

'Must be tough on your family, being here for such a short while.'

'It is,' McBride replied with a curious, almost wistful, look on his face. 'The company looks after us well though; like I said, it schools the kids and things like that.'

Then they arrived at a door marked "Dr Ashok Mahajan, PhD, M.Sc., MBA, FIET, FIEEE – Manager, Control and Instrumentation Department". McBride knocked and opened the door without waiting for a response.

The man inside was grossly fat with glossy, slicked-back, jet-black hair. He was wearing a pale blue suit, a blinding white shirt and a dark blue tie bearing narrow diagonal stripes; their lie from top right to bottom left betrayed its American origin. His suit jacket was buttoned and stretched tightly across his vast belly. He was sitting behind an imposing glass-topped desk on which a small pile of papers lay in front of a computer screen with its keyboard and mouse. One wall of the office was completely occupied by an enormous book-case filled with textbooks and manuals – the huge amount of equipment on the site required many instruction manuals, and while most of these were initially provided on disk, many people liked to keep hard copies in stout binders, so that they could be kept close at hand and copies of selected pages consulted while working out on the plant.

In the centre of the large office was an imposing mahogany-topped conference table with eight chairs down each long side and one at each end. The chair at the end nearest to Mahajan's desk had a high back and carved arm-rests. A modern water-cooler stood in one corner of the room.

The fat man was reading a page at the top of the pile of papers. He looked up as the two visitors entered and his face broke into a beaming smile. With some difficulty he heaved his great mass to his feet to greet them. 'Dr Foster,' he said, his voice curiously high-pitched, his English precise and scarcely accented. 'I am so pleased to meet you, sir. I am Ashok Mahajan, manager of Control and Instrumentation Department here.'

Foster shook his hand and said, 'I'm pleased to meet you Dr Mahajan. A pretty impressive place; it must keep you very busy.'

Mahajan simpered. 'It does indeed do so sir, but please call me Ashok.'

'All right, Ashok, and I'm Dan.'

'Would you like some refreshment, Dan?' Mahajan asked. 'Tea, or perhaps coffee? And you Mr McBride?'

Foster noticed Mahajan's subtle confirmation of a strict pecking-order: only equals were to be on first-name terms; underlings were addressed by their family names. He said tea would be fine and McBride nodded that he would like that too. Mahajan lifted his telephone to give an instruction.

'*Chai-wallah* will bring,' he said imperiously as he cradled the telephone. 'Now, shall we sit?'

They took their seats at the conference table with Mahajan at the head. His bulk scarcely fitted between the arms of his chair and as he squeezed himself into position the action wobbled his enormous jowls. For a moment Foster had the amusing thought that if a fire broke out and a rapid exit was needed the manager would have to make his escape crouching with the chair still encasing his buttocks.

'Now, Dr Foster,' he said solicitously. 'Did you have a good journey to here?'

Foster said he had and they exchanged small talk for a while, until a small wiry man brought in the refreshments. From his very dark skin, Foster guessed this *chai-wallah* was from the far south of the sub-continent, perhaps Chennai or Sri Lanka. The refreshments were laid down on the table in front of

Mahajan. They were on a silver tray with china cups, a teapot, a small jug of milk and a bowl of sugar. A pile of McVities Rich Tea biscuits lay beside them on small plate. *How very English*, Foster thought.

While Mahajan carefully poured the tea for them, and without looking up, he said, 'I have heard much about your work, Dr Foster.'

Foster groaned inwardly. He had hoped that tales of his investigations into power-station accidents wouldn't have reached India. If these people knew his background they would be bound to be extra wary, fearing that he would be asking about the earlier accident at this site. But then Mahajan spoke, and Foster's fears subsided.

'Saburo Mizutani has told me that you are experienced with the control systems of these boilers,' he said as he passed Foster his tea, 'and that you will be able to optimise them for us.' He proffered the plate. 'A biscuit, Dan?'

Foster took a biscuit and passed the plate to McBride, who took two and returned the plate to Mahajan. Foster saw the trace of a frown forming on the Indian's face as he noted this liberty-taking. It passed in a brief moment: the frown was dismissed and the smile returned.

'Well,' Foster continued. 'I'll try. I'm going to have a look at least. I'll be taking some measurements and seeing how the plant responds to changes in throughput.'

The smile left Mahajan's face again and his eyes dropped for a moment. When he looked at Foster again he was frowning. 'That may be ..... a little difficult,' he said hesitantly. 'You see, at present we operate under jurisdiction of Global Consolidated Resources and they are always asking us to generate as much as possible ... and for as long as possible. Their investment must be recovered, do you see. We were hoping you could achieve your .... your aims by employing pseudo-random binary sequence cross-correlation techniques.'

Foster saw McBride wince. The manager was using the high-blown language of the academic researcher, partly to show that he was aware of the latest trends in technology but also to impress his distinguished visitor. It was true that the technologies he'd mentioned might have been able to achieve improvements without necessitating the throughput changes that Foster was demanding. They had indeed been used previously to determine plant characteristics and improve performance, but those studies had been carried out under very carefully controlled laboratory-like conditions, and then only on a small scale; never of plants of this size and complexity. Mahajan's world of complex mathematical control technology was worlds away from McBride's reality of hot pipes and hissing valves.

'I fully appreciate that,' Foster replied with a reassuring smile, 'but that's not my way of working. But never mind that; the fact is that I'll not be wanting any changes at the beginning anyway; I'll just want to see how the systems respond to normal, day-to-day changes.'

Mahajan's frown lessened slightly. 'But in the end you will want large-scale load swings?'

Foster knew that this was the sticking point. If he was to achieve anything he wasn't going to embark on largely theoretical approaches that would be unlikely to yield real results; he needed to see what happened when the megawatts generated by the plant were suddenly reduced. When it was complete, his work would ensure that everything operated ideally in those conditions. He needed to know how well the existing control systems handled such changes: then he'd modify the systems and see if they had improved. It was his way.

'I appreciate the economic realities,' he said, 'but any loss of throughput will be short-lived, and after I've done you should be able to see vastly improved performance. Every tonne of coal you burn will produce more megawatts than at present. That's got to be good.'

Despite this reassurance Mahajan still looked uncomfortable. 'I do so fully understand,' he said. 'I will try to explain to Mr Miller. In the end it is he who must authorise such things.'

'OK. But let's do one thing at a time, shall we? We'll cross that bridge later on.'

Mahajan looked relieved at the postponement of an unpleasant confrontation and promised Foster the assistance of his entire department. Foster told him that he already knew that they possessed most of the specialized measuring and recording equipment he needed and Mahajan agreed to have it made available.

With the arrangements made, the manager offered to introduce Foster to his senior staff.

'I'll come along too, Ashok,' McBride said, and Mahajan nodded his head agitatedly. Foster detected that the Scot had long since decided that he wouldn't be playing Mahajan's game: he would call him whatever he liked and do whatever needed to be done.

Mahajan's state of happiness blossomed as the three of them headed down the corridor. He looked much happier as he said, 'Dr Foster, I would be honoured if you would be my guest at my home one evening.'

'I'd be delighted,' Foster answered.

'Good, good!' Mahajan enthused. 'Shall we say tomorrow evening?'

'Yes, that will be fine.'

'I will ask others to join. Sundip Singh including, perhaps. He is Station Manager.'

A few moments later they reached the door to the commissioning team's office, but before they went inside Mahajan stopped and said, 'I understand you have lady here with you.'

Foster was not surprised at this statement. As Alexis's bungalow had been provided by "the company" – whoever or whatever that may have been – it was only to be expected that news of her presence here should have percolated through to Mahajan. 'Yes,' he answered. 'She's my niece; she's always wanted to see India so when my brother told her I was coming here she asked to tag along.' He smiled inwardly at the irony as he added, 'He's entrusted her to me.'

'That is good,' Mahajan said. 'Has she seen much of interest?'

'Yes, I took her to Golconda Fort last weekend.'

'Ah! That is very good choice, very good indeed. It is a long journey from here but it is one of most impressive monuments in this area – indeed in the whole of India. Even beside the many jewels of our beautiful country, even beside the famous Taj Mahal, Golconda Fort is a unique and glorious relic of past days,' he gave a significant smile before adding for the Englishman Foster's benefit, 'before the Raj even. Yes, certainly you must bring her with you when you come to my home.'

Foster said he would ask her, although he had little doubt that she'd jump at the opportunity to visit an Indian family and see how they lived in their home.

Mahajan turned to McBride and asked, 'Will you and your wife join us also, McBride?'

There was a brief pause, and Foster detected a strange look on the Scot's face – was it wistfulness? Then the reply came: that he'd be delighted to attend.

After that they went into the Commissioning Team office to meet those waiting inside.

Apart from McBride, who was a full-time GCR employee, the commissioning team comprised Indian nationals who would in due time answer to Mahajan. Foster was told that at present the entire team answered to Miller, but when the plant was handed over to NTPC they would transfer to the Indian power company's payroll and administration.

The team comprised five men and, somewhat to Foster's surprise, two women – it was clear that emancipation had finally arrived in India. Clearly all of the engineers had been well rehearsed. Mahajan introduced them one by one, listing their qualifications and specialisations from memory. It was an impressive feat of memory, and the team composition was also impressive. As each was introduced, he or she stood up and politely shook Foster's hand. In each instance the greeting was the same: 'Good morning sir; I am pleased to meet you.' Their command of English was uniformly perfect, but their accents and intonations varied considerably, from carefully enunciated Victorian-Etonian preciseness to what many would call full-blown, Peter Sellers style "Bombay Welsh".

Foster asked each of them a few questions about their day-to-day work, and from their responses he assessed them all as being bright, capable and very enthusiastic. Two of the team were Muslims, but there were no signs of antagonism between them and their Hindu colleagues.

Only one of the engineers asked Foster any question. Mahajan had introduced him as Praveen Jampani and explained that he was the team's principal instrument engineer, and when Foster asked him about his work he answered swiftly and confidently. Foster was particularly impressed; the safety and efficiency of the plant depended heavily on its complex electronic instrumentation, and he was all too familiar with situations where poor performance – and in some cases damage – had been caused by carelessly calibrated, badly installed or poorly maintained instruments.

The two female engineers were young, pretty and slim and both wore beautiful brightly-coloured saris. Foster couldn't help wondering what would happen when they went out on the plant: the saris would be quite impractical and dangerous on the steel stairways and galleries. Men would have donned boiler suits, but for the women things would be more complicated.

Mahajan then led his visitor to the workshop and showed him the extensive collection of instrumentation there, ranging from dead-weight calibrators to the latest state-of-the-art electronic test meters and oscilloscopes. All the equipment, power supplies and tools were placed on long work-benches or stacked on steel shelves over them. Foster asked about and was shown the high-speed event recorders that he wanted to borrow. He recognised them and was impressed: there was certainly no shortage of money here.

From there, Foster, McBride and Mahajan adjourned to the manager's office where they sat at the conference table and began to discuss the detailed plans for the work to be carried out. From time to time McBride went over to the book-case and brought over manuals and drawings which he spread over the table to clarify some detail or other. Foster judged that the Scotsman made much more use of them on a regular basis than Mahajan, though the manager insisted on keeping them in his office.

At one point Mahajan invited Foster to see some software on his computer. It was a heat-balance calculator that Foster recognised but he could see no relevance to their present discussion because its purpose was to calculate the efficiency of the plant. However, he dutifully went to Mahajan's desk and looked as the manager tapped at the keyboard which Foster saw was in the Indian Inscript form, with Hindi symbols engraved alongside the Latin characters on each key.

Then Foster understood. This was Mahajan's toy and his use of it was a demonstration of his command of the plant and all of its operations.

While he watched the demonstration, Foster saw that he had been wrong in thinking the software would not be relevant to his work: it would in fact be very useful to him. 'You keep regular records of the plant performance?' he asked.

'Oh yes, Dr Foster. Indubitably.' Mahajan pointed to a fat lever-arch file on the bookshelf. 'Daily records are kept there. Also on computers.'

'Good. If we compare the results before and after my work it will show what I've achieved.'

'Exactly! My thinking too!' Mahajan enthused, pleased that he was one step ahead of this expert in at least one area.

Demonstration over, they returned to the conference table and as they took their seats on opposite sides of it McBride caught Foster's eye and gave a conspiratorial wink.

It was a long and gruelling session and it was late in the afternoon before all the details had been hammered out and the procedures agreed.

'You were very honoured today, Dan,' McBride said wryly as they left the building. 'That lazy bastard rarely gets off his arse. Stays all day in his office and sucks up to the high and mighty.'

'He seems competent enough,' Foster countered. He had put some highly technical questions to Mahajan and the answers had been correct and had come quickly, 'And he's right about the heat-balance software: it will be very useful.'

'Oh aye, he's bright all right. Just bluidy lazy. Knows the theory, talks Bode Plots and Laplace Transforms whenever he can, but he won't ever touch a valve or a switch. We think he's terrified of it. But when we get visitors he does a great Lord of the Manor act, swanning about the place and pretending that he's in total command and giving the impression that he knows and does everything all on his own;

like he did back there with the heat-balance software. Fact is, it's his people that do all the real work: they know more about the practicalities of the place than he ever will. But he gives them precious little credit for it.'

'I've met the type,' Foster sympathised.

'So have I, but friend Mahajan is the worst I've seen. The fat slob spends all his time behind that aircraft-carrier flight-deck of his. When he does come out of his office he creeps around like some sort of big slug. In fact the only time I saw him move fast was on the day of the explosion.'

Foster's pulse quickened and he tried to stay calm as he asked, 'What – after it happened?'

'No. In the hours leading up to it.'

'What happened that day, Peter?' Foster asked quietly. It was a natural question in the context of their conversation and his asking shouldn't raise any suspicions.

'It was a hell of a day, Dan. In fact it had been a hell of a week.'

By then they had reached the Land Rover. The sun had blazed on it for hours and the interior was unpleasantly hot when they climbed in. McBride tapped at the red-hot rim of the steering wheel but said nothing as he waited for it to cool. After a while he started the engine, and as they set off he sighed and continued: 'There was a lot of pressure on us to get the unit away that day.'

He was referring to the urgency associated with starting up the boiler-turbine unit. Foster knew that extreme management pressures at such times were commonplace and entirely natural. At the same time, much caution was needed as every step was taken: the boiler had to be started safely and then the steam fed to the turbines gradually so that they warmed up slowly. Heating them too rapidly would cause thermal stresses in the metal, resulting in serious damage.

'We were having a lot of problems,' McBride continued. 'All sorts of stupid fucking little things. A lot of the instrumentation kept falling over. And all the time the Assassin was climbing the walls. At one point I actually saw him hit one of the Indian engineers. Physically hit the poor sod – and he hit him hard!'

'No!'

'Och aye! Knocked him down – right to the floor. I thought he'd broken the poor bugger's nose – there was a lot of blood coming from it – but it was OK. Lucky it didn't start a strike. We would have had one in most of the places I've worked, but everybody here's so shit-scared of Miller that we got away with it. No strong union to take up the cudgels either.'

Foster growled angrily under his breath. The more he heard of Mr Sam Miller, the less he liked him. 'And Mahajan?' he asked.

'He'd hardly been in that den of his all week,' McBride answered. 'That was unusual in itself. He was even running around – well, sort of waddling quickly is more like it. He was all over the place; trying to second-guess Sam so he wouldn't be blamed for anything, keeping well clear when trouble started.'

'Sounds like you had all the conditions for something to go wrong.'

'You're right,' McBride replied. 'And then it did. One minute it's all shouting and swearing and chaos, the next thing the whole fucking place shook. It actually rocked. I saw a mug of tea go flying right off a table.' He stopped the car briefly as terrible memories came back. When he spoke again his voice was puzzled and muted, as though he'd suddenly recalled something. 'It's strange, you know: I don't remember hearing a bang.'

They sat there in silence. The car's air-conditioner hissed softly in the background, blasting chilled air at them as the Land Rover baked in the blazing heat of the afternoon.

McBride started the vehicle again, and as they continued the drive along the deserted tree-lined road he continued his tale: 'I was in the main control room. When I went out – God! How I ran – Number One Unit was a mess. There were huge chunks of steel lying everywhere. Everything was covered with the insulation that had been blasted off the thing. That and dust and ash and God knows what else. I ran over .... God I wish I hadn't. I found what was left of one poor wee bugger lying on the ground. He'd lost both legs, and what was left of his body .... it was burned almost to a cinder. I'll never forget the smell of burning hair. He was still alive; he opened his eyes and looked at me and his mouth opened. But no sound came out of it – only a sort of gurgling – and then he died. There was nothing I could do for him, so I went further in ...'

His voice died out as he remembered the horrors of that day.

They reached the bungalow and as McBride cut the engine, Foster asked, 'Any idea what caused it?'

'No idea really. There was an inquest and the coroner said it was because of a leaking gas valve.'

Foster studied his face carefully as he asked the next question: 'Do you agree with that?'

McBride was quiet for a few seconds before he shrugged and said, 'Dunno. Could have been, I guess.'

But from his expression it was clear that he was not convinced.

Foster decided to change tack, and as they climbed out of the Land Rover he said, 'I'm amazed there's no sign of any damage to be seen now.'

McBride walked slowly round the vehicle and looked thoughtfully back towards the power station. 'Those Japanese!' he said pensively. 'Bloody amazing people! They had a crew on site within 24 hours and the heavy machinery they didn't have here already arrived a couple of days later. They attacked the wreckage, cleared it all away and carried out the repairs in a couple of months.'

'Want to come in for a beer?' Foster asked, but McBride politely turned down the offer, saying he wanted to clear up some things back in his office before he went home.

Later, as Foster and Alexis were eating dinner in her bungalow, she told him how she had spent the day. The driver had taken her to some small villages to see how local people lived. 'It's amazing,' she said. 'It's like the suburbs of London or even Houston, with the addition of wandering cows and dogs.'

'The cows are all right,' Foster said, 'but watch out for the dogs; there's a lot of rabies around here.'

'I know. Aadesh warned me.' She bent down to lift a big golden-yellow ball from a carrier bag at her feet. 'Look at this,' she said offering it to Foster. 'It's a kind of sugar ...'

'I know,' Foster confirmed. 'It's called jaggery in the West, but hereabouts it's called *gur.*'

'That's what Aadesh called it: *gur.* He took me to a place where they make it. It was a tiny place right in the middle of nowhere: a mass of pipes, shallow pans of boiling liquid and open conveyor belts – all under a low corrugated-iron roof. There were a handful of men, women and children working there. Nobody spoke English to me but they understood what I was saying all right. Everybody was so nice, so pleased to see me – made a great show, offered me tea and in the end gave me this.'

Foster hefted the ball of sugar in his hand. 'You must have made an impression,' he said. 'This stuff's quite valuable. It's made by boiling sugar cane. They use it in cooking and to make delicious sweetmeats .. and alcoholic drink as well. It's meant to be very healthy stuff.'

'I gave them a few Rupees for it,' she said. 'They didn't seem to want to take it, but I insisted and in the end I think they were delighted to have the money.'

He gave the sugar back to her.

'What am I going to do with it?' she complained.

'I'm sure Aadesh or Shah would take it off your hands.'

He then told her about his meeting with Mahajan and about McBride's story.

'So do you think Desai was right?' she asked. 'That the accident *was* the result of more than a simple equipment failure?'

'Can't say yet. Peter McBride seems to have some doubts too. But there's lots I've heard and seen today that I don't like.'

'Such as?'

'Things like relentless and interfering pressure from senior management who have little or no engineering training or experience. That rarely helps to get a smooth commissioning process running. And an image-conscious, lazy guy in charge, who gets involved only when things go wrong ... it's all bad news. But no, there's nothing I could find in the way of real evidence of a cover-up.'

'But you'll keep looking?'

'You bet! But there's a long way to go yet.'

He told her what he'd planned to do in the line of fulfilling his obligations to Mizutani, and added that this would give him plenty of opportunity to look out for the evidence he needed.

When Mahaan Shah collected their plates and took them away she took the opportunity of leaning over the table to kiss Foster. It was a long, lingering, exploratory kiss.

'Careful,' he said quietly when their lips parted. 'Mustn't give anybody cause for gossip.'

She smiled, looked towards the door and whispered, 'I can't wait to have you to myself. Can't wait for the weekend.'

'Neither can I,' he answered.

She had settled back in her chair when Shah reappeared with the coffees.

'I've arranged to go down to Hyderabad after the party,' she said to Foster, but also for the major-domo's ears as he poured the coffee. 'OK to borrow Aadesh? I'd like to do the tourist thing for a few days. I might even stay there until you've finished here. Is that OK?'

The request was scarcely necessary; Foster had already told her that she would be free to have the services of the driver to take her wherever she wanted. As for himself, the bungalow was near enough to the power station to walk there in the cool mornings and he could always rely on a lift back from McBride in the afternoons if necessary.

'I should be done here soon,' he said. 'A week's pretty tight for all I have to do, but I think it's possible, so I'll confirm our flights for next Sunday. I'll come down and we can set off from there. If I get delayed here I can switch to a later flight, and I'll let you know. Will you do the same or will you go back to London on your own?'

'No, I'll wait for you,' she replied. 'But you don't really expect any delays, do you?'

'You never know what'll happen in this game. The plant could trip out and be off line for a while, and that'll delay things. But everything seems to be running OK at present.'

'Fingers crossed then.'

'Fingers crossed.'

After finishing their coffees, Foster left the bungalow – but not before Alexis had stolen another surreptitious kiss in the darkness.

Chapter 5

Mahajan's home was in the same residential area and built to the same pattern as Foster's and Alexis's bungalows – only much, much bigger. As Foster and Alexis approached the house a strong, enticing odour – a mixture of curry spices and incense – wafted out on the warm evening air, initially blending with and then overpowering the delicate scent of the flowers and shrubs outside. A red-coated flunky opened the door. He was wearing an elaborate turban with a long sash hanging down his back, and his uniform was resplendent with highly-polished brass buttons. He saluted the visitors and ushered them into the main living room where a girl in a blue sari trimmed with gold thread offered them drinks from an ornate silver tray. They both chose flutes of champagne.

The room was a long rectangular space, the walls totally bare except for portraits of Hindu deities painted or embroidered on silk adorning one of them. Brass ornaments stood on various small tables that were dotted along the edges of the room: they were families of elephants, other gods and – incongruously – models of New York skyscrapers, including the ill-fated twin towers.

A couple of musicians were setting up their sound equipment in one corner of the room, the drummer tapping at the taut surface of a *tabla* while he listened carefully, his head bent close to the instrument.

Here the smell of incense became dominant. The room was packed with a noisy crowd; mainly Asians with a scattering of Americans and Australians – and of course one Scot: McBride.

And it was McBride who spotted Foster first. 'Hello Dan,' he said.

Foster shook his hand and introduced Alexis. McBride gave her an appreciative smile before calling to a flame-haired woman who was talking nearby. 'Fiona,' he said, 'come and meet the guy I've told you about.'

At the mention of that name Alexis shot a glance at Foster. She saw the pain cross his face as a memory of his fiancée was brought forcefully to him.

Fiona McBride was slightly plump and jolly-looking. After they had been introduced she was clearly intending to take Alexis under her wing when an unmistakable shape emerged from the crowd and approached them, closely followed by a small shy-looking Hindu woman with a prominent yellow caste mark on her forehead. 'Ah! My friend Dan,' Mahajan enthused, putting his hands together at chest level, elbows out, in the traditional *Namaste* greeting. He shook Foster's hand, turned to Alexis and gave the greeting again. 'This must be your delightful niece.'

Foster wondered if had detected a slight hesitation before the last word, but concluded that he was just becoming paranoid.

Alexis was clearly discomfited by the gesture, uncertain of how to respond, but finally put her hands together to copy him. She then introduced herself.

'I am Ashok Mahajan,' the Indian replied. 'But you must be calling me Ashok.' He turned to the small woman, who was standing slightly behind him, and inclined his head to urge her forward. 'This is my wife, Kajri.' The woman smiled as she gave them a wordless *Namaste* greeting. 'Her name means "like a cloud",' Mahajan continued. 'She will look after you.'

The statement had been a clear dismissal and his wife dutifully took Alexis off and led her to meet the other guests and inspect the house.

Mahajan caught Foster's elbow and escorted him to a tall, handsome, well-built and bearded man wearing a white turban. 'This is Sundip Singh, Dan,' he said. 'He is Station Manager.'

The two men shook hands as Mahajan watched, plainly delighted to be introducing an internationally renowned engineer to his ultimate boss. It confirmed that he himself was a truly important figure: a deal-maker and power-broker, someone worthy of respect.

'I regret that I have been unable to be with you so far,' the Sikh said. 'Unfortunately, there are many matters that demand my attention at this time.'

Foster's response was interrupted by the arrival of Sam Miller. He was all smiles and affability. 'Glad you've made it, Dan,' he enthused. 'You gettin' on OK? Everybody lookin' after you? Anythin' I can do?'

This sudden show of cordial interest and helpfulness was clearly intended for Singh's benefit. Foster said everything was going well and that he'd be sure to call Miller if any assistance were to be needed.

'I trust that Dr Mahajan is providing you with all assistance you need,' Singh said.

'Oh yes, he certainly is.' Then Foster made a decision.

It was inevitable that sooner or later he was going to have trouble with Miller. Now was the time to clip his wings by effectively forestalling him. 'I've got on well so far,' he said to Singh. 'The next thing I want to do is to see how the present control systems handle load swings.'

He sensed rather than saw Miller tense.

'And you hope that your work will make improvement?' Singh asked.

'I certainly do. Most systems work well enough when everything's steady; they just don't handle things so well when they change. And the further you get below full load, the worse it gets.'

Singh smiled. 'I have seen already this happen,' he said. 'But I do not fully understand why. Dr Mahajan has tried to explain, but I am not a control expert. I would have thought the systems could be tuned to give good control over a very wide range of loads.'

'They could,' Foster said. 'But it takes time to tune the systems. And because everybody's in a hurry during commissioning it often doesn't get done properly.'

'I see.'

Foster bit the bullet. 'And to do it the plant throughput needs to be reduced from time to time. A load drop carried out before I do anything will show how the systems react as they are now; then I'll make changes and do it again. Hopefully it'll show an improvement. Then I'll repeat the exercise – again and again – until everything's perfect.'

As he spoke he could sense Miller's increasing agitation and now the GCR executive burst out, 'That's always the problem Foster. Control engineers are geeks who want to tinker forever. They don't appreciate the hard realities of project financing.'

'But surely what Dr Foster says is correct,' Singh interrupted, 'is it not?'

Miller frowned as he gave a grudging admission. 'Yes, but …'

'Then we must accept some slight loss,' Singh observed quietly, 'in the sure knowledge that in the long term the benefits will far outweigh losses during short-term tests.'

Foster thought Miller would explode in anger, but the American constrained himself and gave Singh a bleak smile. 'I shall remind you of that later,' he said mockingly, and Foster had no doubt that, at some time in the future, he would indeed turn the Station Manager's words to his advantage.

Singh returned to the point: 'And the improvements will be what exactly, Dr Foster?'

'Several. Higher efficiency for one, lower emissions for another, and lots more besides. Most importantly perhaps, the life of the plant will be extended.'

Improved control would reduce the range of temperatures that occurred during day-to-day operation of the plant. This would reduce the stresses and strains that contributed to bringing about premature failure of steel turbine blades and the plant pipework. However, the improvements would be of value to the Indians and they would yield benefits only in the long term; they would not be of any significant value to GCR because by then they would by then have moved on to new projects.

'The first two will be excellent by themselves,' Singh smiled. 'Higher efficiency will cut fuel usage and that will save money, will it not Mr Miller?'

Miller growled a sort of grudging acceptance.

At that point they were joined by a striking woman. She was elegant and tall with high prominent cheekbones and cascades of rich, nut-brown hair tumbling to her shoulders. She was wearing a figure-hugging ankle-length black dress with a neckline that dived astonishingly low between her voluptuous breasts. A small jewelled medallion hung on a thin gold chain round her neck, drawing all eyes to the creamy soft flesh of her cleavage. She was holding a half-full champagne flute delicately by the stem in her right hand.

'This is my wife,' Miller said to introduce her. 'Gloria.' There was a dreamy far-away look in her hazel eyes as Foster shook her hand. While looking steadily into his eyes, her attention seemed to be focussed far beyond him – or well into his being. It was unsettling. On taking her hand he found her fingers were slender, soft and cool; she maintained the contact for slightly longer than was strictly necessary.

Just then Alexis returned from her little tour of the house. She was without Mahajan's wife, who had disappeared off to busy herself supervising the servants. Alexis saw Gloria's hand in Foster's and raised one eyebrow slightly at him.

'Sam told me about you,' Gloria said to Foster, ignoring the presence of Alexis. 'Sounds an interesting life you lead.' Her voice was deep and melodic.

He gave what he hoped was an enigmatic smile and she turned her gaze to his companion. 'And this must be your … niece.' The slight delay was more definite this time, and spoke volumes. 'Sam told me about you.'

'Yes,' Foster replied. 'Let me introduce her: Alexis Marshall.'

The two women shook hands briefly as they contemplated each other warily. Like prize-fighters or gladiators.

There was a strained silence as Miller took Singh's arm and led him off.

'Tell me,' Gloria said to Alexis. 'I understand this is your first visit to India. How do you like it?'

'It's wonderful,' was Alexis' heartfelt and innocent reply. 'Really wonderful! It's much more than I could have ever imagined.'

Gloria gave her the sort of indulgent smile that a mother gives to her daughter. 'People, particularly women, come here with all sorts of fanciful ideas about India,' she observed coldly. 'Sometimes the reality comes up to their expectations, more often than not it doesn't.'

'So far it's been everything I imagined,' Alexis replied, 'if not more.'

Gloria smiled and took a thoughtful sip from her champagne. 'Tell me, Alexis, you're American – so how does an Englishman come to have an American niece?'

'Simple!' Foster intruded quickly and Gloria turned to him. 'My brother works in the States and married an American there.'

Gloria looked back at Alexis. 'And you're in England now …. doing what, precisely?'

As Alexis explained about her work Foster became increasingly concerned. He recognised Gloria Miller's type: clever, inquisitive and, he suspected, quite unscrupulous.

'Sorry Gloria,' he interrupted, 'but I'd like Alexis to meet a few people here. Do you mind?'

'Not at all. But ….' and her voice adopted an inviting tone as she turned her attention to him, 'we must talk together more, and soon.'

Then she stopped and opened the tiny jewelled handbag that dangled on a slim black cord from her shoulder. 'Here,' she said. 'Take my card. It's got my mobile number on it. Call me and we'll have a drink together.'

She passed the card to him and walked away to find her husband.

While Alexis and Foster made their way through the crush of people, she quietly said, 'Wow! "Call me and we'll have a drink" – honestly! Where did that come from?'

'I don't know,' Foster replied, 'but we need to be very wary of her, I suspect.'

'Don't worry, Dan. I recognize the type and I'll be very, very careful. But you be careful yourself: if ever I saw a man-eater …. *and* she was giving you a good once-over – I saw her! Oh yes, she's got the hots for you all right!'

Foster smiled, in spite of his fears.

The party continued long into the night. The musicians soon encouraged several people to become involved in a series of vigorous *Bangla* dances, while servants circulated carefully round them with trays loaded with drinks and a seemingly never-ending variety of foods. The noise built up until conversation became a matter of mouth-to-ear shouting. Interspersed with the usual gossip and discussion of national and international politics, references to the power station were frequent.

Foster eventually decided to make his excuses and leave with Alexis. 'I've got an early start Ashok,' he said. 'Can't be too late. And Alexis is off in the morning to look round some of the sights with our driver.'

Mahajan looked disappointed. 'Oh but the party has not yet begun, Dan,' he complained. 'There is much food to come still.'

'I've had my fill thanks. I really am sorry to go, because it's a great party, but I must. Thanks for inviting us anyway.' Mahajan's mood seemed to lighten at the compliment. His wife was nowhere to be seen.

As Foster led Alexis towards the exit, Sam Miller intercepted them.

'Leaving already, you two?' he asked.

'Yes. Sorry Sam, but I've got a lot to do tomorrow ...'

'And I'm still a bit jet lagged,' Alexis interrupted.

Miller ignored her and asked Foster, 'Just what have you got planned for tomorrow, Foster?'

'Well, I've almost finished taking all the measurements I need. Now I have to analyse them ...'

'Remember that if you want any load swings you'll have to clear them with me first,' Miller warned, and the hard gleam in his eye indicated that, in spite of their earlier discussion with the Station Manager, permission would be hard to extract.

'Don't worry, Sam,' Foster said pleasantly. 'I'll be coming to you tomorrow afternoon with a detailed plan.'

Without another word, Miller shrugged and turned away to re-join the party, leaving Foster and Alexis free to leave.

Soon after the couple left the house, Gloria Miller came out into the cool scented air on the veranda and took a cigarette case from her handbag. She leant against a wall, selected a ready-rolled spliff and turned it slowly between her thumb and forefinger before putting it to her lips and lighting it. She inhaled deeply and then watched the smoke thoughtfully as it drifted towards the diamond-bright stars. Out here the noise of the party was muted, the music little more than an insistent thumping in the background. It was almost drowned out by the continuous chirruping song of countless cicadas in the trees and bushes of the residential complex. She listened, enchanted for a while, then she spoke quietly to herself: 'Well now, Dr Dan Foster, you're an interesting man.' And after a few moments she added, 'And that so-called niece of yours .... now, I wonder ...'

The next day, after Alexis had set off for Hyderabad with their driver, McBride collected Foster and drove him to the plant.

There was a lot to do and soon Foster and the small team that had been seconded to him set about installing, collecting and calibrating all the instruments that would provide the information he would need to perform his assignment for THI. Sometime during the morning Foster made up his mind that he would return to his bungalow for lunch. Although there was an excellent restaurant on site the bungalow was quiet and isolated from the eyes and ears of curious onlookers. It would give him an opportunity to make plans and to read and send emails. On those occasions when McBride was unable to give him a lift he borrowed one of the company Land Rovers to make the short journey without having to endure the savage midday heat, and that is what he did that day.

He had told Mahaan Shah not to worry about coming in at those times: he would look after himself. In reality, he valued the chance to get away from the major-domo's admittedly delicious curries and to snack on a sandwich or one of the samosas that were always to be found in the refrigerator.

He had just finished eating and opened his laptop to send an email to Scott Klein when he heard a car draw up outside. Hastily closing the unfinished message and deleting it he went to the door to see who had arrived. The fierce midday heat blasted at him as he opened the door. 'Oh no!' he whispered as the car door opened and Gloria Miller's elegant leg emerged into the blazing sunshine. He had enough trouble on his plate with Sam Miller: he did not need any more – and from the first time he'd met her he knew that Gloria was trouble.

'Hi there,' she called cheerfully. 'I heard you came home for lunch and I was just passing by ... so I thought I'd look in. See how you were coping.' She stood looking at him, those amazing eyes hidden behind fashionable shades. When he made no move she pushed the sunglasses to the top of her head, looked at him, gave a dazzling smile and said, 'Aren't you going to invite me in, darling? It's baking out here.'

'I was just about to go back to the plant,' he lied.

'Ten minutes won't make any difference.'

Foster considered it, and then decided that he had little option but to let her in. Scorning her would put her on her husband's side against him. He stood aside and she entered, passing him in an invisible cloud of expensive perfume. She was wearing high heels, tight-fitting jeans and a blouse of thin white material with too many buttons open at the top. She was bra-less and her nipples made prominent little tents of the thin material covering them.

'This is very nice,' she said as she looked around the living room. 'Exactly the same layout as ours, only smaller.' Another awkward pause, then: 'Your ... niece not here?' She used just enough hesitation to show that she was suspicious of the relationship.

'No. She's got her own place.'

'Oh. Is she in?'

'No. She's gone down to Hyderabad for a few days.'

Walking with a cat-like grace she moved slowly round the room, looking at the papers on the table and at Foster's computer. He was glad he'd cleared off anything linking him with Klein. She left the living room and he could hear the click of her high heels as she looked into all the rooms. When she returned she perched herself on a tall stool and took her cigarette case out of her handbag. She flipped it open and coolly proffered it to Foster. 'Use these?'

He contemplated the case and recognised the contents. He looked up at her and said, 'No thanks, I've got to keep a clear head this afternoon. I've got a critical meeting with your husband.'

She smiled and nodded towards the open case. 'Oh go on,' she said. 'It'll relax you when you confront the great man.' She stood up and offered the case to him again. The action offered him a good view of her breasts and brought her very close to him. She saw where he was looking and smiled invitingly. He could feel his heart beating as she added, 'It's good stuff, you know. You could have a lot of fun.'

He shook his head. 'Where did you get it?' he asked.

'Oh, there's a lot of it around here,' she answered. 'Lots of bored women in an uncomfortable and lonely environment. Their men away all day and nothing much to do.' She looked down at the case and asked, 'Mind if I do?'

'I'd rather you didn't. What you get up to in your own place is your business: here it's mine.'

For a moment she looked crestfallen, but then she shrugged and put the case away.

'You know what?' she asked. 'It took something to make me come here today.'

Another silence, this time longer. Foster didn't know what to say. Eventually words came to him: 'Look Gloria, I really do have to get back to the plant. Did you want anything?'

A bitter laugh exploded from her. 'Want anything?' She shook her head and continued, 'Christ! You know very well what I want. And I suppose it boosts your vanity to hear it. But the fact is I've got no pride left, Dan Foster. The first interesting man comes along and here I am, throwing myself at him.'

Then she turned to face him and he could see that her eyes were wet.

'What's wrong, Gloria?' It was a natural question in the circumstances, but the wrong one to ask at that point, because she slumped down on the settee, put her hands to her face and began to sob bitterly.

Her response was quiet. 'You don't want to know.'

'Probably right.'

'But you look the type who could care.'

He sighed. 'Look, Gloria,' he said quietly. 'It's obvious you've got problems. But I'm not the one to help you. Besides, I'm only here for a few more days.'

But she was not going to be deflected. She took a tissue from her bag shook her head and dabbed at her eyes. 'Oh Dan,' she sobbed. 'My life's a goddamned awful mess; I just don't know what to do. I'm stuck in the fucking hellhole of a place, in the middle of nowhere, with no real friends, no intelligent company and nobody to turn to.'

He recognised the situation. There were no Western-style shops within a hundred miles of Varikhani; the restaurants were small and poky; there were no bars or theatres; and the women were left alone for day after day while the men worked on site. If they did make friends among the local families they entered an alien world where the women were subservient to the men. The fact that their own menfolk were working for them and their families – to make a better life for them – scarcely mattered.

No doubt when the original assignment had been offered to their partners the women had been excited at the prospect of going to a new, exotic country. The fact of the matter was that they very soon became lonely and bored.

'Turn to?' he repeated her words.

'Yes…. I don't know what to do, or where to go.'

When Foster said nothing she continued, 'It's Sam, as I'm sure you can guess. He's … well, you don't know … you can't know what he is.'

In spite of his reservations, Foster felt sorry for her. He sat down beside her to try and talk …

But that was enough. She immediately threw herself at him, holding him tightly, her head buried in his chest. 'You know,' she sobbed. 'You're the first person I've felt … well, the first one who I thought might get me away from here.'

Foster looked at the back of her head in astonishment. On the basis of a single brief meeting she was expecting him to ride to her rescue and carry her off like some hero from a romantic movie? Was she completely deranged?

'Out of here?' he said. 'That's absolute nonsense! I can't interfere, Gloria, you know I can't.'

He started to lift her head away from him and she suddenly stiffened and turned her face to look into his eyes. 'Sam's a sadistic bastard, you know,' she spat. 'He's got no feelings for

me, no understanding of what I'm going through. He can't …
he won't …'

Foster had no desire to find out what it was that Sam Miller
couldn't or wouldn't do, although he could guess. 'Look,
Gloria,' he interrupted. 'Whatever mess you're in I suggest
you sort it out yourself. There must be other women here you
could talk to, surely?'

'Those bitches? They all hate me. Sam's screwed half of them
anyway. That's why he doesn't want me.'

Foster was seriously worried by now, but even as he tried to
extricate himself from her embrace she was suddenly kissing
him passionately, her tongue probing his lips. Her left hand
was between his legs, gripping urgently at his thigh. Her
perfume and her body pressing against him were evoking an
unwelcome response from him.

But somehow he forced himself to break her spell, and he
disentangled himself and stood up. 'Gloria, I can't help you,'
he said, as calmly as he could. 'I really can't. Now, I must go.
Stay here until you've calmed down. Use the bathroom if you
want. But …' he looked hard at her and concluded, 'Go
home, Gloria.'

As he shut the door firmly behind him and climbed into the
Land Rover his heart was beating strongly. He leaned against
the back of the seat and stayed there for a moment, thinking
over what had happened. As he turned the key in the ignition
he could still hear her wails of anguish. He hoped nobody was
in earshot, but it was very still out there; the hot shimmering
air had lulled even the cicadas into a subdued background
murmur and there were no human sounds.

Back at the plant Foster parked the car as close as possible to the instrument department offices and hurried across the hot gap to reach the air-conditioned cool of the building.

He found McBride and said that he had finished his preparatory work and now needed to discuss the programme of changes to the plant output that he would need for the next step.

'Good luck to you,' McBride said, a bleak expression on his face. 'I've heard that Sundip Singh's given you the go-ahead, but I can tell you now that Sam is not at all happy with it.'

'I can guess. But I *have* to do it …'

'I know that, Dan and, deep inside, our friend knows it too; but he's totally driven by the commercial argument. What he'd really like is for the systems to be optimised by someone waving a magic wand over them.'

Foster gave a grim smile. 'Wouldn't everybody?'

'Well OK,' McBride said, resigning himself to the forthcoming battle of wits. 'Let's go beard the lion …'

Sam Miller's office was located in the swanky suite in the administration block at the front of the power-station complex, so the two men had a fair distance to walk in the heat. As they made their way to it, McBride told Foster a little more about Miller.

On the technical side of power-plant operations, he said, Miller was barely literate: he was a commercial man, an administrator who relied on what he was told by his engineering colleagues.

'What always amazes me,' McBride said, 'is that he can listen to a bunch of engineers talking, take in what they're saying and make decisions. He has an uncanny ability to sort the wheat from the chaff.'

'Quite a trick!' Foster said.

'Aye, he's a clever laddie all right. Quite canny, is the Assassin!'

Foster grinned. 'But are his decisions the right ones?' he asked.

McBride thought for a while before responding. 'Strangely enough they are, at least usually. But the ones he gets wrong tend to hang around.'

'What do you mean?'

'Well, if somebody comes to him with a technical problem and asks to spend money on fixing it, Miller won't sanction it unless he has a detailed cost/benefit argument presented to him. And the argument has to be very strong and positive. He sniffs out any weakness and throws out the request if one isn't forthcoming. In theory you can go back to him later with more ammunition, but it's a brave man who tries that! But nine times out of ten, the original problem is a real one; it doesn't go away just because the financial case hasn't been proven.

So those sorts of things hang around and join a pile of other similar ones.'

'You think that someone with some engineering background would be more sympathetic?'

'Aye. Take spares for example. Some of the kit we have here is already bordering on becoming obsolete. We need to keep a few spares on hand, ready to use if something fails.'

'Common sense!'

McBride shrugged. 'To you and me perhaps, but not to Sam. He's a great believer in the Just In Time principle: don't buy anything before you need it – let the suppliers keep it in their inventory, ready to ship when we yell. We've tried arguing that the cost of buying a few spares and keeping them on hand, ready for instant use in an emergency, is nothing compared with the losses of a whole unit being shut down for hours or days, but he won't have it. "When did that last go wrong?" he asks, and we usually say it hasn't yet failed. That scuppers our chances.'

'But because something hasn't failed in the past, doesn't mean it won't in the future,' Foster observed.

'Right! You understand that, I understand that – any engineer would understand that, but Sam isn't an engineer.' He took off his safety helmet and wiped sweat from his forehead before replacing it. 'Spare parts cost money, and money's something he won't spend unless he absolutely gets forced into a corner.' He looked at the footway stretching in front of them and continued, 'But it's even worse than that, Dan.'

'How?'

'When we first started off on this job we got lots of spare parts delivered. Some smart laddie in our Contracts Division drove a hard bargain with the suppliers; got spares thrown in for free. But one day, Sam takes one of his strolls round the place, looks at the stores, sees the racks-full of spares, and tells us to dump it all.'

'Why on earth …?'

' "Inventory costs money", he says, dump it and the balance sheet'll look better.'

'That's ridiculous!'

'Aye, mebbe,' McBride said bitterly. 'But it makes sense to an accountant.'

'Sounds like the heady days of Enron,' Foster said and when McBride gave a grim nod of recollection he continued, 'Remember when they shut down El Paso Electric to drive up electricity prices?'

'I do. And blacked out California in the process.'

'Lovely people!'

By then they had reached the door leading to the administration block and McBride caught Foster's sleeve to stop him entering. 'Look, Dan,' he said quietly. 'You and I think along the same lines … but you have to understand this: the people at Global are my bosses; the company puts food on my family's table. It's a pretty good life for us … but only as long as I keep my nose clean and my mouth shut.'

'OK, Peter,' Foster reassured him. 'I do understand. I won't make trouble for you.'

They entered eagerly, glad to escape the heat. The reception area was a vast, high-ceilinged room – all glass and chrome, cooled almost to the point of being cold, and with two pretty sari-clad receptionists behind the desk smiling beguilingly at all newcomers. Voices and footsteps echoed faintly off the highly-polished walls and floor.

Foster was already wearing the ID tag that had been issued to him when he first came on site, so they were able to pass the security guard waiting by the metal-detecting security gate. They walked through the gate and straight up to Miller's office.

McBride tapped at the door and the Assassin looked up when they entered. He had been writing in a notebook; now he closed it and glared at them.

'Sam,' McBride said. 'Dan's done with his initial measurements ..'

'And now I suppose you want those load tests,' Miller interrupted, addressing Foster.

'In a nutshell, yes.'

Miller spoke through gritted teeth, 'Neat move, that. Getting Singh on your side last night.'

Foster gave a small shrug and Miller said, 'OK then, what do you want?'

It took almost an hour to hammer out the details and get an agreement, and when it was over Miller emailed his staff, with a copy to Sundip Singh, telling them that, on the next day, the plant would be required to reduce power in ten per-cent steps down to half power, and then come back to full power. That procedure would be initiated on the command of Dr Foster and the plant would be under his control for the duration of the test. He added a warning that the plant should be carefully monitored while this went on, and if any mal-operation should occur the tests should be stopped immediately. Also, he added that ultimate responsibility for maintaining generation output remained his and he reserved the right to cancel the tests at any point and restore full output if overriding considerations were to arise.

It was the best Foster could obtain, and enough for his purposes. The copy to the Station Manager would serve to show that Miller was doing everything he could to help Foster.

And although he did not say anything to Miller about it, the programme left him free to wander round the plant for the rest of the afternoon.

As they left Miller's office he disentangled himself from McBride, saying that there were a few things he wanted to look at. The Scot was pleased to be released from escorting him so that he could return to his normal duties, which had been piling up unattended.

And so began Foster's tour of discovery. But even as he went round with his camera and notebook, events were taking place elsewhere that were destined to stop his progress.

Chapter 6

The furnace of a power-station boiler is a gigantic chamber almost entirely lined with closely-abutting steel tubes. Every now and then the tubes are curved to give way to the gaping mouths of the burners. In operation, each of those burners blasts a huge, hellish flame into the furnace. In plants like Varikhani massive roaring machines outside the plant work endlessly, dragging coal from just below the surface of the land and disgorging it onto conveyor belts that lift and carry it to the plant where it is crushed by the rollers of massive mills until it has the consistency of fine black talcum powder. This coal dust – tons of it – is then picked up and propelled towards the burners by powerful torrents of air. By then the mixture of coal dust and air is explosive and when it reaches the burners it is ignited.

The boilers at Varikhani are of the so-called tangential type. If you could look down from the dizzying height at the top of the furnace, and if you could see past the huge banks of the superheater tubes, you would be confronted by a nightmarish scene, with the burners at each corner of the chamber feeding a vast, rotating ball of fire in the centre.

The fireball is the size of a large house. It is a blinding, enormous, roaring, swirling mass of flame, constantly fed by the burners which can be tilted to move this hellish maelstrom of fire up or down, transferring the energy it radiates to different sections of the tubes. The hot gases of combustion released by the fireball are sucked upwards, past the banks of superheater tubes, heating them until they glow dull red.

The fireball is part of the complex and powerful combustion process that must be carefully monitored at every stage and at all times, including the instant when it is initiated. At that initiation, gas is set aflame by electric igniters and when this flame is safely established the first coal comes roaring up to the burner to explode in a release of energy that blasts the whole structure with heat and pressure.

But before that can happen, great care must be taken to make sure that no gas is lurking in hidden corners. During a period of purging, cool clean air is passed through the furnace, thoroughly scavenging it and removing any dangerous gas before the first burner is ignited. Only when this process is complete will it be safe to proceed.

When the purge period is complete a valve opens to allow gas to pass to the first igniter. With a loud parp! of sound, a powerful electric spark leaps across a gap to set fire to the gas. Electronic eyes watch to see that the burner has safely started and although generally this works, occasionally the igniters fail to trigger off the first flame. In this case, and long before a dangerous amount of unlit gas has been allowed to enter the furnace, the whole process is stopped and has to be started again.

As soon as the electronic eyes detect that a flame has been established, and that it is stable, the first coal is blasted into the chamber. Again, the electronic monitors watch to make sure that the coal flame is satisfactory and again if they are not satisfied the whole process must be stopped and re-started.

It is a critical and dangerous phase of the start-up process and has been developed over many decades to guarantee safe operation. The process is defined by internationally agreed safety standards, and no short cuts are allowed.

Crucial to safety are the electronic eyes that monitor the flames. These scanners must react positively to the presence or absence of a flame; each must not get confused by flames other than the one for which it is responsible – a badly-adjusted scanner seeing a nearby flame can signal that all is well, oblivious to the fact that tons of fuel are flowing unseen into the combustion chamber, only to explode later on. The scanners operate in a hot and dirty environment, a severe test for the electronic components within them, and their lenses must be kept free of dirt or oil films. They are normally cooled and kept clean by a constant flow of air.

All of this was what Foster needed to inspect – and he was appalled at what he found. After about an hour's work in the heat of the afternoon, made worse by the radiated heat from the boiler, he returned, sweat-soaked and exhausted, to the instrument department offices. Making sure that nobody was watching, he hooked his camera into a computer there and printed off some of the photographs that he had taken.

Then, as a precaution, he took the tiny memory card out of the camera and put it in his trouser pocket. It held all the images, and he did not want to lose them. He had brought a spare card with him and he now slipped this one into the camera so that a cursory examination would not show that he had removed the card with the photographs.

Then, in McBride's office, he laid the photographs on the desk one by one. As McBride saw them his face turned white. 'Oh God!' he breathed. 'Where …? How …?'

'I've been taking pictures of things I've seen,' Foster said. 'These are just a few.'

McBride picked up one of the photographs. It showed a tangle of cables and dirty pipes – and one of the critical flame scanners completely withdrawn from its correct sighting position and looking uselessly at the floor. The cables coming from it should have been protected by corrugated flexible steel armour: instead, the armour was broken so that, rather than protecting the cable, it was itself being supported by the thin wires inside.

McBride's shoulders sagged and he looked up at Foster wordlessly.

'They're all more or less like that, Peter,' Foster said. 'Every scanner I saw. Some even have polythene sheets clipped over them.'

'They're always a problem, Dan,' McBride protested. 'The maintenance guys have a hell of a job keeping the lenses clean. It's almost a full-time job.'

'Full-time? Then why didn't I see a single maintenance engineer out there. If it's a full-time job then, by definition they should be always cleaning the lenses. I didn't see one – not once!'

'That's because the boiler's running Dan.'

Foster was astonished. 'You mean it's too bloody hot to work out there?'

'Not just that!' McBride argued, plainly becoming annoyed. 'Once the boiler's up and running the fireball keeps the burners going. If we start another one up the fuel's bound to ignite – the burner's got a fucking big ball of fire right in front of it by then.'

Foster continued to stare at him in amazement, and McBride returned to his theme. 'Anyway,' he protested, 'they do go round cleaning the lenses before a start-up, when it's critical. They're at it all the time then.'

'I bet they do,' Foster barked. 'Know why?' he bent down over McBride's desk so that their faces were just a few inches apart, and spoke very quietly and slowly. 'Because the air you use to keep the lenses clean is taken from the instrumentation air supply.'

McBride's blank look told Foster that he hadn't understood. 'Peter,' he elaborated with sympathy. 'The instrument air feeds things that need to be lubricated, like actuators. The air is coupled to an oil-mist lubricator; it's loaded with oil. That's why the lenses keep getting dirty. The oil coats them and then dust sticks to them.'

Sudden realization dawned in McBride's face. 'No wonder! The maintenance guys sometimes have to put polythene sheets over the lenses.'

'I saw that,' Foster barked. 'What does polythene do?'

'I know, I know. The polythene gets dirty too, but it's easier to clean or even change; the lenses are recessed and hard to reach.'

'That's not what I meant,' Foster said, shaking his head. 'Don't you see?'

When McBride looked at him blankly he continued, 'Those flame-scanners are UV types, aren't they?'

An ultra-violet or UV scanner reacts to light in the invisible range of the spectrum; it is unaffected by visible light and so cannot be confused by the glow of hot metal. When it sees intense ultra-violet radiation it is certain that it has positively identified a flame.

McBride nodded, a puzzled look on his face.

Foster looked heavenward, then said 'Polythene blocks UV, Peter. Think of those transparent plastic umbrellas – sun-screens – that let people bask on the beach without getting sun-burned.'

'Oh my God!'

'Exactly!' Foster said. 'Polythene might help to keep the lenses clean, but when it masks the scanners they can't do their job. They're blind to danger.'

There was a long silence, and then McBride said, 'Leave it with me Dan. I'll sort it out. You've got your optimization to do.'

The following morning Foster went to the control room to find Miller and start the tests they'd agreed. He didn't have far to look: Miller was standing at one of the control consoles, arguing loudly with a frightened-looking operator. As soon as Miller saw Foster enter the room he crooked a finger at him imperiously. 'Foster!' he commanded. 'In my office. Now!' He stalked away and Foster followed, wondering what had happened.

'Shut the door behind you,' Miller said as he took his seat behind his desk.

Foster complied and took a chair facing Miller. 'What's up, Sam?'

'Just a minute,' Miller said as he picked up his telephone and spoke into it. 'Miller,' he introduced himself. 'I want a couple of your guys in my office. Right now!'

He slammed down the phone and stared angrily at Foster.

'You asked me what's up,' he said. 'Well, how's about you tell me, Foster.'

'I don't understand ...'

Miller stared at him and shook his head slowly. 'What kind of idiot do you take me for? What kind of a game are you playin', you bastard?'

'Game?'

'Yes. Game. I had a call from my wife yesterday ...'

Foster stiffened. What lies had she told her husband? He cursed and thought: *a woman scorned...* but what else could he have done?

'She's been lookin' up a few people on Facebook,' Miller continued. 'She found out somethin' very interestin' about your .... What did you call her? Your niece, was it?'

Foster groaned inwardly. What had Gloria found?

'Seems you've been telling us a few lies,' Miller said. 'Quite a few, in fact. Gloria looked up Alexis Marshall. That was interestin' enough. Seems your pretty little niece is married – or should I say *was* married? No problem there, but then my darlin' Gloria looked a tad more into the details. She found a couple of "friends" on the woman's Facebook page. She made contact with a couple of these and guess what? One "friend" thought Alexis was …' he adopted a whining tone, 'one of the sweetest people on earth.' Then his normal voice returned as he went on, 'She had a lousy husband; divorced him and went back to her daddy.'

Foster closed his eyes in shock. The deception was over.

Miller continued, 'Oh yeah, you know his name don't you, Foster – her daddy? Sure you do: but still, I'll tell you – he's none other than the great Scott Klein. The famous scourge of Global Consolidated Resources.'

At that moment the office door opened and two uniformed Indian security guards entered, both of them looking puzzled. Before either could speak Miller yelled at them, 'I want this son of a bitch taken off site – right now. I want him taken to his bungalow. Then you stay there with him. I don't want him to leave. Escort him there and keep him there – *malum*?'

Of course the men understood. They looked vaguely puzzled and uncomfortable but they advanced on Foster. As they approached he stood up, gave a smile and raised his hands to chest level, palms out, fingers splayed, to indicate that he wasn't going to make any trouble for them.

When the small party arrived at the bungalow, one of the guards stationed himself at the front door, another went round the back. Foster felt sorry for them in the heat out there, but he certainly didn't want them inside. He had a phone call to make.

Alexis was pleased to hear his voice, but he interrupted her. When he told her what had happened she sounded worried. 'What'll he do?' she asked.

'I don't know, but I want you to call Desai. Tell him what's happened. And get him to call that coroner – name was Gopal, I think, but he'll know.'

'All right, Dan.'

'You'll need to move fast, Alexis. Aadesh is a company man, so they'll soon find where you're staying – if they don't already know. So, as soon as you've told Desai, tell your father. Then get the hell out of India – as fast as you can.'

'But what about booking a flight?'

'Your ticket's open return, so if you present yourself at the BA desk they'll put you on the first available flight. I'm afraid you'll have to stay at the hotel until the morning…' She started to speak but he cut her short, 'Don't argue, Alexis. Get there – and don't forget your passport.'

'But I can't leave you there …' she protested.

'Believe me, sweetheart, you'll be a lot more help to me if you're outside India.'

After a reluctant pause she asked, 'Are you going to be in danger, Dan?'

'No, I don't think so, but I'll be happier if Desai and the coroner know what's going on. And your father.'

As he ended the call the front door burst open and a profusely sweating and very worried-looking guard came in and said, 'I am sorry sahib, but my supervisor has telephoned. You must give me mobile phone sir. Please. Also camera.'

He extended his opened hand and Foster dropped the phone into it. Then he took his camera out of his pocket and handed it over. He was relieved that Miller had been so infuriated that he had not thought things through in sufficient detail: he had not imagined that Foster would phone for help. Neither had he ordered him to be searched – if he had done so the camera would certainly have been found. Realization had come too late.

Foster had won a few vital moments.

It took nearly two hours, but eventually the police arrived – a young constable and a sergeant presented themselves at the bungalow door. Both were wearing carefully-ironed khaki open-neck shirts with epaulettes and rolled-up sleeves. Broad leather belts supported immaculate light-coloured long trousers. They looked extremely embarrassed but the sergeant saluted Foster and apologised for disturbing him.

'I am to take you to police station sir,' he said. 'To see Sub-Inspector.'

'OK,' Foster said calmly. 'Will I need to bring some clothes, toiletries, that sort of thing?

'Clothes sir?' the sergeant queried. 'Toiletries? No, I do not think you will be needing.'

That worried Foster, especially when a picture came to his mind – of him dressed in a shapeless grey all-in-one with broad black arrows printed on it.

The police station was located near the centre of the small community of Varikhani Township, about a mile from the power-station site. It stood behind a line of tall palms: a long, single-storey building with all its windows protected by stout iron bars. The Tata Sumo that had brought them here pulled up in front of the main doors and Foster was escorted into the building.

Although the day outside was cooling off, the building still retained much of the afternoon heat and the air in the waiting room was hot and musty, stirred by a slowly rotating central fan suspended from the ceiling. The foetid air was further circulated by a table fan that whirred quietly and oscillated to and fro on the desk. The front desk was manned by another sergeant who stood up and saluted when Foster was brought in.

'Sir,' the sergeant said, obviously having been primed that an English suspect was to be brought in. 'You are to see Sub-Inspector please.' He pointed towards a door and came round to escort Foster to it. He tapped at the door and after a significant pause a deep voice from inside called, '*Chelo!*'

The desk sergeant opened the door and waved Foster in, closing the door after him as he left.

The man who had been sitting behind the desk rose to greet Foster with a firm handshake. He was well built and neatly moustached and had a straight-backed military bearing accentuated by a crisp olive-green shirt, again open-necked and with rolled-up sleeves. His shoulders bore epaulettes with two stars and red-and-blue stripes and the name badge above his right-hand buttoned-down shirt pocket identified him as being S.I. Harindra Sharma. His large belly sagged over a shiny leather belt.

'I am pleased to meet you Dr Foster,' he said. 'It is unfortunate that there are some small ...' He looked worried as he searched for the right word, then smiled and finished, '... some small difficulties sir.'

'Thank you, Inspector,' Foster said. 'I am sure there's been a misunderstanding.'

'Most certainly there has been sir. But unfortunately I have been asked to keep you in ...' again the worried look, 'in protective custody sir. But you must be assured I have had the room cleaned for you. And it will not be for long time. But first, would you like tea?'

The tea was sweet and came with the obligatory tin of condensed milk. While the two men sat and drank it they chatted together affably, like old friends.

The cell was indeed clean and smelt strongly of disinfectant, but it was a cell nonetheless. There was a small wash-basin on the wall facing the door and a low bed alongside with a rough khaki blanket lying neatly folded on it and a grey-looking pillow on top. Peeping out from under the bed was a white enamelled chamber-pot with a handle. A small window, set high on one wall was stoutly barred. It was already dark outside so the only light in the room came from a single armoured light-fitting screwed to the ceiling. Thoughtfully, the S.I. had given Foster an English-language *Times of India* to read while he waited.

It was a long wait and he eventually lay down on the bed and pulled the blanket over him, because the night was cold and the chill quickly penetrated the unheated cell. He drifted off to sleep, only to be wakened by the arrival of a worried-looking S.I. Sharma.

'I am sorry, sir,' he said. 'But a very serious charge has been raised against you.'

'Oh? How serious? And who's brought the charge?'

'Sir it is Global Consolidated Resources. They have accused you of no less than industrial espionage.'

'What!' Foster exclaimed. 'How can they …?'

'I am very sorry,' Sharma apologised, 'but I am not knowing every fact sir. But I can tell you that the matter has been taken to a very high level.' He shook his head sadly. 'Very high level, sir. 1 am awaiting arrival of Senior Superintendent of Police from Hyderabad. He will be here some time tomorrow.'

Foster groaned. A night in this place with the chamber pot – it was not an appealing thought.

But in fact, it was not the promised Senior Superintendent who arrived at the cell the next morning.

Fortunately, Foster had managed to persuade the Constable on night-duty to allow him access to a wash-room, so he felt relatively clean and ready to receive visitors, even if his clothes were crumpled. He had even managed to shave with a borrowed razor.

He was back in his cell, sitting on the bed and wondering about what the day would bring when a jingle of keys announced the arrival of a visitor.

'Good morning, Dr Foster,' the arrival said. He was short and very dark, with snow-white hair and small, very round glasses. He reminded Foster of pictures he'd seen of Mahatma Gandhi. 'I am Jivas Gopal,' he said.

'Ah!' Foster exclaimed. 'The coroner.' He was relieved. It showed that Alexis had managed to make the contacts he'd requested.

'Yes indeed, that is my post. But I am not here in capacity of coroner, sir. I am coming as lawyer at the request of Kalpak Desai – whom I believe you know – to obtain your release on police bail, which I have paid.' He looked carefully at Foster before continuing, 'Unfortunately, it is a condition of this bail that you surrender your passport. It cannot be avoided. Do you have it with you?'

Foster took his passport out of his shirt pocket and held it out. It went against the grain to let go of it, but he was confident that he could trust Gopal. The coroner took it and said he would hand it over in exchange for a receipt.

Satisfied with the morning's progress he asked, 'We will leave now. Have you had breakfast?'

135

In spite of being told that Foster had been fed, Gopal took him to his home where his effusive wife bustled about, preparing and serving him an excellent breakfast of two boiled eggs standing upright in little silver cups with neat soldiers of hot buttered toast lying beside them. A mug of sweet, steaming tea completed Foster's pleasure.

'I believe that breakfast in the police station would not be very excellent,' Gopal said with an ear-to-ear grin. 'I hope this is improvement.'

'It certainly is!' Foster assured him. 'A lot better!'

'Now sir,' Gopal said. 'We must resolve the matter of your charge. I believe it is industrial espionage?'

'So I'm told.'

Gopal shook his head and rolled his eyes. 'That is very serious. We must deal with it with utmost caution, sir, utmost caution. I am coroner, not lawyer, but Mr Desai will assist.'

'Here,' Foster said, taking the camera memory card from his pocket. 'This might help.'

'What is this?' Gopal asked as he took it.

'It's a memory card with all the photographs I took on site. They're pretty damning.'

'If it is so,' Gopal said, looking seriously at the card and holding between his fingertips as though it was hot, 'then Mr

Desai must receive it.' Then he thought about it a little more and asked, 'Sir, are these photographs the reason why the company has accused you of carrying out industrial espionage?'

'They probably are. But I see them as evidence. Espionage would imply they would be of value to a competitor ...'

'Yes sir, that is correct.' Gopal straightened his back and looked at the ceiling as though recalling lessons from law school. 'Espionage is defined as the act or practice of spying to obtain secret information, to give to another government or a business competitor.' He returned his gaze to Foster and continued, 'There is small distinction between obtaining evidence and spying, I think. It would have to be argued in court.'

'Indeed, but ... would you be compromised if I sent those pictures to Mr Desai.'

Gopal thought carefully before replying. 'No, it would not compromise me. If we say that Mr Desai is acting for you, he is entitled to receive all evidence. Poor fellow, he has no work at present; but he has not been struck off. He is free to act on your behalf, I am sure.'

'OK then, may I ask you another favour?'

'Of course, sir.'

'Do you have a PC here?'

'A computer? Certainly.'

'Can I use it, please,' Foster asked. 'I'd like to send those pictures to Mr Desai. And while I'm at it I'll pull some prints for you – I presume you have a printer here?'

137

Gopal nodded and beamed a smile.

It was not yet 3 a.m. when Alexis came down to the Novotel's reception desk to check out. She was still almost half asleep and she felt rumpled and drawn. Her eyes were gritty and her whole being rebelled at this assault on her sleep, but her enquiries shown that the next BA flight was scheduled to leave at 6:45 and the drive there, coupled with the long check-in time necessitated an early start. She had set her alarm for 2 and had booked a wake-up call for 20 minutes later, to make sure she didn't turn over and go back to sleep.

The hotel was a pillar of light against the black night and the reception hall had the look and atmosphere of all such establishments at such hours. The gentle glow of lights in the hall was reflected in the windows that shut out the darkness outside. The silence was broken only by the soft susurration of the air-conditioning system and the muted drone of a janitor polishing the marble floor in the distance. Seated behind the long, highly-polished desk, the sole checkout girl on duty was bright and cheerful and her yellow sari with its silver trim lit up the room. Clearly such early departures were routine to her.

'Everything was satisfactory madam?' she asked as she swiped Alexis' credit card.

'Yes thank you.'

'There is no problem?' the girl asked. 'You are checking out before you planned.'

'Oh, yes. Everything's fine, thank you. But I've had an urgent call from London. They want me back home sooner than they'd hoped.'

The girl seemed satisfied: the mysterious "they" were pulling hidden strings, and the hotel was not at fault. It was a familiar situation to her, and therefore a relief.

'The porter will put your bags in the courtesy car madam. It is waiting outside.'

As she made her way to the door, Alexis felt for her purse to make sure she had the necessary folding money at hand for when the porter solicitously opened the car door for her.

Outside, dawn had not yet broken and the morning air was pleasantly cool.

A black limousine was waiting and the driver standing beside it asked, 'Mrs Marshall?'

When she nodded the porter opened the door for her and she climbed in. But then she remembered the tip and tried to open the door.

Damned child locks, she thought as she tugged at the ineffective handle. The chauffeur climbed in and settled himself in front of her and she said, 'Just a minute, driver. I haven't seen the porter who brought my bags down. I want to give him a tip.' He ignored her and she pressed the window button as she searched through the glass for a sight of the porter outside, but he was nowhere in sight and the forecourt of the hotel was deserted. She repeated her tap at the button but still the window didn't respond.

Still there was no word from the driver, and the car began to pull away. With a sudden surge of alarm she realized that a safety-glass screen was rising in front of her, separating her from the driver.

She was a prisoner in the passenger cabin.

With his evidence delivered to Desai, Foster felt he could relax a little. He sat sipping sweet tea with Gopal on the coroner's small veranda.

'I think,' Gopal said as he shuffled through the photographs Foster had given him, 'that these will be enough evidence.'

'For what?' Foster asked. 'The Inquiry's closed, isn't it?'

'Yes sir, but – although I am not an engineer – even I can see that maintenance at Varikhani power station is not of good standard. You have explained to me about the vital role these … these scanners play in safe operation. In this case Global Consolidated Resources, or their representatives here who attended my Inquiry, are guilty of perjury and obstruction, because their defence claimed that all equipment was properly maintained. This is perjury, a criminal matter that I can refer to Andhra Pradesh High Court.'

'And will that mean that the victims and their families will receive better compensation?'

'Eventually perhaps,' Gopal replied with a slight smile. Then he gave a sigh and continued, 'But unfortunately in India, sir, these matters can take long time to resolve. Very long.'

'Why?'

The coroner gave a brittle laugh before explaining. 'Sir, Indian courts have large backlogs; even the Supreme Court in Delhi has a backlog of many hundreds of years.'

'Hundreds of years?' Foster exclaimed in horror.

'Indeed sir. And this is despite average case taking less than 5 minutes in court. But I should say that the correct word for the large number of cases pending is "pendency" not "backlog", because the cases are all pending action.'

'Amazing!'

'Indeed it is, sir. Many cases are very minor: abusing, stealing, insulting … There is much time spent, even though sometimes only a few Rupees are involved.'

He leant forward to pour them both more tea. 'And these days majority of cases are motor vehicle offences,' he continued when he had finished. 'Small accidents, wrong parking, not following traffic rules and so on. It is well known.'

'Can't they move them on faster?'

'No sir. You see, people involved sometimes have several driving licences, each with different address. Real address is never given to police officer, so accused cannot be produced before court for years. Often they are never found. But all the time the case is pending.'

Foster sat back in his chair and stared at Gopal.

'Also there is severe shortage of judicial staff,' the coroner continued.

'How does anything ever get done?'

Gopal shrugged. 'Also sir, you must understand that corruption is very common here. My experience with the Varikhani inquiry was that the American company has influence with senior Government officials. They are ...'

He hesitated and Foster suggested, 'Cosy with them?'

Gopal frowned. This was not the word he wanted, but he was working on it. 'They are entrenched. Well entrenched with officials.'

'I guessed that when Scott Klein was denied permission to enter the country – even though he had a valid visa.'

'Mr Desai told me about that,' Gopal said with a slow, rueful shake of his head. 'But sir, I am just coroner in small Indian town. I may not be able to fight very successfully. Even Mr Desai – his recent reputation will be used against him by defence lawyers.' He shrugged his shoulders, a mournful expression on his face as he ended, 'But I will try. I will try.'

Further discussion was interrupted by the ringing of a telephone inside the house. Gopal's wife came out and said, 'It is a call for you, Dr Foster.'

'Oh?' Foster said, puzzled. 'Who knows I'm here?'

But he went indoors and picked up the telephone.

The caller was Sam Miller. 'You should be happy to hear from me, Foster,' he said.

'How did you get this number?' Foster asked.

'Aha! Wouldn't you like to know? Put it down to an efficient intelligence network. But let's cut the crap Foster, shall we? Because I've got good news for you.'

'What's that?'

'We're withdrawing the industrial espionage charge against you. You're clear.'

Foster was dubious. He tried to keep the suspicion out of his tone as he asked, 'Why the change of heart, Sam?'

'We're nice guys, Foster. We reckon you were just pokin' your long nose into things because you're an engineer, and engineers like diggin' into these things. You saw some things that gave you the impression that … well, you think we're sloppy here. But you're wrong. We know we're clean and can prove it. So no harm done. We've called off the dogs.'

Something in his tone alerted Foster that there was more in the offing, and then it came. 'Oh, there is one thing Foster. I gave you the good news, but there's some bad news too.'

Foster could sense him enjoying this game, playing with his quarry before reeling him in for the kill.

'You showed McBride some pictures,' Miller said slowly and when Foster was silent he said, 'We'd like the prints back. We've got your camera and we'll give it back to you … but naturally, without the memory card.'

So they haven't checked it yet! They thought the images were on it. They were getting sloppy.

'All right,' Foster said. 'I'll give you the prints. When and where do we do the handover?'

'You come back to my office at the plant tomorrow morning at nine. We'll do it then. And don't worry, Security will let you in.' Then his voice became icy as he added, 'Oh, and don't think of makin' any copies. You'll find out why, but I assure you that you'll regret it if you copy them.'

True to Miller's word, Foster was allowed in past the gate and escorted up to the American's office.

Miller lolled in his chair and didn't stand as the secretary showed Foster in and left. He dangled Foster's camera from a finger wordlessly. Foster sat down in front of him, reached into his pocket, withdrew an envelope and tossed it onto the desk. 'It's all there: the photographs,' he said as he lifted the camera and put it in his pocket.

Miller opened the photographs and slowly examined them all. When he finished he put them in a stack and looked at Foster. 'You still think we're idiots, don't you, Foster?'

Foster felt a chill creep up his spine as he asked. 'Idiots?'

'Yup.' Miller reached out his hand, palm up and said, 'Come on. Give.' His tone was cold.

'Give what?'

'We're not idiots, man. Where's the card? The right one this time: the one with the pictures on it.'

Foster shrugged innocently – an action that ignited Miller's pent-up rage. 'Don't fuck with me, Foster!' he exploded. 'I want that card, and I want it now.'

Foster shrugged again and said, 'OK Sam, you've got me.'

Then he reached into his shirt pocket, retrieved the memory card and handed it to the American.

Miller tossed it on his desk and said, 'OK, wise guy. I'll get it checked out. But I know you've probably sent those pictures to Klein. That's why you don't mind givin' me the card.'

He stood up and walked over to the window, where he stood looking out in silence for a full minute. Then he turned and looked hard at Foster. 'I warned you Foster, I can't take any risks. I have to be sure that you don't do anything stupid.'

The chill at Foster's spine intensified.

'I have to be one hundred per cent sure that you don't do anythin' that could harm my company,' Miller continued. 'So I'll give you a deal.'

'A deal?'

'Yup! There's a little weasel of a lawyer who's raised an allegation of perjury against us. He's involved the coroner who bailed you out today. Until that's resolved I need to be sure you won't spoil things. And neither will Klein.' He intensified his search of Foster's face before continuing. 'That's why we're holdin' his daughter – your so-called niece – as a guarantee.'

After the shock hit him, red-hot rage welled up in Foster and he stood up to take a step towards the American but Miller held up his hand. 'Stay cool man,' he said. 'Don't worry.

145

She's fine. Fine and dandy, in fact. The thing is, we know where she is … and you don't.'

When he had calmed down sufficiently, Foster asked, 'You don't think we'll take that lying down, do you? For a start, Scott Klein will go ballistic. You may have stopped him coming here once but you're really going to get him riled now and he won't stop. He'll bring in the US Embassy here, for a start. And I'll get the British High Commission to act too.'

'No you won't!' Miller's smirk showed that he was confident that he had the upper hand. 'Like I said, Foster, she's safe; but you won't want to take any risks, will you? When the case goes to court you're goin' to back us, aren't you? You're goin' to say that you've had a good look round, and everythin's fine and dandy.' He sat down curled his fist, looked down at it and appeared to examine his fingernails very carefully before concluding, 'And we don't want the police involved, Foster. Understand?'

Foster sat down again and inhaled deeply as he considered all the possibilities. Then he remembered what Gopal had said about the Indian judicial system. Surely it was inconceivable that GCR were going to hold her until the case against them was heard – it could take years.

Chapter 7

'I am sorry, Scott,' Foster said. 'You asked me to look after her, and I failed.'

He was sitting on the edge of his bed in the Hyderabad Novotel, cradling the hotel telephone against his shoulder while he scrolled through the addresses on his smartphone. He had returned here to try and find out if anyone had seen anything that could help him find Alexis – a car registration plate, a recognised face, anything. But he had drawn a complete blank.

The hotel manager had been seriously worried. A guest, kidnapped from his premises! With much hand-wringing, he had told Foster that the bell-boy had been delayed when he took Mrs Marshall's luggage to the service lift. Somebody had engaged him in conversation, asking many questions, and when he reached the ground floor she had disappeared. Initially puzzled, he had asked the receptionist what had happened to the guest and it was only when she said she'd been taken off by car that both of them had become worried. The receptionist had called Security and the night manager.

They suspected that a friend or colleague must have collected the guest, but were at a loss as to why her luggage had been left behind. At that time they had not called the police, feeling that they had insufficient cause for concern. It had been a relief when Foster arrived and asked for a room. Perhaps he could explain.

At Foster's insistence the hotel's security staff had played through the CCTV images for him. These had confirmed everything the porter had said: the interception at the lift, his

147

amazement at finding her missing, his increasingly frantic discussion with the receptionist and finally, the limousine drawing away into the night with a pale face looking anxiously out of the rear window. There was much shaking of heads when Foster asked if anybody recognised the man who had intercepted the bell-boy, or if the limo looked at all familiar.

'I shall call the police now,' the manager said, reaching for the telephone, but Foster stopped him with a gesture.

'No, don't,' he said. 'I'm sure it's a mistake.'

The manager looked puzzled and frightened. 'But sir, this is serious problem for us ...'

'I'll take responsibility,' Foster said. 'I need a few hours. I need to talk with some people. I think I know somebody who might know.'

The manager had finally agreed – very reluctantly – to take no further action for a few hours, until Foster returned to instruct him one way or another.

When he telephoned Klein it had been midnight in Houston. The American had been shocked at what he heard, giving rise to Foster's apology.

Then, after a very long silence, Foster heard a sigh of resignation. 'No Dan,' the voice came slowly. 'I know how those bastards work. You were on your own against all of them. And they play dirty. You were on a loser – whatever you did.' Then he added an afterthought: 'I should have stopped her going.'

'But you said it yourself: she's a determined lady. She'd do her own thing.'

148

'Yeah, I guess you're right.'

Foster was grateful for Klein's understanding. 'All the same,' he said, 'I feel bad about it, Scott. And the worst thing is that I don't know what to do.'

'They said not to call the police?'

'Yes, but the hotel says somebody ought to. I'm stalling them, but they won't hold out forever. In the meantime I've decided to call Gopal. Tell him what's happened. I need advice from somebody local, with experience of the legal process in India.'

'Yeah, good idea,' Klein agreed. 'See what he says.'

Foster hung up and dialled the number he'd found for the coroner in his phone's address book.

When he told Gopal what had happened the Indian was horrified. 'Sir, you must definitely tell police,' he said. 'You must be involving them very urgently. At once. If not sooner.'

Foster wasn't sure if that was a joke, but Gopal's tone showed no trace of humour. 'Miller says harm will come to her if I do – at least that's what he implied.'

'Then that is direct threat sir; a criminal offence.'

'But you yourself said that GCR has friends in high places.'

Gopal hesitated before replying, 'That is indeed true, and with police too, I think.'

'We've got no choice then. The thing that's really worrying me is what you told me about the delays in the Indian courts system.'

'Yes sir, that is also true.'

'I can't believe they're seriously planning to hang on to her for any length of time.'

Gopal's silence confirmed his agreement. Then he said, 'Sir, I shall make discreet enquiry at court. I have friends there.'

'OK,' Foster said. 'But go easy, won't you. Meanwhile, what do I do about the hotel? The manager's very unhappy at leaving it there. I can't hold him off forever.'

'Can you not tell them it was mistake? That you have found her and it is all … all right. They will be relieved at that, surely.'

Foster smiled at Gopal's wily cunning. It was indeed a good idea, and he was surprised that he hadn't thought of it himself.

By the time he reached the hotel's administration suite he had worked out the details of his story. He told the manager that he had called a friend who confirmed that their first guess had been right after all. There had been a simple mistake: the friend had sent his personal driver to pick Mrs Marshall up and take her to the airport. It was a generous act of hospitality to a friend who was a guest in his country. But the driver had been stupid: inexperienced at such things, he had misunderstood the instruction and had assumed his task was merely to transport the woman – not any baggage that she might have had with her. Alexis had misunderstood herself: she had thought the friend's driver had been the hotel's and that her luggage had already been stowed in the boot. When she arrived at the airport and discovered the mistake there hadn't been enough time to send the driver back for her bags, so she'd now asked Foster to bring them with him when he went back to London. The message had taken a long time to get through – hence the confusion.

The manager's face lit up with relief when he heard the explanation. Clearly, losing a foreign guest was something of a disaster, but having to call in the police was an action he'd rather avoid having to take. Police cars outside his establishment and officers buzzing around inside were not good for the image. But now: guest found, police unneeded – he was a happy man.

It was early the next morning when Gopal called Foster and asked if they could meet. Clearly the matter was too important and sensitive to trust to an open telephone line.

They met in the Novotel's bar. Gopal sat nervously sipping a cup of Darjeeling tea while Foster played with his coffee.

'I have made enquiries,' the coroner said. 'I have discovered that the company has applied pressure to have case advanced through system, but at present they are not succeeding. Now they have brought in hot-shot legal firm and I am sure they will be forceful.'

'But at the moment a quick hearing's not on the horizon?'

'No, sir. At present a wait of at least several months is to be expected.'

'Christ! And while we all wait, Alexis is locked up somewhere. How can I tell her father that? And what happens afterwards?'

He was really speaking out his own thoughts but Gopal sat there, his head pivoting in sympathy. 'GCR Company will surely wish to discredit all evidence against them,' he offered. 'They hope that, once High Court has heard case – and if the evidence you possess is not available – then the charges of perjury and obstruction will be quashed. Case cannot be re-opened after that.' He looked at Foster and gave a reassuring smile. 'After that time, sir, then they can allow her to go free.'

Foster looked at the Indian's face, seeing worry clearly visible in his eyes – perhaps there was even fear there. 'Maybe. But what about you? Surely if the case is quashed you will be in a difficult position,' he said.

Gopal nodded vehemently. 'Oh yes, sir. You see, it is I who brought the matter to High Court. My judgement would be questioned. And I am fearful that Global Consolidated Resources will take revenge. They are so powerful here that they could ….'

As his words trailed off, Foster could see the risks. 'You think they could jeopardise your career?'

'Oh yes. I could even lose job. I, the Coroner. It is unthinkable.'

His face looked bleak and Foster remembered how the lawyer Desai had been treated.

And as he remembered him, Foster had an idea.

'What about Kalpak Desai?' he asked.

'Sir?'

'Do you think he could help?'

It was a little while before Gopal replied, 'Perhaps sir. Perhaps he could. But I am not seeing how.'

Neither did Foster, but some instinct told him that it was a slim chance at least, and the only hope he had.

When Foster telephoned Klein that evening and reported on his meeting, the American's voice sounded weary and strained. 'So we're no further forward,' he said.

'Afraid not. There's a chance that Desai could bring something to the table. It's not very likely, but I don't have any other options that I can see, so I'm meeting him here tomorrow. But quite honestly, Scott, I've no other ideas. I feel I've simply run into a wall.'

'What about the police, Dan? I know Miller warned you not to involve them but is there a chance you could get them involved without him knowing?'

Foster smiled to himself. 'Anywhere else and I'd agree with you. Give it a try at least.'

'But not in India. Is that what you're saying?'

'Well it's not just India, though we know there's a lot of corruption here. No it's because we know GCR have their contacts in the police administration – look how they got you stopped at the airport. I just wouldn't know who to trust.'

In the long silence that followed, Klein's distress was palpable. 'Christ, Dan!' he said eventually. 'She's my daughter. She could get hurt.'

'I don't think they'd be so stupid, Scott. As long as they keep her safe there's a chance we'll play ball. If she gets hurt ..'

'Or killed?'

'Yes – if they do that they know we've got nothing to lose and we'll come after them – hard. No, while they've got her safe they're in control.'

'Is that why you want to involve Desai? You think he'd know?'

'Could be that, Scott. But I don't really have a definite plan; just a feeling.'

There was another long silence before Klein spoke. 'Look Dan. I think the time's come when we should involve the US Embassy – perhaps even the British High Commission in Delhi.'

'No Scott,' Foster said quickly. 'Those people can only work through their own established contacts, and they're bound to be at a high level. We need to work quietly around the lower levels of the administration; find who we can trust. Let's try Desai first anyway.'

Klein agreed reluctantly and then added, 'I guess this guy could use some money?'

'Desai? Yes he certainly could. He's lost his job and from my meeting with him I gathered he's pretty desperate.'

'OK Dan. When you see him tell him I'm prepared to engage him to represent me. Work out how much he'd expect to get paid and I'll wire the money over. In fact, I'll wire some out now, as a retainer.'

'That's very generous of you, Scott. And though I hate to push a point there's the matter of my bail bond.'

'Right! Who's paid it?'

'Gopal did.'

'Well, I'm happy to underwrite it. Meanwhile, take the bail money out of the funds I'm wiring. You should have it by tomorrow night.'

It was indeed a generous offer, but Foster's researches had shown that Scott Klein had made considerable money from his pursuit of GCR, and these payments would be chicken feed to him. Also, even chicken feed would look like a lot of money in India.

Desai looked ill at ease as he sat opposite Foster in The Square, the Novotel's swanky restaurant. He was wearing the same brown suit that he had worn at their first meeting at

Golconda Fort. His plain white shirt had been carefully ironed, but the open-necked collar showed signs of wear at the points and he kept tugging self-consciously at the sleeves of his jacket to cover his frayed cuffs.

After greeting him at reception, Foster had led him to the restaurant where the maître d' sat them at a table in the corner of the room. Foster said they wanted to talk for a few minutes before ordering their food and the maître d' went off to bring their drinks. Desai had asked for a bottle of mineral-water, while Foster had his usual malt.

'I'll come straight to the point, Kalpak,' Foster said. 'I want you to take on a small job for me. Or rather, for Mr Klein.'

For a moment he thought the Indian was going to choke on his drink, but he recovered his composure and carefully set the glass back on the table before speaking. 'I would be pleased to consider this proposal, sir. What is it?'

Foster explained about Alexis being kidnapped and Miller's implied threat.

Desai's eyes widened at the GCR's boldness. 'That is terrible,' he exclaimed. 'But what can I do about it, sir?'

'That's the problem, Kalpak. I don't really know. In due course we'll probably ask you to act for us in a legal sense, but for now I'd like you to see if you can get any clues as to where they may have taken her.'

Desai considered that carefully. Then he smiled. 'In the course of my work I have met many miscreants in this town, sir. I think if I ask among them, perhaps one or two of them may know a little.'

'Good man!'

The Indian smiled. 'There are many that I shall ask sir. They are not really bad people, not criminals, but they …'

'They sail close to the wind?' Foster offered and Desai nodded enthusiastically.

It was at least a beginning. If Desai managed to find where Alexis was being kept it may just be possible to engineer her escape, and in that circumstance they could even consider using the resources of Desai's 'miscreant' contacts.

Foster smiled at the thought. 'Shall we eat now?' he asked and when Desai nodded he called over the maître d'.

As they ate, Foster told Desai as much as he knew. When he explained about the pictures on the Novotel's CCTV system, the Indian asked him if he could describe the person who had intercepted the bell-boy. 'No,' Foster answered. 'It was a very short glimpse and the image was fleeting and blurred.'

'And the car?'

'I couldn't read the number plate. But the car was a BMW 760. Black.'

'That should help us locate car. It is not very common hereabouts.'

After they had finished eating, Foster reached into his inner coat pocket and took out a white envelope bearing the Novotel logo. 'This is something to tide you over until we are active,' he said as he put it on the table between them. 'Scott Klein wired it over today.'

The Indian left the envelope there for a while, but his eyes never left it. Then, with what seemed to be a slightly shaking hand he slowly reached over, picked it up and put it in his own pocket. He didn't even open it to count the contents but Foster could see that he knew he had just been thrown a badly needed lifeline.

'Thank you, sir,' he said quietly. 'And thank Mr Klein. I am indeed grateful.'

The gratitude in his words was as nothing to that in his eyes.

It was two days before Desai called Foster again and asked to meet.

They sat drinking tea in the bar and Desai took a small spiral-bound notebook from his pocket. After opening it and carefully reading its contents he looked across at his new-found friend and said, 'I have had some little success, sir. After asking many questions and meeting many people I have gleaned some information that may help us to find location where Mrs Marshall is held.'

'Great!' Foster exclaimed as hope surged again.

'But there is bad news too, Dr Foster. From my contacts I have found that Global Consolidated Resources company has obtained assistance from very bad people.'

'How bad?'

Desai sighed and then explained. 'I am afraid it is the D-Company.'

'Who the hell are they?'

'They are our Mafia, sir. They have many … friends, in high positions. Some perhaps in the police services as well. They have interests in legitimate businesses like movies – Bollywood. But also you see, India is important transit point for drugs. Heroin coming from our Golden Triangle is sent to Europe. My country is also world's largest legal grower of opium, and some of this is converted into illegal heroin. Also, Mandrax …'

'What's that?' Foster interrupted.

'It is, how do they say it? – a recreational drug. It is called happy tablets and is popular in South Africa. It was developed here in India, and pharmaceutical industry is responsible for much illegal production.'

'Christ!' Foster exclaimed. 'You're saying Global's mixed up with that?'

'Not directly, sir. But the bad fellows who run these very profitable businesses see value in alliance with them. We call these people *goondas*. It means ruffian. And there is more.'

Foster was horrified. 'More?' he asked.

Desai rolled his head. 'Money laundering, sir. Government has made it illegal in 2003, but *hawala* – which is the name – is big business here. It is useful to drug runners and also to al-Qaida.'

Foster drew in his breath. He could see the value of such ruthless people to Global. The company could use them to carry out dirty business on its behalf.

And no doubt the benefits were mutual.

'So we are dealing with drug smugglers and money launderers?' he asked.

'Yes sir. D-Company is involved in all these enterprises.'

'Can it get any worse?' Foster was almost thinking out his thoughts.

'It depends on viewpoint, sir. Drugs and money-laundering are important sources of income, but diamond smuggling makes more. The gems are shipped via South Africa. Diamonds are also sometimes used to disguise shipments of heroin. It is all closely interlinked.'

'So what are you saying?' Foster asked, his mind cold and bleak with concern. 'That this D-Company has helped Global to kidnap Mrs Marshall?'

'I am not sure, sir. But my informant has seen some activity that may indicate complicity. And they have a BMW car as you described.'

Foster punched his fist into his open palm. 'Got 'em!' he exclaimed.

He took stock of this new knowlcdgc. After a while he asked, 'Can we find where this car is?'

'I am hopeful.'

'How?'

Desai leaned back in his chair and pursed his lips before replying. 'One of my informants thinks he has seen much activity in a house that we believe is used by D-Company. He is asking friend to observe.'

'Good! And if this friend wants to be paid it won't be a problem.'

'Thank you, sir. I will make enquiries.'

After Desai had left, Foster telephoned Klein and told him about the progress that had been made. The American sounded delighted. 'That's great, Dan,' he said. 'Just great! Where now?'

'I'm afraid we're in the hands of Desai's buddy – the one who's watching the house. Once he reports back we can make a move.'

'Can't we plan ahead?' Klein asked. 'So we're ready to jump when the time comes?'

'I've been thinking about that. The trouble is that we daren't involve the police; but I'm not a one-man army – I can't go storming in and rescue her.'

Klein allowed himself a brittle laugh. 'I guess not. Anyway, from what you say these guys are seriously bad cookies.'

'That's putting it mildly, Scott. The main thing is that I'm not going to do anything that'll put Alexis at risk. So at the moment I'm stuck for ideas.'

After another long, expensive silence, Klein said, 'Dan. I'm glad you're there. If she's in trouble I need to know there's someone I can trust.'

'Thanks, Scott,' Foster replied. 'And there's one thing I need to do.'

'What's that?'

'I need to know that she's OK. Really all right.'

'How'll you do that?'

'I'll put on the pressure. They must be ready to talk; they need reassurance that we're keeping our side of the bargain and that we'll keep our mouths shut until the case is finished. As I said before, they need to keep us in line by keeping her alive and well. I intend to test them.'

'How'll you do that?'

'I'll ask to speak with her. I'll try to make it face-to-face, but I doubt they'll agree to that, in which case a phone call will have to do.'

'OK Dan, but take it easy. After all, they could decide there's another way of keeping you quiet.'

Foster gave a grim smile. The implication was clear. 'Possibly. But they can't get at you so easily, can they? I guess they'll rely on keeping her locked up and me worried enough to keep my mouth shut.'

'Yes, but what happens when the case is over?'

'That's what worries me, Scott. That's why I'm not going to wait for it to happen.'

'You've gotta be jokin'!' Miller said when Foster telephoned to say that he wanted to see Alexis.

'No I'm not, Sam. I need to know she's OK, and so does Klein. We're only going along with this thing because we want her to be safe. If you've already hurt her the deal's off, and I'm sure I don't need to tell you the consequences.'

Miller was silent for a moment and when he spoke again he sounded thoughtful. 'I'll see if we can allow you to speak with her on the phone.'

It was an interesting choice of words, implying that Miller was not totally in command of the situation. Foster shuddered. Could Desai's warning have been right? Could the D-Company be more than mere assistants to Global? He needed to know, one way or another.

'There's no choice Sam,' he said, hoping to tease some information out of the American. 'I want to see her, and see her soon.'

'I told you Foster: the most you'll get is a phone call. But, tell you what, I'll fix that to happen in the next hour. Hang around.'

Foster grudgingly agreed to wait for the call, although he cursed silently that he wouldn't be able to see Alexis face-to-face. But at least he'd won something – and he was now confident that it was Global in the driving seat, because Miller had not asked for time to get the D-Company's approval.

He thought he'd try one more shot. 'All right Sam, where can I reach her?'

Miller laughed. 'I'll give you this Foster,' he said. 'You're a trier. But it's no dice – as they say in Hollywood: don't call us, we'll call you.'

Well within Miller's promised hour his phone rang and an obviously excited Alexis said, 'Oh Dan! I've been so scared.'

'Don't be, sweetheart. I'm here and I'm going to get you out of wherever you are.' He heard a coarse male chuckle in the background: he was obviously on speakerphone and her captors were listening in. 'But I need to know: have they hurt you in any way?'

'No, they've been OK. I can't get out of this house but ..'

The line suddenly went quiet. He guessed that her guard had cut her microphone in case she divulged more – bad enough that she's mentioned a house.

Then her voice returned. 'It's all right, Dan. They're treating me well. I've got food and water and everything's clean. They've even got me some nice clean clothes. Will you let Dad know I'm OK?'

'Yes of course. I speak to him every day and he's up to the minute with the news.' A rustling sound came to the fore and then she concluded, 'They're telling me that's it, Dan. I have to go.'

And with that the line went dead.

Foster ran over the call in his mind. She'd confirmed that she was being held in a house, which indicated that Desai's informant had been right. But there were no clues to its location; apart from that brief chuckle there had been no background noise to provide any clues, no sound of traffic or passing trains.

Was there anything in her words? Apart from the mention of the house, had she said anything else?

And then he realized that she had possibly given him a clue: the reference to clothes. He had to call Desai.

Desai was positively animated when they next met

. 'Sir, my friend has found that somebody did buy Western ladies clothes in the bazaar yesterday.'

Foster could have hugged the little Indian. When he had told him about his conversation with Alexis Desai's face had broken into a huge smile. He saw Foster's point: it was unlikely that anybody would set out to buy a complete set of such clothes in this area – all in one purchase.

Desai explained to Foster that he had set his small army of helpers into action. They had painstakingly toured dozens of shops and bazaars in the locality, but for all their work they had drawn a complete blank in and around Varikhani. But then they had struck gold in Hyderabad itself: an emporium in the General Bazaar which specialized in Western clothes. The owner, who by chance turned out to be a distant cousin of Desai, cheerfully reported that just such an order had been made by a man who had aroused the interest of the serving staff because of his anxiety to keep a low profile. This *chaprassi* had paid for the clothes in cash and insisted on collecting them himself. But the store had been unable to provide tee shirts of the right size, and in the end the *chaprassi* had reluctantly agreed for these to be delivered to an address in Varikhani.

It was the same house that Desai's contact had been watching,

I bet the chaprassi gets a bollocking for that! Foster thought wryly. It was the vital link they needed, and a stupid error by a low-ranking gofer had exposed the prisoners' location.

'I'd like to see this house,' Foster said, and his words were met by a furious shaking of the Indian's head.

'No sir,' he exclaimed. 'That would be very dangerous for madam – and for you. My people can watch without being noticed, but a European? No sir, you would be instantly noticed – very instantly.'

'Not if we went after dark. All I want to do is drive past the place – to check it out.'

Desai's eyes widened in horror. 'To check it out sir? Are you planning to make an *attack* on the house?'

Foster frowned. In a way it was exactly what he had been contemplating; every nerve in his body urged him to get her away from her captors. But simple logic told him it wouldn't be so simple: if this was indeed a D-Company operation, and if they were the Indian Mafia as Desai said, they were extremely dangerous people, and he was entirely on his own. Desai and his small retinue of helpers were unlikely to be anything like a fighting force, ready and able to take on a powerful band of ruthless criminals.

'No, my friend,' Foster said very quietly. 'Not an attack. We'll have to be far more subtle than that. It would be foolish to try and take them on with a frontal assault.' He tapped the side of his head and winked. 'We will have to use our brains instead.'

Chapter 8

Foster had difficulty sleeping that night. He tossed restlessly, his mind busily exploring all the options and the risks attached to each of them. His suggestion that they should use their brains had been an obvious one: there was no realistic alternative. But those were just brave words; it was by no means clear to him exactly how they should proceed.

He had finally drifted off to sleep when he awoke suddenly and sat up in the bed. 'God!' he exclaimed to himself. 'Of course! You stupid arse! Why didn't you think of it before?'

He switched on the bedside lamp, scrambled to his feet and went to the dressing table to find his wallet. He pulled a small collection of business cards from it and spread them out on the bedside table. There it was – Gloria Miller's card! He looked at the display on the alarm clock; it was almost 3 am – not the time to call anybody.

He left the card on the table, turned off the lamp and was soon fast asleep. This time the restlessness was gone; he fell into a deep, restful sleep, his mind reassured that another small step had been taken to resolve his dilemma.

The next morning he called her.

'Why Dan! I never thought you'd call.' Her voice was sultry, melodious and inviting as she added, 'Now what can I do for you?'

'I need to talk with you, Gloria. Face to face.'

She gave a deep, bubbling laugh. 'That would be fun! Your place or mine?' Somehow, from this woman it was more than a cliché.

Foster thought about it. He was in Hyderabad, a good four hours' drive from her and his use of the company vehicle was severely restricted. Basically he had to ask Miller every time he wanted a car.

When he told her where he was she swore. 'Shit! I can get down there but it won't be until tomorrow. And then not before 2.'

He could guess that her boredom at Varikhani meant that she made frequent trips to the high-life of Hyderabad. 'That'd be fine,' he said. 'I'm in the Novotel.'

When she arrived at the hotel he was sipping a coffee in the bar. He stood to greet her and she offered her cheek to him. Again, her perfume was overwhelming.

'Darling, you look wonderful!' she enthused.

She put a small grip on the floor and perched herself on a bar stool beside him and asked for an iced tea.

When the glass of tea arrived she said, 'I heard what happened, Dan. I'm sorry. But then, I did tell you Sam was a bastard.'

'What have you heard, Gloria?'

'That you've been drummed off site.'

He searched her eyes. 'Do you know why?' he asked.

She said nothing, but her face coloured slightly. She obviously felt some guilt over having told her husband about Alexis's link with Scott Klein.

'Well, I'll tell you,' Foster said. 'You did some checking and told Sam that Alexis was Scott Klein's daughter, didn't you?'

'Yes.' She shrugged. 'I thought he'd find it interesting.'

Foster's eyes blazed. 'Interesting?' he barked. 'Do you know who Klein is, Gloria? Have you any idea what you've done?'

'Not really. I'd just heard Sam mention the name a couple of times. That's why I thought he'd be interested.'

Foster leaned back in his chair and stared at her. Her face looked innocent; either she was a very good actress or she really didn't know how big a thorn Klein was in GCR's side.

'Let me explain.'

It took a few minutes to disabuse her, and her horrified expression showed that she suddenly realized the implication of what she'd told Sam.

'Oh my God!' she whispered. 'I'm so sorry. I really am.'

'The damage's done now,' he said ruefully. 'He thinks I'm spying for Scott Klein.'

'And are you?'

He decided to come clean; after all, he wanted to use her help. 'Yes. I'm trying to find out what happened when the boiler blew up.'

'Oh, that!' she exclaimed with a shrug. It was as though the incident, with its horrors and the loss of life had been something in a TV soap opera. 'But that was months ago. They said nobody was to blame.'

'Yes, that's what they said.'

'But you don't believe it; is that it?

'I think there's something else. I think the poor devils who died, and their colleagues who were injured, deserve more than the paltry compensation they got – much more.'

She was silent for a few minutes, her face a mask as she sipped her tea and looked into a distant corner of the room. Then she snapped free from her thoughts and asked, 'So what're you going to do now?'

'There's not a lot I *can* do. Sam's tied my hands, and Scott Klein's.'

'Tied your hands? Just by getting you sent off site?'

'Oh no. Far more than that. Sam obviously hasn't told you the full extent of his skulduggery, has he?'

She shook her head.

'He's had Alexis kidnapped,' Foster said.

Her eyes snapped wide open in shock. 'Kidnapped?'

'Yes. He's holding her hostage until the trial's over.'

'*He's ... holding* her?'

'Not him personally. But he's got some pals to do his dirty business for him – and they're a very dangerous bunch of nasties.'

She shook her head slowly in disbelief, then looked down. 'You fucking idiot, Sam Miller,' she breathed, addressing her half-empty glass. 'What have you got yourself into now?'

Foster answered the question. 'He's enlisted the help of the Indian Mafia.' He waited for the impact of this new shock to subside before he continued, 'Although I suspect that while he thinks he's using them, in fact they're using him – if not now, they will in time.'

She shook her head again, then drained her glass. 'Can I have something a bit stronger?' she asked and he signalled to the barman.

This time they both ordered whiskies: his a malt, hers a Jack Daniels.

'All right,' she said as she sipped at her drink. 'You said you wanted to talk. I suspect you want more.' She gave a small smile and her eyes sparkled at the implications.

He ignored the innuendo. 'Yes. I want you to find out where she is, and then tell me.' Although he was pretty confident that Desai's accomplice had identified the place where Alexis was being held, he wanted to get her to confirm it. In the process, it would show that she really was on his side.

And a plan was forming in his mind: a plan that would require Alexis to play a carefully-orchestrated part. 'And I want you to give her a message,' he concluded.

'Is that all?'

Foster nodded silently. 'What I want you to do will be a betrayal of Sam.'

She gave a small laugh and then there was silence while she contemplated the request – and its consequences for her.

'I've got a feeling that what you're about to ask will really finish it for me with Sam,' she whispered, shaking her head. 'You know that, don't you?'

'You're probably right. But you did say you wanted to get away from him, didn't you?'

She nodded. Her expression was sad. Resigned.

'Yes. I knew it would come to this someday, but still … now I'm there … it's a hell of a big step.'

'I know. But, as you said, you were going to take it anyway. And I really do need you to do this for me, Gloria.'

She stared at him and asked, 'For you, or for that girl?'

'For both of us.' Then he added, 'Really, for all three of us.'

She stared at him for a long time before asking, 'So what do you want me to do?'

'First, are you sure Sam hasn't told you anything about the kidnap? No hint of where Alexis might be?'

When she shook her head he continued, 'OK, do you think you can get it out of him?'

She thought about it and said, 'I can say I've heard he's up to something. It'll start a row – God, won't it just?'

Foster guessed that rowing was a normal state in the Millers' relationship. 'He's bound to ask how you found out.'

'Absolutely.'

'Tell him I rang. Tell him I told you.'

She stared at him in horror. '*You*? Rang *me*?'

'Yup! What've I got to lose?'

She looked startled, and then a smile broke on her lips. 'That'll certainly make him think!'

'Think what?'

'That you and I …'

'So what? Give him back a little of what he's handed you.'

'I'd like that.'

He leant forward and held her wrist. 'He might get violent,' he warned.

'I'll say I don't care what he gets up to, as long as it isn't murder. I'll demand proof that she's OK. I'll say I want to see her.'

'Do you think he'll go along with that?'

She shrugged. 'I can try.'

Foster sighed. She was a fragile reed. But she was all he had.

She seemed to push the thoughts from her mind and focus elsewhere. 'Can we eat now?' she asked. 'I'm famished.'

'Yes of course. Sorry, I should have thought of it.'

'No matter. But I need to change; can I use your room?'

He gave her the card key and the room number and she click-clacked away towards the elevators.

Foster was cooling his heels, turning over the recent events in his mind while he waited for her in the hotel lobby.

When he had been ejected from the site he had reported the fact to Klein, and then to Mizutani.

Klein had been philosophical. 'At least we've got the pictures, Dan,' he said. 'Even after you've got Alexis out of there, I'll still need you to hang around until the case comes up.'

Foster wished he had Klein's confidence in his ability to rescue Alexis. He saw the sense of staying on afterwards. Klein had confirmed his room at the Novotel for two more weeks. If the hearing was delayed beyond that they would have to think again.

Conversely, Mizutani was appalled. He obviously thought that, at a stroke, his company's business relationship with their best client had been thrown into jeopardy. From the outset he had made it clear that he considered Foster's taking

175

of Alexis Klein to India would be a foolish and dangerous act, but he had been persuaded to go along with it – even to the extent of obtaining accommodation for her. He had been reassured that the use of her married name would conceal her relationship to Klein. In essence, he trusted Foster.

But now her unmasking had threatened to expose them all.

Nevertheless, any sign of annoyance was hidden. The Japanese believe that showing obvious anger is a loss of face – it is always better to work with and around any situation, however complex or frustrating. Now Mizutani became cool and respectful and Foster could sense the ice that had developed between them. He knew that he had lost a good friend, ally and supporter.

But then Foster's thoughts were interrupted by the arrival of Gloria Miller. She was dressed in a figure-hugging white dress with a skirt that showed off a considerable amount of her tanned legs. She gave him an inviting smile and took his arm.

They took lunch at The Square. Conversation was animated and ranged over many subjects. To Foster's surprise she had a great love of opera and a wide knowledge of music generally. Although still wary of her, he felt himself warming to her. In spite of her trim waist, she had a huge appetite and when they had finished eating she stretched back luxuriously and looked at him, a slight smile on her lips.

'It's getting late,' she said. 'I haven't booked a room,'

Alarm bells immediately rang in Foster's head. 'You're not going back today?'

'What? Endure that dreadful journey twice in one day? Not on your life! I've sent my driver back; he'll come for me tomorrow.'

'Ah!'

'I could stay in your room,' she suggested. She leant forward, rested her elbows on the table so that she was very close to him. Her marvellously luminous hazel eyes blazed as if she was trying to mesmerize him.

'Not a good idea, Gloria,' he said quietly.

'Why not?'

'For a start, I wouldn't want to antagonize Sam any more than I've done already. And you need to keep on his side for a bit – at least until you've seen Alexis.'

She shrugged, dismissing the thought and then, without changing her position she said, 'Now, about Alexis.'

'Who you're going to try and see,' he reminded her.

She nodded. 'Don't worry, I'll see her. I know my Mr Sam Miller too well. But that wasn't my point: she's a nice, pretty young thing. You *are* lovers, aren't you?'

He shrugged non-committedly and she snorted. 'I thought so. But isn't she a bit young for you?'

'That's none of your business, Gloria.'

'Perhaps not, but I just think you're the kind of man who needs someone a bit more … mature, should I say – more experienced.'

This development wasn't altogether unexpected. Foster had seen it coming, but he hadn't thought of a way out of it. He needed to keep her on his side, and she knew it.

'What do you do when you come here usually, Gloria?' he asked in a weak effort to deflect her.

'I stay here.'

'So you could book a room.'

'I could.'

'It would be safer. Once you make the break from Sam you need to make sure he hasn't got anything he can use as leverage.'

A small frown crossed her face. 'That's right, I suppose.'

'And if you spent the night away from home with no proof of where you'd stayed it would look bad for you. Especially as I'm in this hotel. Someone's bound to notice.'

She gave an exasperated sigh. 'Do you know if any rooms are free?'

'No, but I can find out.'

'No. I should ask. As you said, someone's bound to notice and it'll be more obvious if you make a reservation for me. I'll go down.'

Luckily, a room was available, on the floor below Fosters. She rang his room from there and gave him the number.

'I'm going down to the pool as soon as it's cooled off a bit,' she said. 'Join me for dinner?'

Foster consented, but he was deeply unhappy about the way things were developing. From the outset he had recognised Gloria's type: dangerously voracious and manipulative, a man-eater. But he was trapped; she was the only key he had to finding and – hopefully – rescuing Alexis from her abductors.

He gave a grim smile. As a young man he would have fantasized about the situation he was in: forced to succumb to the lustful desires of a beautiful woman. But now, faced with the reality, he was faintly repelled by the prospect. But could he persuade Gloria to help him without giving her what she so obviously wanted?

To avoid being too obvious by eating at the Novotel, they took a taxi to a restaurant in the upmarket quarter of Banjara Hills. They were enjoying their desserts when Gloria finally returned to the subject of Klein's daughter. She asked, 'This Alexis, your girl-friend – are you in love with her?'

He stared levelly at her. 'I told you before, that's none of your business.'

'Perhaps not, but it matters.' She leant forward and gave him the full benefit of a view down her cleavage while her eyes challenged him. 'I'll come to the point right away. I haven't got room for time-wasters in my life. The question is this, Dan Foster: are we going to bed or aren't we?'

Foster thought about it. She was very beautiful, and he was sure that sex with her would be wild and passionate, but indulging in it would undoubtedly draw him even further into her trap.

He parried her question. 'What about Sam?'

She laughed. 'I told you. There's nothing between us anymore. He's screwing around everywhere anyway.'

'He's a piece of work, isn't he?'

Before answering, she leant back in her chair again and looked into the distance beyond his shoulder. When she spoke her voice was very quiet. 'You don't know the half of it, Dan.' There was a look of anguish in her face and suddenly Foster felt sorry for her.

'Hurting him won't solve anything, Gloria,' he said sympathetically.

Her eyes returned to him. It was an unsettling experience, as ever. 'You mean by being unfaithful?' she asked, and before he could respond she said. 'It wouldn't be the first time, and it's never changed anything.'

'Does he know?'

'Of course! I make it a point of telling him.'

Foster decided that he couldn't even begin to understand the Miller's relationship.

'But we're fencing with each other, aren't we,' she said, and there was a hard edge to her tone. 'Are we going back to the hotel now, to your bed or mine, or are we going to sit here talking through the whole bloody night?'

He sighed, and then made up his mind. He signalled to the waiter, asking for the bill and when he looked back at Gloria she was smiling triumphantly.

Sex with her was as wild and uninhibited as he had imagined, and when he finally subsided beside her, exhausted, she gave an enormous sigh of satisfaction. They lay together for some time, letting the cool draughts of the air conditioning waft across their sweating skin. There was no touching of hands together as lovers do; there was only the heat of sheer animal passion, now slowly subsiding.

'You know,' she said finally, 'you're quite something.' She gave a grin and added, 'I'm tempted …'

Her voice trailed off and he asked, 'Tempted?'

'To keep you… for myself.'

He tensed and she rolled over to face him. She ran a finger through the thick mass of dark curly hair on his chest. 'I'm tempted to keep you my prisoner, my slave, for as long as I can. I'll tease you, dangle you from my finger, make you

satisfy me as long as I can. To do unspeakable things to me …
for me.'

He raised himself on one elbow and stared at her. He
desperately needed her to play her part, to lead him to where
Alexis was hidden. But suddenly she had turned into
Scheherazade, spinning out her fate – and his – with endless
promises.

But then she smiled and her finger came to his lips. 'Don't
panic, my love. I'll do what you want. I'll find her for you.'

He kissed the tip of her finger. 'I need that,' he said.

Again they lay down in silence until eventually she said,
'What'll you do, Dan? When you know where she is.'

His answer was a long time coming. 'I don't know. I really
don't know. I wish I could raise an army, but … Well, that's
not going to happen, is it?'

'Whatever you do, you'll need to get her away quickly.'

'I know.'

'Where's her passport?'

'Don't know. I asked her to take it with her. And since they
lifted her on her way to the airport I assume she had it with
her.' He shrugged and added, 'But then, they might have
taken it from her. I just don't know.'

'I'll try and ask her if she's got it. When I see her. That is, *if* I
see her.'

He gave a grim smile. 'You have to, Gloria.'

She pursed her lips. 'And what about her ticket?'

'Same thing. But this time there's an option, at least: if she hasn't got it I can just buy her one at the airport.'

'That girl's going to be travelling light,' she observed. 'Really light.'

'Mmm.'

She propped herself up on her elbows. Without looking at him directly she said, 'You know, Dan, I'm scared.'

'Scared? Of what? Of what's going to happen?'

She sighed. Then, still avoiding his eyes she answered, 'No. Not just that – although that's scary in itself. It's me… You…' She turned her face to his. 'I guess I thought I had everything under control – myself, my feelings, and my life. And then you happened. And now I don't know what's happening to me. I'm not in control of myself any more. *That's* what scares me.'

He looked at her and shook his head. Then he reached across, pulled her face to his and kissed her gently.

She smiled as their lips parted and then said, 'Alexis… She's just a girl, Dan. You know that.'

'I know.'

'You need someone more experienced – a woman.'

A long silence followed. When he eventually spoke his voice was drowsy. 'Go to sleep, Gloria.'

Her driver called to collect her in the morning. But before she left, one small thing happened that puzzled him at the time, although everything became clear some days afterwards: as she left the shower room, drying her hair, she was smiling broadly and her eyes were dancing.

'What?' he asked, looking at her quizzically.

'Never you mind!' she said. 'I've just thought of a way to tell Alexis.'

In spite of his questions she refused to say any more and eventually Foster gave up. After she had dressed and packed he kissed her lightly and then left to return to his room. There was to be no public display of fond farewells in the hotel lobby, in case inquisitive eyes were watching.

Back in his room, Foster threw himself on the bed, folded his arms behind his head and lay there thinking for some time. His thoughts were a confused jumble: Gloria, Alexis – what had he done and what was happening to him? He felt vaguely guilty about spending the night with Gloria, but he realized that he had had little choice. It had been a duty, but he could not deny that it had been pleasant, and the experience had made him think about his feelings for Alexis.

Eventually he sat up and found his mobile. Before Sam Miller had found him out, it had always been painful having to remember Klein's number each time he wanted to call him, but now he only had to look up the number in the phone's address book. When he got through he explained – in the barest outline – what had happened.

'She straight up, Dan?' Klein asked. 'Can you trust her?'

'I hope so. Fact is, she hates her husband. It's real she-cat, scorned-woman hatred, believe me. She's ready to leave him, and if she can hurt him she will.'

'This'll sure do that!' Klein agreed. 'But isn't it stretching things to expect her to find Alexis, tell her when you're coming for her, and then to pass the information to you?'

'Probably. But she's going to try. And, besides, remember that it's the only card I've got in my hand.'

'I guess so.' Klein still sounded unhappy, but then he turned to other matters. 'What about that guy Desai? Anything new from him?'

'Not yet, but it's early morning here still.'

'Jeez! I keep forgetting the time zones.'

Almost as soon as the call ended, Foster's mobile rang. It was Desai. 'I have confirmation, sir!' he said, sounding excited. 'My informant has seen a lady in that house. She is European. She never leaves house, but he has seen her at window.'

'Great!' Foster exulted. 'Any idea of how she's being guarded?'

'Oh yes sir. It is mostly two fellows in the day and two others at night. They are bad men – *goondas*.'

'*Mostly* two?'

'Yes sir, sometimes another man comes. He is some sort of supervisor, I think.'

'Does he ever come at night?' Foster knew that if he was going to release Alexis, his only hope of escape would be to take her directly to Rajiv Gandhi Airport and get her on a flight as quickly as possible. Since the London-bound flights left early in the morning, and because he might have to buy her a ticket, he would need to get her to the airport before 4 a.m., which meant he would have to get her out of the house by 3 at the latest. It would be hard enough with two guards on duty; his only hope was the element of surprise; the presence of any more guards would make the task just about impossible.

'We do not think so,' Desai replied. 'He seems to come only in the middle of morning.'

Foster thought for a moment. All the half-constructed plans that had been forming in his mind over the past few days now needed to be finalized. 'Kalpak,' he asked. 'When the time comes I'll need a driver to take us to the airport. It'll be early in the morning. Think you can arrange that?'

Without any hesitation Desai said, 'Yes, sir. I will myself drive.'

Foster wondered if the lawyer would be up to any rough-and tumble: he didn't look the type. But he asked anyway. 'Do you think you'd be able to help me get her out of the house?'

It was a while before Desai replied, and then his admission came in a sad voice: 'Sir, I think I would be an encumbrance to you.'

'Don't worry,' Foster said, although he knew the task ahead of them did really need more muscle. 'Hopefully I'll be in and out before they realize what's happened. But if anything goes wrong and somebody spots you – or gets sight of your car's number-plate – they'll come after you. And they take revenge very seriously, these guys.'

Desai was again silent before he smacked his forehead as if an idea had suddenly occurred to him. 'I have it, sir!' he exclaimed. 'If we use third-party driver he can say he knows nothing; that he was hired for just that one task. And I know just the right fellow. He is reformed *badmash*, but he would be useful to you in other ways as well as driving. He could go with you when you enter house.'

'Good! Tell him he'll be paid well.'

Gloria called him the next morning. Her voice sounded strange, though he couldn't be sure what was odd about it. 'I've found her,' she said. 'You were right. Sam's hired some goons to keep her locked up, but I told him I knew all about what was going on.'

'And what did he say?'

Her reply sounded as though it came from a tight throat: 'He went ape, Dan. Totally, completely berserk. Told me I was a stupid interfering bitch who didn't know what was good for me. Then he asked me how I'd found out. I said what you told me to say: that you'd told me.'

Foster could scarcely begin to imagine the scene that must have followed: the blind fury, the resentment, the hatred … and what else? 'What did he say?' he asked.

'Better I don't say. But then I told him I wanted to know that he hadn't done anything even more stupid; said I wanted to see her – to prove to myself she was OK.'

'Did he agree?'

Her long silence spoke volumes. Then she said, 'Yes, finally. But as I suspected, he's going to take me to see her and he'll be standing right beside me every second.'

'Oh bugger! I should have worked that out when I said you should tell him I'd phoned you.'

'Don't worry about it,' she said. 'I know him, remember? I expected it, so I've worked out how to do it. I told you I had. But you need to tell me what the message will be.'

Foster thought for a few seconds, and then he asked, 'When're you going to see her?'

'He said tomorrow.'

'OK. Then tell her – I don't know how you'll do it, but tell her – that I'll be coming to get her out at 2 a.m. the next morning. She's to be ready, dressed and with her passport and ticket.' Then he remembered and cursed, 'Sod it, they won't be there, will they? We don't know where they are.'

He thought he detected a chuckle as she replied, 'Think again!'

Foster could have leaped with joy. 'You've found them?'

'I've found the passport.'

'Never mind. That's enough! How did you do it? Where were they?'

This time her chuckle was clearly audible as she answered. 'Sam Miller may be a clever, devious, calculating bastard,' she said, 'but his one weakness is that he always underestimates me – as he's done this time.'

'How?'

'He's got a safe at home. But I learned the combination of that many months ago. The stupid bastard wrote it down in a notebook and I found it. As a result I know a lot of his dirty little secrets.'

'The passport was there?'

'Yes indeedie! And don't worry, it's still there. I didn't want him to find it missing before we're well and truly ready. He'd guess what we're up to and, more importantly for me, he'd know I knew the combination. That's why I'm very careful to put everything back exactly as I found it, every time I take a look.'

'Attagirl! All you need to do now is to give her the message and her passport.' Then another thought hit him and he added, 'Tell her to leave her light on. It'll help me find the room she's in. But tell her to turn it off as soon as I tap on her door – we don't want light flooding out and alerting anybody.'

He was still hoping to snatch Alexis while her guards were asleep.

'Is there anything else?' Gloria asked.

'No. That's all.'

Chapter 9

It was the night of the planned rescue. The moon was half full, the three men who had gathered in the garden were surrounded by buildings and trees that were little more than featureless grey shapes. Desai's reformed *badmash* was called Ram Lal. He was dark-skinned, tall, bearded and muscular and as Foster sized him up he judged he would be more than useful in dealing with Alexis' abductors – should they wake. In the pale glow of the moon the broad grin that Ram Lal gave Foster exposed a set of brilliantly white teeth. The two men exchanged silent *Namaste* greetings while Desai hovered excitedly nearby, a dark shadow against many others.

Foster strained his ears to find any human sounds above the pervasive music of the cicadas, but all seemed quiet. The three men began to creep stealthily towards the house, placing their feet on the ground with cat-like stealth.

It was a sprawling single-storey building, surrounded by rough hedges of shrubbery. All was dark except for a line of light lining the edge of a blind at one window. Foster gave a grim smile: it seemed that at least part of his message had got through to Alexis.

Ram Lal got to the door first. Foster half expected to hear a soft click as the Indian picked the lock open but to his surprise the door swung silently open without any coercion. It was apparent that the D-Company's known links to the house afforded it considerable protection from petty thieves of the district, Moreover, no rescue mission was expected. Who would be foolish enough to tweak this particular tiger's tail?

The trio crept carefully through the door and looked around in the pale glow of moonlight that filtered through the simple blinds at the windows.

They didn't have to look far. Loud snores pinpointed the location of the two sleeping occupants. One was sprawled on a simple *charpoy*. The rough blanket that covered him was drawn up over his shoulders and head so that only a mop of long black hair was exposed.

The second man was lying in a deck-chair, his head tilted against his shoulder. A thin line of spittle trailing from his open mouth down his beard glistened in the moonlight and his chest rose and fell in synchronism with his loud rasping snores.

Foster was undecided: should they leave the men undisturbed while they searched for Alexis, risking a commotion if the guards woke, or should they deal with them now? But the decision was taken for him by Ram Lal, who tiptoed behind the chair. He stood there for a second or two and then slowly lowered his hands until they were alongside the guard's head. Then suddenly, in a single smooth movement he grasped the head and violently twisted. There was a small, muffled snapping sound and the suddenly lifeless body slumped into the chair like a heavy bag of laundry. It was all over before the guard was fully awake and no sound had escaped his lips. Foster drew in his breath in shock but before he could speak or act, Ram Lal put his finger to his lips and beamed. Then he crept to the charpoy and meted out the same violent punishment to the second guard.

'Christ!' Foster whispered. Desai had said the man was reformed, but he had just casually murdered two men.

Foster looked at Desai. 'That was not what we agreed,' he whispered, but he saw from the little lawyer's round eyes that he was equally shocked and surprised.

'These men are devils,' Ram Lal said with a shrug, as though his victims had been less than human. 'We must not take risk. Now nobody can identify us.' Seeing his words had not adequately consoled Desai he added, 'We will be going away from here in few moments. People will say afterwards that some *chota* thief broke in and did this, not knowing all facts. D-Company will look everywhere, but they will not see us.'

Desai was visibly trembling by now and Foster thought he could hear the faint sound of chattering teeth.

'Come on,' Foster commanded. 'Let's find her and get away from this place – fast.'

But suddenly they all froze. A faint sound had come from the door they had just entered. It was just a tiny, momentary clink of something metallic. And then silence returned.

Ram Lal's fingers shot up to his lips, signalling the need for silence, and he put out his other hand, palm down, to indicate that they should not move. They held their positions for a moment, scarcely daring to breathe, while the bearded Indian glided toward the door. His movement was stealthy and he covered the distance without any sound until he was standing just inside the door, waiting.

After a few tense seconds a shadow blocked the moonlight and then a figure appeared in the doorway, moving slowly and cautiously into the room. Ram Lal moved swiftly, expertly. In a blur of movement he had the newcomer in his grasp from behind, his hand over the mouth to suppress any shout of alarm.

Foster started in amazement: it was Gloria Miller.

Her head was held back by the Indian's grasp across her mouth and she struggled vainly against the muscular arm that pinioned her to her captor's chest. Foster saw that, amazingly in the darkness, she had been wearing large sunglasses, which were now tilted at an absurd angle across her cheek.

'Don't move, Gloria,' Foster breathed. 'Don't make a sound.'

She shook her head and the Indian released her. Gloria readjusted the shades across her eyes. Ram Lal looked bewildered as he whispered, 'A lady sir? You know her?'

Foster nodded and then Gloria' caught sight of the two bodies and her hand flew to her mouth. She looked horrified. 'Are they asleep?' she whispered and Foster shook her head and drew a finger across his throat.

'Dead?' Gloria gasped. 'Oh Christ! How horrible. Did you …'

Foster shook his head. 'No. Let me introduce Ram Lal; my helper, driver and now my tame assassin.'

The Indian beamed cheerfully, but Gloria's expression didn't change. Clearly, she had never encountered violent death before and the proximity of the two corpses was horrible for her.

'Let's find Alexis and get the hell out of here,' Foster said, turning towards the door behind him. There was a pale line of light at its threshold and he pointed at it. Gloria nodded and Foster tapped gently on the door. There was a short delay, then there was a quiet click and the light went out.

Foster smiled; she had received all his instructions and was following them to the letter.

But then he realized that, with both guards dead, there was little need for creeping around in the dark. He reached over to the switch and turned on the light. As the room was illuminated he looked at Gloria – and immediately saw why she had been wearing those dark glasses. Her left cheek was bruised and swollen. He reached over to her. She caught at his wrist but he lifted the shades.

Her eyes were almost completely closed by folds of heavily bruised skin, the whites bloodshot.

'Sam?' he asked and she nodded.

They were losing precious minutes and sympathy could be left to later. Now he needed to get to Alexis. He turned back to the door and saw a key protruding from the lock. Foster turned it and opened the door.

Alexis was sitting on a bed, cowering and visibly shaking from fear. She recognised Foster immediately and flung herself into his arms with a sob and said, 'Oh Dan! It *is* you.'

'Yes, sweetheart. I've come to get you out.'

'I've been so scared...' She stopped suddenly as she saw the two corpses and gave a sharp intake of breath. Foster turned her head so that she was shielded from the sight. She recovered her thoughts and continued, 'I just didn't know what was happening. I still don't understand at all. But when Gloria got that note to me ...'

'A note!' He swung round to look at Gloria. 'How on earth?'

Gloria looked down at her fingernails. 'Clever, aren't I?' she said, smiling. 'I told you I'd thought of an idea when I was in the bathroom at the Novotel.'

Foster felt Alexis tense in his arms but before anything more could be said Desai was pulling at his sleeve. 'Sir, we must get away from here.'

'Yes sahib,' Ram Lal agreed. '*Juldi.*'

Foster and Alexis went in Desai's car, a Honda. Gloria piled in behind Ram Lal in his vintage Ambassador and the two vehicles started for the airport.

Sam Miller turned over in his bed and opened his eyes. He had been tossing and turning all night, sleeping only fitfully. He had drunk two or three litres of beer before falling naked into bed and now his bladder was driving him. He struggled to his feet and headed for the bathroom.

When he returned he rubbed at his face and eyes. Then he went to the door of the separate bedroom where Gloria slept. He could hear his own breath snorting from his nostrils as, with his first need assuaged another one grew.

Two needs, in fact. First he needed sex: hot, hard and violent sex. Then, he hadn't adequately dealt with his wife for her earlier misdemeanours, her undoubted fling with that interfering Limey. Now he would address both needs. Her screams of terror and pain would not be heard by anybody else.

He opened the door and walked towards the bed. The sheets and duvet were piled in a heap which he first mistook for her body.

When he realized the bed was unoccupied he swore loudly.

He spun round and stormed through the house in a fruitless attempt to find her. Then, careless of his nudity, he burst out into the small garden that led to the road. He stood there for a moment. Her car was missing.

He ran back into the house and went to her wardrobe. He flung open the doors and looked about. He rarely took any notice of her possessions and couldn't be sure, but he suspected that some clothes were missing. He snatched at dresses, skirts and blouses, careless of tearing them off their hangers and flung them to the floor.

'You fucking, crazy bitch!' he exploded into the void. 'What've you done now?'

He whirled round and ran back to his room to dress, all the while ranting, 'I'll find you! I'll find you, you whore, and when I do you're going to pay for this.'

He flung on shorts and a shirt and pushed his feet into a pair of trainers and was about to leave the house when a sudden thought stopped him. He kept a pistol in his safe; he'd take it – perhaps only to frighten her, but …

He ran back to the safe, dialled the combination and swung the door open. Then he stared in amazement. The weapon wasn't there.

Unwilling to believe what he saw he grabbed at the papers in the steel chamber and tossed them on the floor. Then he froze.

The passport! The fucking American woman's passport. Where was it?

He scrabbled at the heap of papers on the floor in case he'd missed it and then sat back on his haunches. His body was tensed with rage and frustration but his mind was suddenly icy calm.

Now he knew where she'd gone.

Then he ran out to his car.

Dust and dirt erupted out from behind the Range Rover's tyres as it surged away from the house into the night. Blind fury was driving his actions now and he swung the car violently through the narrow streets, oblivious of any person or animal that may have tried to cross his path. The house was only a mile or so from his bungalow, but he had no way of knowing how much of a head start she'd had. As he roared towards a crossroads he dropped his eyes to his watch … and at that moment when his attention was distracted a Honda shot across his path. He looked up in horror and instantly slammed on the brakes.

With a scream of protest from its smoking tyres his car started to slow its onward rush. He swung desperately at the steering wheel until he was almost broadside on to the other car, but by then the Honda had almost cleared the junction and they passed, flank to flank, within inches of each other.

Then Miller's eyes widened in horror as he realized that he was now heading straight into the path of a battered Ambassador that was hard on the heels of the Honda. For a moment he was looking straight into the startled eyes of its driver, and then the two vehicles collided head on.

By then Miller's Range Rover had almost come to a standstill, but the Ambassador slammed into it at almost 40 miles per hour. There were no such things as air bags to protect the driver, and Ram Lal had not been wearing a seat belt. He was catapulted through the windscreen, head first. His skull was shattered like an eggshell by the glass and the cruel shards shredded his flesh and muscle as his body was propelled by inertia out of the car.

The two vehicles came to rest in a steaming heap of tangled metal, shards of glass and the bleeding fragments of a dark body.

Alexis gave a short sharp scream of horror at the sight of the carnage. Then the Range Rover driver's door swung open drunkenly and Sam Miller fell out of it. He stumbled to his feet and staggered towards the Ambassador's rear door. He yanked it open – and found himself staring at the broken body of his wife. She was badly injured but conscious and when he recovered from the shock of the accident and his surprise at realizing that it was her he screamed, 'You fucking crazy bitch! What have you done? Where is she?'

His words woke Gloria and she stared at him uncomprehendingly. Then he reached forward and he tugged at her, regardless of the further damage he was inflicting on her maimed body. She gave a single short scream of agony.

Inside the Honda, the three occupants stared at the unfolding drama. Then Foster turned and thumped Desai's shoulder.

199

'There's nothing we can do here,' he yelled. 'But we have to get away from this. Now!'

Desai came to his senses and started the car.

Behind them, people had started to emerge from the nearest houses to investigate the commotion that had interrupted their sleep.

'But Dan!' Alexis cried, 'We have to do something. We must help. She's hurt.'

Foster shook his head. 'It's too late. She's going to need an ambulance and by the time it gets here, and when the police have stopped questioning us you'll have missed your only chance of getting away from here.'

In fact, as the scene disappeared from their view, Gloria Miller died. But she died smiling. The last words from her bleeding mouth were venomous: 'I've done it at last, you bastard,' she breathed into her husband's face. 'I've really fixed you up this time.'

They encountered no more traffic until they neared the perimeter of Rajiv Gandhi International. As the lights of the airport appeared they were joined by a few cars, buses and trucks converging on the airport like so many moths attracted to its bright lights.

By then Alexis had fallen asleep against Foster's shoulder. He guessed she was exhausted, having waited up through the night for her rescue.

Desai looked over his shoulder and saw that she was asleep. 'I will leave you here, sir,' he whispered to Foster. 'I must go home, in case people start asking what I am doing driving around city in the night.'

'Yes, that's fine,' Foster said. 'I can get a cab back to the hotel. Anyway, their shuttle may still be around.'

'You will take lady away from here, sir? It is vital she does not remain. She must stay nowhere in India.'

'Don't worry. She'll be on the first flight I can get her on.'

The attendant at the British Airways ticketing desk was able to find a seat for Alexis in Business Class. She was puzzled that there was no baggage to be checked, and that Alexis had no handbag. She checked her passport over and over again, but everything was in order and she eventually returned it with the ticket.

They picked up her boarding pass at the check-in desk where the attendant informed them that the flight was expected to leave on time.

Foster looked at his watch. Two hours to wait! He would keep her with him until the last minute.

They found the cafeteria and sat at a table where Foster could watch the airport entrance. He was pretty sure that Miller wouldn't be able to get away from the scene of the accident in a hurry, but it was best to be sure. He could even telephone for some goon to come after them.

As they sat there, he explained as much as he could to her. She listened in wide-eyed horror as he told her about Sam Miller's involvement with the D-Company.

And suddenly she understood. Until that moment she had no inkling of why she'd been kidnapped.

'What did she mean?' Alexis asked as she drank her black coffee. 'Gloria – when she said something about the Novotel bathroom?'

Foster thought carefully. He suspected that Alexis would eventually find out that he'd slept with Gloria, and he didn't want her to be hurt.

'Look, Alexis,' he said very gently. 'Yes, she came to the hotel. She agreed to help. I told her that Sam had had you kidnapped and that he was holding you as ransom, to stop your father queering his pitch. That lawyer Desai was going to bring a charge of perjury against Global and Sam didn't want anybody helping the case against them. I had information that was pretty damning …'

'And the price?'

'Price?'

Her voice was cold. 'Yes. I'm sure Gloria would have wanted something in exchange for helping you.'

Foster shrugged.

Alexis' eyes blazed. 'I knew it!' she spat. 'You slept with her.'

He reached over to hold her wrist but she shook free of his hand. 'How could you?' she snarled.

Foster made another effort to hold her hand, and this time he succeeded, though she was clearly tense. 'There was no other way,' he explained. 'I had to have somebody on the inside.'

'Yes,' she snapped, 'and having sex with her was no doubt a truly unpleasant experience. But you just had to endure it, didn't you?'

He released her hand and put his head in his hands. Eventually he looked up at her and said, 'Look, Alexis. Do you remember, at the beginning, what you said? Something about your generation seeing sex as something enjoyable – with no hang-ups.'

'Something like that.' She admitted quietly. She looked miserable, but much of the anger had gone out of her tone as she continued, 'Look, Dan, I've been through hell over the past few days; I've been terrified, and tonight I've seen some horrible things. But always, always you were there in my mind. I knew you'd be there for me. I knew you'd find a way of getting me out.' She looked into his eyes before continuing. 'Yes, you're right; it did start off as a bit of fun. But it became much more. I began to trust you … and now you've betrayed that trust.'

He couldn't defend himself. So much had happened. His emotions were confused, tossed about like so much flotsam on a stormy ocean.

He took her hand again, and this time she didn't try to pull away. 'Alexis,' he said, 'you have to understand something about me. You know I was married once, had two wonderful kids, loved them and loved my wife. But then I found out that she'd been sleeping with someone else. All the time I was working hard to build a good life for my family … it took me away from her … too much. She found companionship with someone else. So I lost everything. My wife, contact with my kids, eventually my job.'

Now there was returning pressure on his hand from hers.

He looked towards the airport's entrance doors before continuing, 'You know, I thought at one time that I could forgive her. Felt I'd brought it on myself, I guess. But what I couldn't come to terms with was that… well, she'd fallen out of love with me. It just wasn't the same any more.'

Again, her clasp of his hand increased.

'And then there was Fiona,' he continued. 'Lovely and full of joy at life. She showed me that I could trust a woman again. It took a long time. Mainly, I guess, I was afraid. She was so much younger than me.' He stopped and looked at her closely. 'Younger even than you, Alexis. But once I let myself go I never stopped to think. I never wondered what it would be like when I was really old. Somehow, I thought her love would keep me young. Preserve me.' He closed his eyes and was quiet for a moment, memories flooding back. Finally he continued, 'And then it got blown apart. She went into the Underground one day, and never came out again. At least, not alive. My lovely Fiona, so full of happiness and excitement... and sheer joy. Snuffed out. All extinguished. Gone.'

'Oh Dan,' she whispered. 'I know. I'm sorry, but ...'

'Nothing to be done, Alexis,' he said. 'In the end I got over her ...'

She decided to change the subject. 'This high-flyer you told me about...'

'Yeah. She'd been hurt too. Was fighting back at life, I guess.'

He fell silent and she continued for him, 'And then there was me.'

'Yes, you.' He squeezed her hand. 'I didn't want to lose you too, Alexis. I know you said it was just one of those things: just a fling. And that's how it started, but something was beginning to grow from it.'

'I felt it too,' she said quietly. 'I didn't want it to happen, but ...'

'Then when they kidnapped you I was desperate,' he said. 'Didn't know how to save you. And then Gloria gave me a chance to get you out of wherever they'd taken you.'

A long silence followed. They each avoided the other's eyes.

'It's all right,' she said finally, 'I'll get over it.'

He let out his breath. 'Gloria,' he said. 'Her husband, Sam ... he was a bastard.'

'I know.'

He changed tack. 'But how did she get the message to you. Sam must have been watching every move.'

She gave a little laugh. 'Clever, really. She'd written a note,' she said. 'When she went to the loo in that house she must have unwound the toilet roll, slipped the note in and re-rolled it. I found it when I went later. It fell out when I pulled the roll.'

'Sam must have checked the toilet,' he said.

'He did. I heard him moving things around, lifting the seat even.'

'He just didn't think of unwinding the loo roll.'

'It was so clever,' she smiled. 'She must have even noticed that the bathroom floor was white, and written the note on brightly coloured paper so that if it fell on the floor I'd be bound to see it.'

Foster smiled grimly. *You were a clever bitch, Gloria,* he thought. Then he spoke to Alexis: 'Anyway, you'll be safe soon. As soon as you board your flight. They won't be able to get to you then.'

'You think Sam might still come after me?'

'I'm sure he'll try. I don't know how long it'll be before he can get away from the accident scene, but he's bound to make another try.'

'It's over then,' she mused. 'At last.'

'I'm afraid not. There's quite a way to go yet.'

She frowned. 'Why? Once I'm away from here surely they've lost their hold on you. You can spill the beans to the court.'

'Yes. But we're not at that stage yet.'

He repeated what Gopal, the Coroner, had told him about 'pendency' and the interminably long-drawn-out legal procedures in India.

She looked horrified. 'So we've got to wait, what, *years* for the case to come up?'

He shrugged. 'Depends. Gopal's set the ball rolling already. If he collects enough evidence and if he can persuade the High Court officials to look at it, than it could come sooner.'

'Meanwhile we all sit and wait?' Her voice sounded angry.

Foster grinned. 'Not exactly. You see, I want to do a bit more digging.'

'Why?' she asked. 'Surely the evidence you've already got is enough.'

'For this case it is.'

'There's something else?'

'Yep! I'm not sure exactly what it is, but there's something else going on – or something's already happened – that's causing everybody to be very panicky. From all the trouble the company's taken, I suspect it's something really big. Bigger even than being accused of perjury. Bigger than being shown to have flouted safety rules.'

She gave him a wide-eyed look. 'What? Worse than being blamed for an explosion that killed people?'

'Yes. I'm sure there something else. They could deal with the explosion easily enough – just cough up more compensation. In fact, they should've done that at the beginning. Then none of this would have happened. Their secret would have remained safe. The point is that they didn't deal with it. And I want to find out why.'

'It was them trying to duck that issue that brought my Dad in,' she agreed, 'and eventually you.'

'Exactly! So why did they take that risk? There's something bigger going on, much bigger, and that's what I'm going to find out.'

Just then he looked at the entrance doors again and as he did he stiffened. Because through the glass he saw Miller climbing out of a taxi that had just drawn up outside.

Foster leapt to his feet. 'He's here,' he cried. 'Get moving. Go to the boarding area. Now!'

Alexis looked alarmed. 'Where? Where is he?'

'Never mind where. I've seen him. Get moving. Once you're air-side it'll be much harder for him to get to you.'

Sam Miller was badly out of breath: panting with the exertions of the past hour. He'd had a hell of a time getting away from the crash site. The police had arrived and thirty or so minutes later an ambulance wailed to a halt beside the wrecked vehicles. The police seemed to want to arrest everybody in sight and it was only when he managed to make a phone call that things started to get resolved. He had called the same high-ranking officer in the Central Industrial Security Force who had arranged for Alexis Klein to be kidnapped. This time though, the officer had been somewhat reluctant to help – being roused from his sleep at almost 3 a.m. hadn't helped – but in the end he was persuaded to act and within ten minutes the traffic police were ordered to let Miller go free. He had then got the cops to order him a cab.

Now, as he paid off the driver he looked furiously around the terminal building.

Had he failed? Had Foster managed to get the Klein woman away?

And then he spotted Foster walking casually towards the bus terminal. He pushed his way through the burgeoning crowd of travellers and the usual meters and greeters. 'Stop!' he yelled. 'Foster! Stop!'

People were staring at him with curiosity but he didn't care. Foster was in his sights and he was going to deal with him. The only thing was that there was no sign of the Klein/Marshall woman.

Foster heard his shouts and stopped. 'Why, if it isn't Sam Miller!' he called jovially. 'How are you, old man?'

Oblivious of the watching crowds, many of whom were beginning to show real interest in this unfolding drama, Miller ran up to him and grabbed his arm. 'Don't fuck with me, Foster!' he shouted. 'Where is she?'

'Where's who?' Foster asked innocently as he pulled his arm free of Miller's grasp.

The watchers' eyes swivelled from one man to the other and silence fell on them as they strained to hear what was happening. Miller looked as though he was on the point of having a heart attack. 'I told you, you bastard. Quit horsin' around.'

'Do you mean Mrs Marshall?' Foster asked, as though he'd only just realized who Miller was wanting. 'I'm afraid you've missed her, old boy.' He looked at his watch before concluding, 'She must be boarding right about now.'

At that, all the fight went out of Miller's eyes and his shoulders sagged. He looked from side to side, over and through the interested onlookers as though they were invisible, obviously seeing nothing at all.

'I'm sorry, Sam,' Foster said, though there was no sorrow in his expression – only triumph. 'Look, why don't we go and have a coffee. We've so much to tell each other.'

But Miller simply walked slowly away, his shoulders sagging, his face lined with worry and – something more, much more: sheer terror.

It was all unravelling and he had two masters who would each be calling for his blood.

Chapter 10

A lthough it was still early, the blazing summer heat of the Deccan Plateau had already started to burgeon. Through the heat haze, the onion domes and towers of the Andhra Pradesh High Court, set amid luxuriant gardens and tall palm trees, looked cool and inviting and Foster went gratefully into the shade with a beaming Desai trotting alongside him.

'It's a big day for you,' Foster said.

'Oh yes, sir,' Desai agreed, 'and for Mr Gopal. And for you too, I think.'

It had been a long, hard battle, with GCR's lawyers fighting every inch of the way, desperately unwilling to concede any ground. They had clearly been instructed to keep the case away from the High Court but they had failed.

And then – quite suddenly – they backed down. Desai had rung Foster and told him that the hearing was to be preponed.

'Preponed?' Foster asked. 'What the hell is that?'

'Ah, it is an Indian extension of English,' Desai said seriously. 'When an action is postponed it is delayed; so when it is brought forward it is preponed. Yes, the hearing has been preponed.'

Foster sensed that the lawyer was entirely serious. Clearly, "preponing" was not an unusual term here. Still reeling at the strange but irrefutable logic of the Indian mind, he brushed these thoughts aside and began to consider why the court hearing should have been brought forward. The rapid change of heart was puzzling. Why the change? And how was it that the normally ponderous, slow process of the Indian judicial system had been suddenly galvanized into action? It was as if a turtle had taken up sprinting.

The change renewed his suspicions that something far bigger than the Varikhani incident was being carefully concealed; something that would be infinitely more damaging to the company if it were not dealt with quickly. When he telephoned Scott Klein and told him about the change the American had agreed, and set about probing through his own contacts and informants in the States, to see if an explanation could be found.

So far it had proved futile, and now matters had rolled on to this point – and led to Foster's presence being required at the High Court.

Both Gopal and Desai had reassured Foster that proceedings in the High Court were always conducted in English. In fact, in an attempt to further reassure him, they stressed that even the barristers' robes were based on the British equivalents. Nevertheless he was still worried, fearing that he might make a serious blunder because of a failure to understand some critical point expressed in sing-song Anglo-Indian patois or because of unfamiliarity with the court procedures.

He had tried desperately to stay away from the court. 'I'd love to be there through it all,' he had lied, 'but Scott Klein wants me to do some other work for him on an urgent basis. But don't worry; I'll stay in touch. If they need me to present evidence in court I'll be here.'

'But you *must* attend,' Gopal had pleaded, supported by much vigorous nodding of Desai's head. 'If High Court calls on you as a witness you must be there. Failure to attend would prejudice the case against GCR … and could even lead to your arrest.'

And so he had resigned himself to sitting through days or weeks of interminable court proceedings, probably understanding only a small fraction of what passed.

The case was to be heard in No 4 Court Hall and they milled around in the crowded corridor. Desai had just said that the hearing was to start in fifteen minutes when they were approached by a barrister wearing a black court coat with a white neck band. He had a whispered conversation with Gopal and Desai and then swirled away to enter the court room, leaving the two Indians to break the news to Foster.

'This is most unusual,' Gopal said agitatedly, as much to Desai as to Foster.

'What's happened?' Foster asked.

'Sir, that gentleman is Mr Chandra Vasant, acting for the prosecution against GCR. He has told us that the judge has ruled that defence will be heard first.'

'This never happens,' Gopal elaborated, looking amazed and worried at the same time. 'Always,' he emphasised, 'always, the prosecution case is heard first,'.

'More GCR string-pulling?' Foster asked.

'Most certainly,' Gopal replied and Desai nodded sadly in agreement.

'This case is being heard under Public Interest Litigation,' Desai said. 'Nevertheless, I understood that normal court procedure was always to be followed, even under PIL.'

'But not today,' Foster said. 'Why?'

The answer to that question emerged quickly enough when they went through the doors and took their places in the court.

After the normal preliminaries, the judge called the two barristers to his bench. Following a preliminary whispered conversation, the two lawyers returned to their seats. Chandra Vasant whispered something to Gopal and Desai, who immediately paled.

Before either man could tell Foster what had happened, the judge addressed the court.

He spoke in impeccable, if still sing-song and over-elaborated English. 'The court has been presented with information,' he said, 'and it is information that throws into question the Public Interest aspects of this case. I have consequently asked that crucial evidence is heard first. This may alter the *modus operandi* of this case. And now, as the matter in question was originally put forward by Dr Foster, I shall ask him to take the stand.' He smiled indulgently before adding, in a kindly manner, 'Dr Foster, at this stage there will be no need for you to confirm your credentials. Both parties are aware of them and their value is accepted by this court.'

Foster stood up and walked over to the witness box. From there he looked across at a thinly populated courtroom.

GCR's defending barrister introduced himself as Ravinder Vempati. He spoke with the air of a man who clearly enjoyed the dramatic potential of his profession. He was wearing a black robe over a dark grey pin-stripe suit and, like the judge and the prosecution barrister, he too sported a white neck band. He was tall and immaculately groomed and his English sounded as though he had read law at Oxford or Cambridge. As he addressed Foster, his demeanour grew even haughtier. 'Doctor Foster,' he said in a deep, resonant voice. 'I understand that you have provided the prosecution with information that is claimed to show a laxity of management supervision at Varikhani power station.'

'That's right. I gave them photographs …'

'Ah! The photographs.' He paused for several moments, with the clear intention of increasing the dramatic effect before he continued, 'Tell me Dr Foster, before we come to the matter of those photographs, for the benefit of the court may I ask you to clarify certain technical matters?'

'Yes of course,' Foster answered, sensing a trap.

'Good!' Again a pause. 'Well, would you agree that power stations all over the world are built to broadly similar designs?'

'No. Not really.'

Vempati frowned. 'What do you mean? Surely, in simple terms, it is a matter of fuel going in at one end and electricity coming out at the other?'

'In simple terms, I'd agree with that. But well, some plants burn gas, others oil; some, like Varikhani use coal. Those factors have a considerable bearing on the nature of the plant and its layout …'

Vempati's frown eased. 'Oh I see,' he said. 'But in very general terms – shall we say to the eyes of the layman – would you say that they could look broadly similar?'

'Well, I guess so. But, as I've just said, they are all different in detail.'

'Perhaps so. Then tell me, Dr Foster, how can we be sure that the photographs you produced were in fact taken at Varikhani and not at another power station? Perhaps one in another country.'

Foster was nonplussed; he could see Vempati's point, but it was like saying that, to a tribesman in some remote jungle community, all cars looked the same. 'Well,' he said eventually, 'I guess the only way to be sure would be to go to each and every point where one of those photographs was taken and compare it in detail with the reality.'

'Exactly so, Doctor.' Vempati gave a broad smile. 'And that is why I took a party of court officials to the power station just two days ago. We went from one of your claimed photographic viewpoints to another and examined each one of the pictures very carefully with what lay before us. Everybody agreed that the images you have presented to court bear no relation to the plant here. They were obviously taken elsewhere.'

'That's ridiculous!' Foster snapped, 'Let me take you round there. I'll show you.'

'Are you suggesting that it takes a power-station expert's eyes to see such things? Such small differences that make one power station different from another? Perhaps the colour of the paint, eh?'

'Yes. I guess that's what I am saying.'

'Perhaps you are correct. But we anticipated that possibility; our party was taken round the plant by a very experienced manager, Dr Foster: no less than Mr Sam Miller, Project Director at Varikhani.'

Foster looked at Miller, who was sitting near the front of the room. The American's reaction to his recent bereavement had been to wear a gaudy yellow tie. Now his face bore a triumphant smirk.

'Mr Miller has intimate knowledge of the Varikhani plant,' Vempati continued, 'with which he has been intimately involved for several months.'

Foster looked at the barrister without responding. He remembered McBride telling him how Miller, while having no technical qualifications had an uncanny ability to understand engineers and engineering matters. No doubt he had led the party round and showed them what he wanted them to see.

Vempati smiled and signalled over his shoulder. A small folder was handed to him by an acolyte. He opened it and took out two sets of photographs, each held with an elastic band. Holding onto one set, he passed the other to Foster who removed the elastic and fanned the pictures out to look at them. They were the photographs that he'd laid on McBride's desk some time before: the same ones he'd shown to Desai and Gopal.

'Do you agree, Dr Foster,' Vempati asked, 'that those are the photographs you have offered as evidence of poor practice at Varikhani power station?'

Foster examined the prints and nodded.

'Let us consider the picture that have been labelled on the back as "1A(f) burner",' Vempati asked gently.

Foster found the picture and studied it. He nodded and Vempati continued, 'Now let us examine a photograph taken two days ago during our inspection. It shows that same burner.'

He took a photograph from the second bundle and handed to Foster, who saw that it was indeed the same burner assembly. But this time it looked entirely different: instead of being filthy and covered in coal dust, everything was spotless: the flame scanners that had been dangling down uselessly when he had seen them were properly installed, the armour protecting the cabling that had been broken was now intact.

Foster looked at the barrister and said, 'It's been tarted up.' He handed the photograph back to the barrister.

'What do you mean by that expression, "tarted up", Dr Foster?' Vempati asked, smiling indulgently.

'Cleaned, dusted, polished-up, repaired. You name it.'

'No, Dr Foster, not "tarted up" as you say. Let me put it to you that the two photographs were of two entirely different installations. The one I have just shown you was taken at Varikhani two days ago and its taking was witnessed by several legal, management and engineering personnel. The one you put forward was taken with no such witnesses present ...'

'Of course not,' Foster interrupted. 'I was meant to be investigating how the plant performance could be improved, not digging about in an accident that happened months before I arrived here. I wanted to be sure that nobody was watching me.'

'I see,' Vempati murmured. Then he looked up and stared directly at Foster. 'Or perhaps the picture was taken at another power station, Dr Foster. How can you prove otherwise? There are no witnesses to support your version of things.'

Foster snorted in frustration and Vempati turned to the judge and said, 'Your honour, as you know, there is considerable doubt about the authenticity of the photographs offered as evidence by the prosecution. Dr Foster claims that they were taken by him at Varikhani but he cannot prove that claim. Be that as it may, if he did indeed take photographs at the power station here, photographs that he admits he had to take surreptitiously because he was intending to use them against the interests of Global Consolidated Resources, then that action is a clear violation of GCR's interests and indeed could be regarded as being no less than ...' he turned to look malevolently at Foster before concluding, 'industrial espionage.'

Later, outside the court, Foster found Gopal and Desai deep in conversation and looking extremely dejected. He decided to adopt a light-hearted approach in an attempt to cheer them up.

'Look on the bright side, lads,' he said. 'At least the judge didn't have me arrested and banged up in jail.'

The two Indians looked at him in astonishment and it was left to Desai to comment: 'Sir this is not a matter to be taken with a light heart. Indeed it is extremely serious that judge has dismissed case. Gopal-ji's reputation is impaired sir, seriously impaired. Moreover – and you do not yet know this because you left court beforehand – I was summoned in front of judge. He has fined me for breach of confidence.'

'What?' Foster exploded.

'Judge said that as GCR company was client of my practice at the time, I had a duty of care not to divulge confidential information to others: specifically to you sir.'

'Good God! How much was the fine?'

Desai's face was bleak as he answered, 'It was five lakhs, sir. I do not know where I am finding such a large sum.'

Foster shook his head, five lakhs was five hundred thousand Rupees or almost £7,000 in English money. There was no way that the advance that Scott Klein had paid Desai so far would cover such a large sum.

'I'll have a word with Klein,' Foster said. 'Perhaps he'll cover it.'

Desai shook his head and protested, 'No sir, I could not ask Mr Klein for that.'

'You haven't asked, and I haven't promised anything. All I said was that I'd see if he will cover it.'

Desai looked at him with tears of gratitude brimming at his eyes. Foster looked at Gopal and saw that he was pendulemming his head and smiling abstractedly.

'What about you, Mr Gopal?' he asked. 'Mr Desai said your reputation had been impaired ...'

'It is of little concern,' Gopal gave a small smile as he answered in a subdued voice, 'but thank you for asking, sir. I have been thinking about it for some time and am resigned to my fate. If I was a young man, perhaps it would matter; but I am no longer young. I have reached top of my professional tree. I am not looking for career advancement – which today's action would indeed have badly affected. I have already made decision: I shall be retiring.'

Back at his hotel, Foster telephoned Klein and outlined the day's proceedings.

'The bastards!' Klein said. 'They've done it again, Dan. They've screwed us.'

'Looks that way, Scott.' There was a long silence while the two men considered the situation. Finally, Foster asked, 'But tell me something: the other day you said that you were probing around Global's other operations, to see what they may be trying so desperately to hide. Did you get anywhere?'

'Well, I don't rightly know yet, Dan. But there's something in the wind.'

'Tell me?'

'You ever hear of Ocean Venture Gamma?'

'Yes I have. It's a gas platform – or at least it was. Didn't it blow up a couple of years ago?'

'Got it! It was a gas and oil platform, a big one, off the coast of Vietnam. When it blew – and it was three years ago – it killed around 40 people working on it, and caused a lot of pollution.'

'Ah yes! I remember it now. I remember being puzzled that there was no real fuss about it in the media. No banner headlines. Not like Piper Alpha in the North Sea or Deepwater Horizon in the Mexican Gulf.'

'Too far away to concern folk hereabouts,' Klein said, cynicism colouring his words. 'No oil on American beaches, no American fishing jobs lost.'

Foster sighed. Klein was right.

'Are you saying that Global was involved there?'

'Sure were,' Klein replied. 'Not directly, so that's why I didn't make the connection at first. It was a subsidiary of a subsidiary, or they were joint-venture partners; I don't know which, right now. But the fact is they were involved.'

Foster gave a low whistle. 'If that's right, and if we can find some connection … then you'll have a field day, Scott. You'll be able to show that they routinely flouted safety rules and procedures, and did it across the board, across all their operations.'

'Won't I just!' The exultation in the American's voice was palpable.

The call had barely ended when Foster's mobile rang. It was Peter McBride, Global's Commissioning Engineer at Varikhani. His voice sounded strained.

'Are you all right, Peter?' Foster asked.

McBride ignored the question. 'We need to talk Dan,' he said. 'Can I come over to Hyderabad? That's where you are, isn't it?'

'Yes. At the Novotel. What's up?'

'Can't tell you right now. I can be there tomorrow afternoon; is that OK?'

It was mid-afternoon when McBride arrived at the Novotel. Foster met him in the lobby and the two men went to the bar and ordered drinks.

'OK, Peter,' Foster said. 'Tell.'

McBride looked moodily at his glass, twirling it slowly in his hand before speaking. 'It's a lot to confess, Dan. I've been an idiot. Got into a real mess. But now that's been resolved – at least for me.'

Foster couldn't understand. 'Resolved?' he asked. 'For you? What do you mean?'

Again a long silence and a pensive sip before the answer. 'You know Miller's wife was killed in a car crash?'

'Yes,' Foster answered, wondering how much was known about his own involvement in that night's tragedy.

McBride took another long sip of his drink. 'The bastard killed her, you know?'

'What? It was an accident. Surely ...'

'It was an accident all right. But she was still alive afterwards. But then Sam arrived on the scene. I don't know what he was doing there at that time of the night. I don't know what she was doing there either, for that matter. Or why she was being driven around by some low-life thief ..'

'What happened to him?' Foster asked. 'The thief, as you call him.' For the few minutes he had known Ram Lal he had come to respect him, perhaps even like him – in spite of his thuggish ways.

'Apparently he was killed outright,' McBride said. 'But the point is that Sam pulled Gloria out of the wreckage.'

Foster was saddened. 'A natural thing to do,' he observed. 'To try and rescue his wife.'

'No Dan, it wasnae like that. Apparently he hit her across the face. Can you believe that? The bastard hit her, his own wife, while she was lying there, seriously injured. Then he just hauled her out. It made everything worse. I heard that the paramedics said they might have been able to save her if he hadn't just manhandled her like that. It made her injuries worse.'

Suddenly, as he looked into McBride's grief-stricken face, the connections clicked in Foster's mind, and he began to understand.

'Good God!' he began, 'You're saying that … you and Gloria …?' And then McBride gave a sad nod of acknowledgement.

Foster remembered McBride's wife, Fiona, standing beside her husband at the party in Mahajan's house: a short, cheerful woman, full of bubbly excitement.

'I was a bloody idiot, Dan,' McBride said quietly. 'My boss's wife too, would you believe?'

While Foster slowly shook his head in disbelief, the Scotsman continued his sad confession. 'It began a few months ago. Things hadn't been right between Fiona and me – they haven't been right for years – and living out here, well it just made it worse. She felt isolated and began to focus more and more on the kids. I was incidental to her life.'

'You poor sod!' Foster said. Between the two normally taciturn engineers it was a rough sort of sympathy.

'Aye,' McBride said with a grim smile. 'I don't think Fiona knew what she was doing to me but, slowly but surely, bit by bit, she was … well, she was emasculating me.' He paused as bitter memories came to him. Eventually he continued, 'I tried to do something about it, Dan, but …' He closed his eyes as he came to the pivotal event. 'Anyway, the night that we went to that party at Mahajan's was the first time I'd been able to persuade her to come out with me, almost since we arrived here. We didn't seem to be able to share things any more, and whenever I tried I'd get rebuffed. I thought the party might get us together again – re-kindle the old fire. I knew it wouldn't be easy – Gloria'd told me she was going to be there …'

'You'd been screwing her before that night?'

'Aye. For about two months. But she promised me that she wouldn't make a fuss at the party; wouldn't rub Fiona's nose in it.'

'It was a risk, though,' Foster said. 'If she wanted to she could have dropped you well and truly in it.'

'Aye. But she could've done that at any time.'

'I suppose so. But in my experience things like this can jog along quite well for a long time … until the two protagonists come face to face.'

McBride sighed, but said nothing.

'I know how tough it can get, living in these places,' Foster said in an attempt to break the Scotsman's gloom. 'They're pretty isolated. People in a closed community can get up to strange things.'

McBride nodded. 'Back home in Edinburgh, I suppose we'd have gone to a marriage guidance counsellor …'

Foster gave a wry smilc. 'I don't suppose,' he said, 'that GCR's comprehensive care policy extends to that sort of service out here.'

McBride gave a bitter laugh. 'Indeed not! So there was nowhere for us to turn. Well, for me to turn: Fiona didn't seem to think there was any problem.'

'I guess you felt pretty low,' Foster said. He felt vaguely uncomfortable discussing McBride's personal affairs with him like this, especially in view of his own relationship with Gloria, but the man was clearly distraught. He needed to unload the hurt and bitterness – and the ultimate tragedy of it all.

226

'Aye, that was it,' McBride continued. 'Anyway, when Gloria first came on the scene she was all the things Fiona wasnae.' Suddenly an unfamiliar eloquence came to this normally taciturn man as he added, 'She was vibrant, alluring – exciting. And it seemed she wanted me.'

Foster could well imagine it; Gloria was good at making her men feel alive.

As if he'd read Foster's thoughts, McBride said, 'Och! I have little doubt I wasnae the only one in Gloria's complicated life. There were no illusions about that between us but, in spite of that it was a grand feeling, Dan. After all those years – and believe me they were empty years – it felt good, really good. Gloria made me feel like a man again.'

'I'm sure she did,' Foster mused. He could see Gloria beguiling McBride and taking advantage of his loneliness. No doubt he was no more than a plaything to her; but on the other hand it was very clear that *she* meant something important to *him* – something very important indeed. Foster could imagine the rough Scottish engineer naively thinking that he might even make a break from his loveless marriage and somehow persuade the beautiful, vibrant but fickle Gloria to settle down with him.

McBride looked into the distance as a new thought came to him. 'Strange thing,' he said. 'But I think Fiona knew.'

'She did?'

'Well, suspected's more like it. I never said anything but I found her sniffing my shirt one evening when I'd just left Gloria. I think she smelt her perfume on it.'

Foster remembered the heady perfume she used to wear. 'How did she react?' he asked.

'She was strange about it. I began to think she was almost …
well, proud of me. I think she was relieved that I'd found …
an outlet, I suppose.' He looked at Foster and gave a sad
smile. 'I'd never leave her and the bairns. I think she knew
that. And with that strength she could accept what was going
on.'

Foster frowned a question at him.

'Aye. It was as though she knew I was a real man again.' He
shook himself clear of his dark thoughts. 'Well, in the end,
when I heard Gloria'd been killed it changed everything,' he
said. 'I began to think more clearly about things. Decided to
get a grip on my life.'

He sighed and looked hard at Foster. 'Dan,' he said
hesitatingly. 'I've quit.'

Foster stiffened. This man was giving up a very good job with
an array of valuable fringe benefits that would make most
people's mouths water. After that, it would be hard to return
to a normal life. No other job could offer the same salary or
perks. 'Really?' he asked. 'You've resigned from Global?'

When McBride nodded, Foster asked 'Where will you go?
Home?'

'Aye. Fiona and the bairns are quite excited about it. Seems
it's what they wanted all along.'

'When do you go?'

'At the end of the month. The company's agreed I can
terminate my contract with no loss of benefits.'

'Meaning?'

'A nice farewell handshake – in cash. No questions asked, no tax authorities knowing – plus full pay for six months and no loss of pension rights.'

'That sounds pretty good.'

McBride gave a grim smile. 'Indeed it is,' he said. 'But there's a price to be paid.' Then he added an afterthought: 'With Global there's always a price.'

'And that price is …?'

McBride gave a broad grin. 'That I keep my mouth shut.'

'Which you've just failed to do,' Foster observed with a laugh.

McBride smiled. 'I guess so, though of course I'll deny everything if anybody asks.'

'So why tell me, Peter?'

'Because I trust you and I know that you'll do something about what I'm going to say – although God knows how you'll manage it – and that you'll not drag my name into it.'

Foster lowered his head and thought. Then he looked up and said, 'OK. It's a deal. Let's hear it.'

McBride took a deep breath and then started: 'You know the pressure we work under, Dan.'

Receiving Foster's nod of assent he continued, 'Everything was done at breakneck speed. Corners were cut, safety procedures largely ignored. Oh, we paid lip service to safety issues all right, but only as long as it didn't delay anything. Take the HAZOP meetings, for instance.'

He was referring to "Hazards and Operability studies" which were widely adopted around the world. During the design and construction phases of any large, potentially dangerous project such as that at Varikhani, HAZOP meetings were required to be held to discuss all hazardous operations. They would normally be extremely painstaking and rigorous; examining each and every operation and what the consequences would be if something didn't function exactly as required, when required.

'Well, we held the meetings all right,' McBride continued, 'but with Sam Miller heading every one of them they were a farce, a complete sham. For example, when we got to a stage where we considered a valve jamming open when it was commanded to shut our friend would say something like, "Has anybody ever experienced such a thing happening?" and if nobody had, we'd simply move on. But if somebody was brave or foolish enough to say that they once experienced a similar failure he'd be called in to Sam's office the next morning to have the riot act read to him. A couple of laddies were even fired: sent home; put on a plane within a day or two. The same thing would happen if an engineer tried to protest about corner-cutting.'

'Ye Gods!' Foster breathed.

'Aye, if anybody asked the company could show that they'd held regular HAZOPs. Nobody would ever go through all the records to find all the little corners that had been cut, all the assumptions that had been made. And it gets worse. You saw some of the things yourself: you gave me photographs to prove it.'

'Yes, those photographs …'

McBride laughed. 'I know,' he said. 'You've probably worked out what happened: a couple of days before the people from the court were brought round we were ordered to clean it all up. Sam looked at each picture and made sure that every shred of evidence was removed before the visitors came on site. It was stupid: those loose cables that you spotted were disconnected and removed, the flame scanners cleaned up and put back in their proper places.' He laughed at the memory. 'As a result, when we finally got round to trying to start up the plant it just wouldn't work – kept tripping out before we'd got anywhere; there was no hope of getting it to run.'

'Didn't the legal boys spot that it wasn't operating when they came round?'

''Course they did but, you see, they weren't *expecting* it to be running. Before they arrived they were told it had been shut down …' he lifted both hand and wiggled his first and second fingers to indicate quotation marks, ' "because of lack of demand". Can you believe that? *Lack of demand!* Here, in India! It was a joke, and it must have cost the company tens of thousands of dollars. The time and money they spent on covering up the deficiencies was one thing; the cost of lost output was another.'

'But it protected their arses,' Foster growled. 'And since there were no engineers around nobody would spot the obvious.'

'Aye. Oh Mahajan was there, but all he did was bow and scrape to the judiciary and say "yes sir" and "no sir" at the right moments, with Sam pulling his strings all the time.'

He looked at Foster and asked, 'Do you think you'll be able to do anything about all of this, Dan? Because something has to be done, before anything else goes wrong. Before more people are killed.'

231

'I'm going to give it a damn good try, Peter,' Foster answered. 'But I do need proof. Would you be prepared to stand up in court to repeat what you've just told me?'

McBride pursed his lips and then gave a firm shake of his head. 'No chance, Dan. I'm sorry. For a start I'd lose my pension rights. What's more, they've made it clear that they'll tell Her Majesty's Revenue and Customs about the cash payment – and not just the one they're going to make to me: it's the payments they've already made to all the others here as well. So if I say anything against the company I'll be selling some of my colleagues down the river. And you won't find anybody else willing to help either, for much the same reason. We've all got too much to lose.'

Foster drained his glass. Without the help of McBride or his colleagues he would stand no chance of persuading any court that the company had been wilfully negligent. It was hearsay; at best his word against Global's.

But then, just as they stood up to leave McBride gave a sheepish grin and, after a brief hesitation, he took something out of his pocket. He kept it hidden in his hand as he spoke. 'I know you think I'm letting you down, Dan,' he said, fingering the object thoughtfully. 'But I hope you see my position.'

'I guess I do, Peter. Sadly, I do.'

'Well, you may like to take a look at this,' the Scotsman said and opened his fist to expose a memory stick.

Foster took the stick and looked questioningly at McBride.

'You didn't get that from me, Dan. But it may help you.'

'What's on it?' Foster asked.

'Apart from being something I didn't give you, it's a dump from the data logger for the day of the accident. I think you'll find it interesting.'

Chapter 11

When he phoned Scott Klein and reported the details of his conversation with McBride, the American asked, 'What was on the stick?'

'It's all the plant data from around the time of the explosion; from before it happened to a few minutes afterwards.'

'What's that mean?'

'They're like aircraft flight recorders,' Foster explained.

'Oh, the black boxes!'

'A bit like that,' Foster agreed, restraining himself from explaining that aircraft flight recorders were bright yellow and not black at all. He went on to say how the plant's event recorders and data loggers, monitored everything that happened on the installation. Every operation was recorded there: every alarm, every deviation from normal of hundreds of temperatures, pressures and flows. The recording systems did this with great accuracy: events that happened within a few thousandths of a second of each other could be resolved to determine the exact order in which they had occurred.

'Did you learn anything from that information?' Klein asked.

'Not yet. But there's a lot of stuff there to go through. I'll get to it.'

Klein moved on and asked, 'If only we could get someone to stand up and give us evidence, Dan ...'

'I know. But McBride's right, nobody'll do that.'

'Pity. We need people to sign affidavits. I can use them in court here in the US.'

Foster knew the term, but not the full implications. 'What's that involve?' he asked.

'Well, it's a list of claims, called "averments" with a statement of truth, generally stating that everything's true, under penalty of perjury, fine, or imprisonment. It also has an attestation clause at the end certifying the affiant made the oath plus the signatures of the author and a witness. It should also be authenticated. Oh, and Dan, if you can get anyone to make one out it'll have to be authenticated by an independent lawyer who's not involved with this; in other words, not Desai.'

'OK Scott. I'm sure we can find a lawyer here somewhere. But I'm not so optimistic of finding someone to make out the affidavit itself. Same reasons as McBride's.'

There was a long pause while Klein considered the facts. Then he said, 'OK Dan, keep looking will you? Because I can't help thinking that McBride would be willing to make out an affidavit if somebody else filed one first.'

'On the basis that the prior statement would bring the company down anyway? Well yes, you may be right: it could happen.'

'Great! Because the more statements we get, the stronger our case becomes.'

There was a moment's silence and then Foster asked if Klein had had any luck with his enquiries into the Ocean Venture Gamma incident.

'Sort of, Dan,' the American replied cautiously. 'That's not to say that it ain't provin' to be a mite interesting, in fact it's mighty interesting indeed.'

'In what way?'

'Well, as I said, Global controlled the platform through a chain of subsidiaries. Made it that much harder for me to track all the connections, but I'm getting' there.'

'Do you think that Global's approach to safety was equally bad there?'

'Could be; though I need more information before I can be 100 per cent sure.'

'All right. Is there anything else I can do while I'm here, or should I head home?'

'I'd like you to hang around, Dan. Somethin' might turn up. Keep nosin' around if you can. But call me every day at around this time. If I don't hear from you I'll send in the Cavalry!'

'OK,' Foster agreed. 'And I'll take a look at the memory stick. See what's on it.'

After the call ended, Foster took out his laptop, booted it and inserted the stick.

At first it was a meaningless jumble of figures, but after an hour of study he worked out the implications. Then he scratched his beard and said to himself, 'Well, Peter my lad. What have you given me here?'

While he was getting dressed the next morning, his mobile rang. It was Desai. 'I am having good idea, Dr Foster,' he enthused.

'What's that?' Foster asked, sensing a slight lifting of his gloom. He had been getting depressed about the chances of making any further progress and Desai's optimistic tone hinted at good news.

'It is concerning gentleman who gave me copy of report at the beginning, Mahajan-ji.' He used the "ji" suffix of respect. 'I have spoken with him and put great pressure on him. He is insisting that he will not give me name of engineer who wrote original report.'

'That's progress?'

'Not of its own accord, sir, but Mahajan-ji is saying that engineer is no longer working for company.'

'They fired him too?'

'Yes sir. It was immediately after I told Mr Miller about the report he had written for Mahajan-ji. But …' his tone lifted even more in his excitement, 'sir, I have found him for you.'

Foster's hopes soared. 'Wonderful!' he said. 'That's great!'

He could sense Desai's pleasure at the praise.

The Indian continued: 'His colleagues at power station were very displeased when he was sacked. He was a popular colleague. I am visiting some of them and obtaining his name and address. I have spoken with him and I think he may be willing to help us.'

'Does he know the risk?'

'Sir, he feels he has nothing further to lose. He is very angry with company; he has lost good job at Varikhani and now has low-paid employment: he buys and sells home computers in a small village shop.'

'Good man, Kalpak!' Foster exulted. 'When can I see him?'

With financial assistance from Scott Klein, Desai had rented a small office in the business district of Varikhani Township and it was a formidable party that assembled there the next day. First to be introduced to Foster was Mohan Rao Prasad, the engineer that Desai had recruited to their cause. He was a tall stocky man with a luxuriant black moustache. Then the others arrived: Chetna Bhaabi, Desai's sister-in-law who had been persuaded to type up the affidavit, then Ravinder Gandhi, the independent lawyer who had been brought in – at Klein's insistence – as an independent witness.

They sat at a rectangular table on which Chetna Bhabi had placed cups, a tea urn and a plate of samosas. 'Thanks for coming, Mr Prasad,' Foster said as they settled down at their places. 'I understand that you're willing to provide us with information that can be used in court.'

'Yes sir. Indeed.'

'Do you understand that the document is an affidavit?'

Prasad looked puzzled, so Foster explained the implications to him.

The answer came quickly: 'Yes sir, I will sign.' There was a glint in his eye that told Foster that this man would be more than delighted to play a part in bringing down the architect of his downfall, Sam Miller.

Foster then set about questioning Prasad. The answers he got confirmed everything McBride had said. Prasad had sat in on some of the HAZOP meetings and could remember clear examples of Miller forcing difficulties into the background. Prasad explained that, as a low-ranking engineer he was unable to appreciate the full implications of these actions, but he had been uneasy over some decisions that had been taken. He had an excellent memory and Foster wrote down all the key points in his notebook.

After the explosion, Mahajan had asked Prasad to carry out an on-the-spot investigation and compile a report. It was a damning document that laid the blame for the incident firmly at Global's door.

'That's the report that Mr Desai took to court?' Foster asked.

'Yes sir. I gave it to my manager, Mahajan-ji, and he gave it in turn to Desai-ji when he came to power station.' He hesitated as a memory came to him. 'Then Mr Miller found out. I was fired, sir. I was escorted off site that day.' His face showed that his memories of that incident were still raw and painful wounds.

Foster gave him a sympathetic smile. 'Are you aware that another report was produced in the court?' he asked.

'Yes sir. Desai-ji told me. The court was told that it was mine … but it was not my report; some *badmash* had forged my signature on it.'

Foster consulted his notebook. He decided his notes would be adequate as an affidavit and passed it to Chetna Bhabi.

After they had paused for tea, Desai's sister-in-law returned with the typed affidavit. Foster handed it to Prasad who read it carefully. 'Yes sir,' he said finally, 'this is correct.'

'And complete?' Foster asked. 'Nothing missing?'

'Absolutely complete, sir.'

Foster watched while the document was signed by Prasad and witnessed by Ravinder Gandhi.

Foster gave a sigh as the affidavit was handed to him. 'Thank you gentlemen,' he said. 'With this bit of paper we can begin to get justice for everybody who has suffered at the hands of Global Consolidated Resources. Now I have to get moving.'

He looked at his watch and calculated the time overseas. It would be too early to ring Klein in Houston, but it was mid-morning in London.

Alexis sounded excited on the telephone. 'Oh Dan!' she cried. 'It's so great to hear your voice again. I'm missing you so much. When are you coming back?'

'Not for a while, sweetheart,' Foster replied. 'There's a bit more to be done here, and things can move pretty slowly in India.'

'My experience is that they can move pretty damn fast,' she joked bitterly. Memories of her abduction, imprisonment and release were obviously still painful.

'Yeah! But that's the bad boys; unfortunately the good ones take things much more slowly. But I think we're getting there. I've already got one affidavit to start the ball rolling and I'm sure others will follow. But meanwhile, have you heard from your father?'

'Yes. I gather he's hit pay-dirt too. As I understand it, his spies have found out quite a lot. You should call him.'

'I will,' he said. 'Right after this.'

'But Dan …' she started.

'What? Something up?'

He could hear a rustling sound; he could imagine her curling up in her armchair. Then with hesitation in her voice she said, 'Well … yes and no. You see, I've been thinking things over and … well, I'm worried.'

'What about?'

'Remember right at the beginning, when all of this started for me? Dad's call in the middle of the night? He warned me to watch out for somebody tailing me.'

'Yes, I remember. What about it?'

'Well, I've been wondering about that. Why would he think that somebody might be trying to follow me?'

'What do you mean?'

'Well, I've been working it out. At that time it seemed he was just trying to recruit you to find out what had happened at the power station. He was hoping to get another bit of ammunition to hit Global with.'

'Yes, that's right.'

'He wouldn't have known about Sam Miller's involvement with the Indian Mafia would he? Not then.'

'The D-Company; yes, that's right – he wouldn't have known.'

'So why would he have been so desperately worried about somebody following me? Especially in London.'

Foster was silent as he thought about it. She had a point: at that time Klein may have suspected that Global was attempting to conceal what had happed at Varikhani, but why would that have made him fear for his daughter who, living and working in England, was far away from the US or India?

Eventually he asked, 'What are you saying, Alexis?'

'I wish I knew. It just doesn't make sense; which makes me wonder if something else is going on – something he's not mentioned to me … or you.'

'Mmm. OK, I'll ask him.'

As soon as he judged that Klein would be awake Foster rang him. He decided to talk about his success first, before he taxed him on Alexis's fears. He told the American about getting the affidavit from Prasad.

'That's amazing Dan!' the American said. 'With that affidavit in our hands we've got undeniable proof not only that the explosion was directly the result of Global's methods of working, but also that they committed perjury in substituting a fake report with a forged signature. We've got 'em Dan! We've got 'em!'

Foster smiled as he said, 'Yes, I think you're right, Scott. I don't see how they can get out of this one.'

'Will you try McBride again?' Klein asked. 'If he backed it up it would be the icing on the cake.'

'Yes. I'll give him another try. But first of all there's something I want to know.'

'What's that?'

'Right at the beginning of this, when you asked Alexis to find me, did you know something else; something you haven't told either of us about?'

There was a long pause before Klein replied evasively, 'What sort of thing?'

'I don't know, but a few things don't stack up. Alexis thinks there's more – that there's some information you haven't favoured us with.'

Klein gave an audible sigh. 'OK Dan, there *is* more…' Foster waited for the continuation. 'You see,' Klein said, 'the thing at Varikhani … it was part of a pattern.'

'You mean sloppy engineering practice? It was happening at other sites? You told me about the gas platform.'

'Yeah! But that wasn't all.' There was another long delay before he continued, 'You remember Enron?'

'Of course I do.'

Foster remembered it very well indeed. Back in the 1990s the Chief Executive of a small utility company in Nebraska, guided by a major consultancy practice, had renamed his company Enron and moved it to Texas. He promised investors that the company would "turn gas into gold" and that it would revolutionise the global energy market. With the help of friends at the highest levels of Government, Enron quickly became the fourth largest company in the USA, employing over 20,000 people. Its top executives were all paid million-Dollar salaries. But it all went belly-up. When it filed for bankruptcy in 2001 the company was shown to have been defrauding investors and manipulating the market in which it operated, and doing so on a colossal scale.

'I think it's happening again,' Klein said; 'but this time with Global.'

'No!' Foster exclaimed. 'You're not serious.'

'I am, buddy! Oh, they're not using exactly the same tricks as Enron did but, believe me, tricks there are aplenty. And there's an even more interesting parallel with what's happening in India right now.'

'What's that?'

'You'll remember what brought down Enron's fantasy creation?'

Foster put his free hand to his head. 'Of course!' he said as he remembered, 'It was India!'.

'Right! It was when the Indians cancelled a massive power-plant project in one of their states. Enron had pinned everything on that project coming to fruition...'

'They were hoping it'd help cover up their losses elsewhere.'

'Got it!'

'When the Indians cancelled,' Foster said, 'it was as if somebody had kicked the legs out from under Enron's already shaky chair.'

'Yup! It all came tumbling down. The whole rotten thing. The shares dropped from a hundred dollars to just a few cents.'

'And you think it's happening again now?' Foster asked.

'Damn sure of it,' came the reply. 'We're a tad short of facts right now, but it seems they've been piling up massive debts all round the world. And a load of their projects are either running way behind schedule or not at all. They're not paying bills, their suppliers are refusing credit – we've even heard takes of people having to go round to warehouses with stacks of bills in their hands, to pay cash for vital parts or supplies.'

'Making the whole thing shaky.'

'Yes. But they have one last chance of coming out of it, and coming out squeaky clean.'

'What's that?' Foster asked.

'They've been putting major efforts into a plan to build a huge number of power stations... guess where?

'Now let me think,' Foster joked. 'Could it be India?'

Klein chuckled. 'Got it in one!'

'I see. With the economy in India growing as it is, it's common knowledge that the country desperately needs a huge expansion of their power-generation capability. Christ! Do you think they're going for the lot?'

'Absolutely! Incredible as it sounds, they're doing just that. Seems they've made the Indians an offer they can't refuse.'

'Appropriate that they're tied up with the Indian Mafia then!' Foster mused bitterly.

'Yep. Global's put together a consortium to build several big power stations: coal, gas, nuclear. And they're all tied together in one massive deal. Global's oil and gas platforms will supply some of them with fuel, their coal ventures will supply the others.'

Foster couldn't believe what Klein was saying. 'But surely the Indian government wouldn't hand all of that to a single company, would they?' he asked. 'Putting all their eggs in one basket?'

'Look,' Klein said. 'Global's one heck of a giant outfit. Perhaps they've never taken on something quite as big as this, but the deal they set up in China last year comes pretty damn close. And India's just as desperate for the power as China.'

'Yes, but the Indians are usually averse to using large-scale overseas operators, aren't they?'

'Used to be, Dan. But now they're finding their feet on a global scale, buying companies like your Jaguar car company and your steel producers. They're far more open to new thinking these days. Far more self-confident.'

'Yes, but there's a pretty bad track-record of relationships between India and big US companies.'

'What do you mean?' Klein asked.

Foster's response was one word: 'Bhopal.'

'That was a while ago, Dan.'

'Perhaps,' Foster said. ' But not *that* long ago: it was 1984.'

'I'm kinda hazy on what happened there, Dan.'

'I remember it only too well,' Foster said. 'A subsidiary of Union Carbide built a plant in Bhopal. There was a serious leak of some really nasty chemicals and a lot of people died as a result.'

'How many?'

'Between three and fifteen thousand.'

'Oh fuck!'

'Exactly!' Foster continued. 'But there's worse to come. The company's CEO was arrested, but it was done at the airport to protect him from the Bhopal community, who were naturally pretty damn worked up about what had happened. He was released a few hours later on a couple of thousand dollars' bail and flown out on a government plane.'

'A *government* plane?'

'Yep – the US Government! You can read what you like into that.'

'So he got away with it?'

'Well, the Indians did try in the end. They summoned him a few years later, to face homicide charges in the Indian Supreme Court.'

'But I guess he wasn't tried,' Klein said. He was getting the hang of things.

'That's right. The company claimed that they were outside Indian jurisdiction.'

'So what happened then?'

'The Indians declared the CEO a fugitive from justice. They pressed for his extradition from the United States but they failed. He never returned to India.'

'Jesus!'

'So do you still think that they'll press on with the deal with Global?'

'Yeah,' Klein said. 'I don't think it'll faze them. Everybody's trying to put all that bad stuff behind them so that they can start again. It's mind-blowing but, like I said, Global have made the Indians an offer they really can't refuse: low down-payments, easy stage-payments, extended credit, the lot. And the scuttlebutt is that they've greased lots of palms. Plus, they've tied up the financing, everything. They've even offered comprehensive training, so that the Indians can move on to the next stage and do it all themselves. To the Indians it must look like an answer to all their prayers.'

'And to Global it *is* the answer to all their prayers,' Foster said.

'Right on! With a project of that scale, the up-front payments alone look like wiping out all of Global's accumulated losses … and doing it at a stroke.'

Foster thought about all the implications for a while; then he asked, 'You knew about this at the beginning, didn't you? When you set Alexis off to look for me?'

Silence, and then, 'No, Dan. Not really. Not all of it anyway. I'd gotten a few hints, but I never thought it was this big. But then, what finally got my suspicions going was when things began to turn real nasty over here.'

'Nasty? In what way?'

'Small things first. It began as soon as my people started diggin' around Global's operations. One day I found out that they'd brought in a firm of legal hot-shots to have me arraigned on all sorts of things, from invasion of privacy to conspiracy.' He gave an amused snort before continuing, 'Then I found that they were bugging my office and tapping my telephone calls. And I was pretty sure I was being followed.'

'So that's why you warned Alexis to watch out.'

'Yeah.' The confession sounded rueful.

'But you chose not to tell her what was going on.'

'No,' Klein admitted. 'Perhaps I should've… But we all make mistakes, Dan.'

'But putting that aside for now, if you thought your telephone calls were being monitored weren't you putting her at risk when you called her,' Foster said bitterly, 'and me?'

'Never! I knew which of my lines and numbers they were bugging and I knew the email accounts they'd compromised. So I used other cells and other accounts. By maintaining the usual levels of traffic on the lines and accounts that they *were* watching, I fooled them into thinking they knew everything I did.'

'But you couldn't be completely sure ...'

'No, of course not. That's why I warned Alexis to be careful. Just in case.'

A sudden thought hit Foster. 'And the phone we're using now?' he asked.

'Look: how do you think I found out about the bugging?' Klein responded. 'I hired a security consultant – a top-flight guy that I've used before – to do a complete sweep or our offices, my car, my house. Believe me, I know exactly where I'm being monitored, and where I'm safe. This line is a hundred per cent secure.'

A thousand thoughts were whirling through Foster's mind as he cut the call. Now, at last, he understood the fear that had driven Global, and their agent Sam Miller. When Global's machinations had first begun to fall apart they must have started cutting corners here, there and everywhere. Some cuts could possibly have been implemented with few detrimental effects, but others would have had more serious consequences.

It could have been going on for years. At first it would have been small things, then bigger ones, until suddenly a huge avalanche of catastrophes would have begun to menace them. As engineering resources were cut on one project after another the consequences would have begun to pile up inexorably. What would have started as applying sticking plaster to a few problems would have turned to needing huge resources to rectify massive failures. And with India being the source of their future salvation it would have been vital that nothing should happen to prejudice their chances of winning the big contracts there that would end their ills.

The explosion at Varikhani must have been a hammer-blow to their hopes. No wonder they were so keen on a cover-up, no wonder hard-man Miller had been so concerned.

The implications of what Foster had just heard were terrifying. Once Klein took Global to court in India – and won, which now seemed inevitable – any shred of hope that the company may have had held for its redemption would be irretrievably destroyed. With the lessons of the Bhopal incident still raw in many minds, the Indian government would not – could not – allow an American company with serious failings of safety procedures to take on a scheme of building multiple power plants. Global's loss of those lucrative contracts would in turn destroy any hope of them paying off their multi-billion dollar debts; and that would destroy them. A trillion-dollar, corrupt and dangerous organization would come crashing down.

And who would fall with it? Certainly many of their highly-placed friends and benefactors in positions of power all round the world, but also – and this gave Foster pause for thought – the collapse would bring hardship to hundreds of thousands of innocent and hard-working employees, let alone the pensioners and their families. It was a terrible dilemma but he had no option but to act, because if he didn't he would be jeopardising far more than people's incomes. Lives would be in great danger.

Chapter 12

Those thoughts worried him over the next couple of days while he continued to study the data-logger printouts. And then, at a very early hour, Klein telephoned.

'Hi Dan!' The American's voice came through loud and clear. 'How're you doin' this fine mornin' buddy?'

Foster looked at his clock and did a rapid calculation; it was 6 a.m. there in Hyderabad, which made it evening in Houston. 'I'm fine, thanks,' he replied, trying to keep the early-morning gruffness from his voice, 'but it must be late in the day for you.'

'No buddy! It's 6 a.m.'

The last vestiges of sleep left Foster's mind. 'Where are you?' he asked.

The American laughed. 'About two doors along the corridor from you, buddy!'

Foster laughed exultantly. 'So you finally made it! No problems this time?'

'Nope. Nothing except for lack of sleep. GCR called off their dogs and suddenly it's all sweetness and light between me and the Indian government. Guess they knew I'd create Hell if they stopped me again. And any kind of stink is not what they want right now.'

253

'Great! I could need support over the next few days. When can we meet?'

'You'll be wantin' breakfast, I guess,' Klein replied. 'I'm gonna need dinner. Say we meet in the coffee shop and compromise.'

'OK. Twenty minutes all right?'

'Yup. See you down there. Let's make it 6.30.'

After a moment or two of thought Foster climbed out of bed and went to the window to look over the shadowy city that was just awakening outside. The first pink traces of dawn had faded and now a brighter light had started to flood into the sky. He pushed thoughts of Global's coming demise to the back of his mind as he headed for the shower.

Although they had never actually met, Foster had no problem in picking out the American: he had close-cropped fair hair and his footballer's frame towered over everybody else in the room as he stood up. To help complete the identification he was wearing plaid golfing trousers.

'Glad to meet you, Dan!' he said as they shook hands. 'After all this time.'

'Likewise.' Foster sat down and the waitress took their orders. Foster had his usual breakfast, Klein ordered "ham and eggs with strong black cawfee, as hot and black as you can make it". The waitress went off and the two men sat down to discuss the momentous events they were about to precipitate.

'And this guy, McBride?' Klein asked. 'Think he'll come over now?'

'Pretty sure. I was planning to call him later today.'

The waitress reappeared with their coffees and they were silent as she set the cups in place and poured. As they sipped at the steaming liquid, Foster filled Klein in with the few details he didn't already know.

As he ended, Klein nodded and then stared into his coffee for a while; then he looked up and said, 'There's more, Dan. And you're in for a little surprise.'

'Oh?' The American's turning up here in India was surprise enough; what else could he have up his sleeve? What bit of information could he have found, to add into the pile of evidence that they had already stacked up against Global?

'Yeah. But before I tell you, let's talk about you.'

'Me?'

'Yeah. I wanna know somethin' more about you.'

'Like what?'

The waitress re-appeared and set their food in front of them. As she left, the American looked thoughtfully at his plate before hefting a forkful of ham to his mouth. Then he said, 'Personal stuff. Y'see, we've been workin' on this thing for a time now, and yet I still don't know much about you really.'

'OK,' Foster said warily. 'Like what?'

'Alexis said that you're divorced.'

Foster nodded his response, wondering how much she had told her father and whether he should tell him – indeed *how* he could tell him – about his relationship with her. What would he think of a man who had slept with his daughter, a woman decades younger than himself? But then Klein took the initiative as he said, 'Don't worry, Dan. She's told me. I know about you two.'

Foster was unsettled by this, but Klein seemed relaxed. No doubt he had had plenty of time to think about it and had got used to the idea.

'Look Dan,' Klein continued, 'she needs a break. The bastard she married … well, I saw through him right from the beginning, but the more I tried to warn her, the more determined she seemed to get. He drove a wedge between us. Then, when she found out about him it really broke her up. She came back to me then and in spite of her hurtin', it sure was a good feeling, I can tell you.'

'She told me about him,' Foster said.

'Yeah,' Klein said, looking thoughtfully across the room. 'And believe me, she knows only a part of it. I'd had him watched and it nearly broke my heart seeing what he was up to, and not being able to do anything about it. It's terrible these days, Dan; there are so many bad things…' the words tailed off and he seemed to be lost in thought for a few moments. Then he came back to the present and continued, 'He could have given her HIV, anything.' White-hot anger showed in his face as he spat out the next words: 'That bastard! I swore I'd kill him if I saw him again.'

'I'd be happy to help,' Foster joked. But was it really a joke?

256

'She was real hurt, Dan. So going to London was good for her.'

'And for me,' Foster agreed.

'Yeah,' Klein said quietly. 'But now let's turn to you, Dan Foster,' Klein said as he put his empty plate to one side and picked up his coffee. 'I admit it came as a shock when she told me about you. The age thing and all. At first I was scared she'd jumped out of the frying pan …. But … well, I got over it. I guess I didn't want to make the same mistake again; I didn't want to drive her away. Anyway, from the little I knew about you, I was pretty sure you'd look after my girl.'

Foster smiled. He suspected that trust had very little to do with it: most probably Klein had had him checked out too, just as he'd had her husband checked. But in his case, clearly he'd passed all the tests. 'That's for sure, Scott' he said sincerely. 'I never thought I'd feel this way about anybody again. And I intend to look after her for as long as I last. Oh sure, I wish I was thirty years younger; but I am what I am, and there's no changing that.'

'And who'd want to change that?' The question came from behind him and he jumped up to look at her. She was radiant, and beautiful as ever. Regardless of the attention they attracted, regardless of her father looking on, they hugged and kissed each other in wild excitement.

Eventually, Foster extricated himself from her embrace and, with his arm still wrapped round her slim waist, he looked at her father. 'Your surprise, I presume?' he said.

Klein nodded, looking very pleased with himself. 'Good one, huh?' he said.

'Scott, I could hug you too,' Foster said.

257

'Easy on, feller!' Klein protested, 'You just stay right there, right where you are. I've got a reputation to maintain, you hear?'

Foster pulled out a chair out for her and held it for her as she sat down. 'See Dad?' she asked pertly. 'A real gentleman! He knows how to treat a girl.'

A waitress appeared and Foster asked Alexis if she'd eaten. 'Yes,' she replied. 'I had room service bring something. Dad said he wanted time to talk with you. But another coffee wouldn't be bad.'

Foster tapped at the empty cafetière and the waitress took it away for re-filling.

'I'm hoping for a quieter stay this time around,' Alexis said. 'No abduction, no imprisonment, no murder, no rapid exit without bags … Oh yes, a lot easier this time I hope!'

'You've got the two of us to protect you this time,' Foster said and Klein nodded in agreement.

'But what happened last time,' she asked, 'after I made my exit?'

'Miller went off with his tail between his legs,' Foster replied.

'And what about his wife?'

Foster looked at her and shook his head. 'I didn't tell you?'

'No.'

'I'm afraid she died.'

Alexis curled her knuckles put her fist to her mouth. 'What? Oh no.'

'Yes. Apparently she was still alive after the crash, but she died when Sam pulled her out of the wreckage. Seems he was none to gentle.'

'You mix with a nasty bunch of folks,' Klein said thoughtfully.

'Not from choice, I assure you. But ..' he turned back to Alexis. 'That's what finally brought McBride on board.'

'Oh, how come?'

'They were lovers.'

Her look moved from shock to bewilderment, so he told her what he had learned.

'But when Sam Miller sat there in court,' he concluded. 'You'd never have thought he'd as good as killed his wife. He was totally focussed on rubbishing our case against his employer. It was as if she'd never existed.'

'The bastard!' she observed. 'The out-and-out bastard!'

'Right on!' Foster said. 'But he must be in a very dangerous place right now. He's not only allowed Global's reputation to be destroyed, he's also upset the most dangerous set of brigands in this country.'

Klein laughed. 'Brigands! That's not a word I hear often. But what do you mean about him upsetting them?'

'He involved them in kidnapping Alexis – and God knows what else as well. Then two of their men who were guarding her were murdered and his wife was killed nearby. They'll realize she was the one who helped Alexis escape and I suspect they'll blame the whole balls-up on him; unfairly perhaps, but they'll want a very visible scapegoat. These people rely on fear to maintain control. They won't care too much about the details or the facts.'

'What do you think will happen to him?'

'Can't really tell,' Foster replied. 'The D-Company may decide to get rid of him, or Global might just bundle him off back to the States, to live out the rest of his days in poverty and obscurity.'

'Get rid of him?' Klein asked. 'You mean murder? You think this Indian Mafia outfit would resort to killing him?'

'I wouldn't put it past them. They must be pretty mad that he allowed things to get to this state. I wouldn't put it past them to make sure he was out of the way.'

'But what about the explosion? Alexis asked. '*Was* it his fault?'

'I'm sure Global will see it that way,' Foster answered. 'It was on his watch that the explosion happened; it was the pressure he applied that made somebody …'

His voice trailed off, and the two Americans looked questioningly at him.

'I hadn't given it enough thought,' he explained. 'But something happened that day, and I've missed out on following it up. I'm an idiot!'

'Why?' Alexis asked. 'What do you mean?'

'I've been so focussed on what happened afterwards that I forgot to look at the actual events that day.'

'The day of the explosion?' Klein asked.

'Yes. You see, although I saw plenty of examples there of shoddy construction, lack of attention and bad operational practice, none of that actually explains the explosion. There's no smoking gun.'

'But what does explain it?' Alexis asked.

'I don't know yet. But I'd told you I was going to take a look at the memory stick that McBride gave me.'

'Did you?' Klein asked.

'Yes. I had a quick look but there's yards and yards of data there. What with one thing and another I never got round to a more detailed examination. And now I'm going to look for something specific. It'll make it easier to get some sense out of it. I'll take another look today. See if I can find what I'm looking for.'

'What do you hope to find?' Alexis asked.

'Just now, I started to say that the pressure from Miller had made somebody do something stupid. I think that was right. I hope that stick will tell me who it was and – probably – what he did.'

Klein looked thoughtful. Then he asked, 'Do you really need to go after him Dan? After all, the case we've got now is pretty damn water-tight. In fact I'd say it's perfect. What more do you want?'

'Legally, nothing,' Foster said. 'I'm sure you've got enough to nail them. But what I'm after is an explanation of what happened. I want to make sure I'm right about the cause of the explosion, and then I want to make sure it won't happen again.'

'But how'll you do that, Dan?' Klein asked. 'After all, you're *persona non grata* at the power plant. They'll never let you on to the site, let alone talk to anybody.'

Foster winked at him. 'Perhaps. But people don't stay on site all day. They go home every day.'

They were all silent for a while, thinking about all the things that had happened to them and to all the others involved. Then Alexis spoke. 'Dad,' she said with a shy grin at Foster. 'I haven't seen Dan for some time. Do you think …?'

Klein shrugged. 'You two go off now, I want to take a look round this city.' His voice was gruff.

Much later, while Alexis was sleeping exhausted on his bed, Foster went over to his desk, took out his laptop, booted it and inserted the stick into a USB port.

Gradually he untangled the messages. And suddenly he saw the full implications. 'I'll be buggered!' he swore.

His words woke Alexis. 'What did you say?' she asked sleepily.

'Nothing for you really. But I think I've found what happened.'

She climbed out of bed and stood beside him as he looked at the screen. He slipped his arm round her naked waist and with his free hand he pointed at a line on the screen that said:

08:57:00:03:01   DI 079 closed

'What's that mean?' she asked.

'At three minutes to nine that morning,' he replied, 'somebody put a key into a locked switch on the control desk, and turned it. "DI" stands for "Digital Input" – that means a switch in this case.'

'And what did that do?'

'Look here.'

He pointed to the next line on the screen:

08:57:02   DO 254 closed: Scanner master override

'That means that a signal was sent to something a couple of seconds later,' Foster explained. 'Without access to all the drawings I can't tell exactly what it was: it could have been a lamp or an audible alarm but either way, at that instant the flame scanners were blocked from doing their job. And they were never reinstated.'

'And?'

He gritted his teeth. 'What it means is that somebody who had a high level of authority – somebody who had been entrusted with the key to operate that switch – used it to blank out all the flame scanners. From that moment, all the essential protection was effectively disabled. The safety system was running blind.'

'Are they allowed to do that?' she asked.

'No. But somebody had built the facility in; probably because they were having a lot of trouble with the flame scanners. I suspect it was a late addition, because I'm sure the Japanese boilermaker would never have given them that facility. It's extremely dangerous.'

'Then why …?'

'I suspect that whoever turned that key fully intended to turn it back later. But he never got round to it. Either the explosion happened before he could do it or he forgot, and the explosion happened as a result.'

'How long a gap was there?' she asked. 'I mean between the turning of the switch and the explosion.'

'Can't really say. Not with 100% accuracy. But look at the flood of alarms that breaks out just after 9 a.m.' He scrolled down the screen and pointed to the hundreds of alarm messages that appeared at that time. 'Up till then we get one alarm or two every few seconds – that's not abnormal – and a scattering of other data. But suddenly, after 9 there's a whole raft of them. Each line on this print-out represents an alarm signal that appeared on the operators' consoles; the messages must have simply flooded onto the screens. They would have appeared so fast that there would have barely been time for one to flash up before the next one came on. I can't make much sense of it, partly because I don't have all the drawings but mainly because when the plant went to buggery all bets were off. I suspect some of the alarm devices were still screaming out warnings while they hurtled skywards.'

'Is that the information you needed?' she asked. 'Is that enough evidence?'

'Partly. It's pretty damning. But I'd prefer it if I had the drawings, or at least if I knew for sure what those few inputs and outputs were; that way I'd be confident that I couldn't be shot down in court by some smooth-talking barrister.'

'Do you think you'll be able to get them? The drawings, I mean.'

He shook his head. 'Not a cat in hell's chance!'

'So what'll you do?'

He looked at her, grinned, and lightly slapped her naked bottom. 'I'll do what a good poker player always does: bluff!'

Having been to Ashok Mahajan's house once, Foster knew exactly where it was located. After a degree of hard bargaining, he had hired a car and driver for a few days at a ridiculously small fee and now, after the long ride from Hyderabad he sat behind the driver and watched the house as the first of the power-station workers began to arrive home. Then a huge black Chrysler swayed to a halt on the manager's drive and Mahajan appeared, heaving his great bulk out of the door with considerable difficulty. He was still sitting, half in and half out of the car, panting from the exertion, when Foster strolled over to him.

'Good evening, Ashok!' he called cheerily and the Indian's eyes opened wide in surprise.

DAVID LINDSLEY

'Mr Foster!' he exclaimed eventually. 'What … what are you doing here?'

'I've come to have a little chat with you. Mind if I come into your house with you?'

Mahajan's eyes swivelled from side to side as he desperately searched for someone to help him, but nobody was in view.

'Oh come on,' Foster cajoled him. 'It won't take ten minutes.'

'Very well,' Mahajan replied in an admission of defeat, and then he finally extricated himself from the car and led the way into his home.

His wife came scurrying up as they entered, smiling broadly to welcome their guest. 'Can I bring tea?' she asked.

'Thank you,' Foster answered, 'That would be very nice.'

She bustled off and the two men went into the main living room where the party had taken place. Mahajan gestured to the settee as he slumped his frame into an armchair. The chair emitted a groan of protest under the strain.

The Indian settled his bulk into the chair and asked, 'What is it that you are wanting, Dr Foster?'

Foster gave him a long hard look and was rewarded by Mahajan visibly squirming in discomfort. 'I'll get straight to the point,' Foster said. 'It's about the furnace explosion: I believe you'd been having some problems with the flame scanners at that time.'

Mahajan nodded silently.

'When I looked round the plant I could see that the flame scanners were in a mess. But when the legal boys were shown round the plant all the scanners were in place, all neat and tidy, all cables in place.'

'That is right.'

'I'd like to hear your explanation of that. But let's leave that aside for a minute.' Mahajan's look of relief faded when Foster continued, 'I understand you couldn't start up the boiler afterwards.'

Now sheer panic appeared on Mahajan's face. 'It is always a problem,' he said. 'Those instruments … they are always very unreliable.'

'I bet they bloody are! If you cool them with lubricated air their lenses are going to be permanently oiled up. Who the fuck dreamt up that abortionate arrangement?'

'It was as THI supplied.'

'Oh no it wasn't,' Foster growled. 'I know them and they'd never have done anything as crazy as that. My guess is that Global cobbled it together themselves – to save a few pennies. And you must have agreed to let them do it.'

Mahajan's head rocked from side to side, admitting nothing, denying nothing.

'So I have to ask myself this question: if the scanners weren't working how did you get the boiler started on the day of the explosion?'

'We cleaned lenses that day. They saw flames and let us start the boiler.'

'Oh yeah?' Foster's tone was accusing. 'You sure about that?'

'Yes sir, absolutely sure.'

But Mahajan's expression said otherwise. His face was beaded with sweat and he was licking his lips nervously.

Relief came at that moment in the form of his wife entering the room with a tray of tea. She set it on a low table between the two men and poured out two cups of black tea. Then, as she she smilingly pointed to the milk jug and sugar basin she saw the expression on her husband's face and her smile turned to a worried frown.

Her husband waved away her obvious concern and indicated that she should leave the room. With just a brief, questioning look at Foster she turned on her heel and left.

As Foster bent forward to put milk in his tea he said, 'You know, I've got the data logger and event recorder information from that day.'

Rebellious anger flashed in Mahajan's eyes. 'How did you obtain those things?' he asked. 'They are confidential company information. Strictly secret.'

'Perhaps. But, secret or not, they should have been made available at the time of the inquest, shouldn't they?'

Mahajan's one-word reply was surly: 'Why?'

'Because they provide damning evidence of what happened.'

The anger in the Indian's eyes was instantly replaced by fear, but he remained silent.

'Tell me,' Foster asked, now venturing onto less secure ground. 'Did you have a key for the flame-scanner override switch?'

Even though he was sitting down, Mahajan swayed. He gripped the arms of his chair until his knuckles turned white. The fear written on his face was now overtaken by stark terror.

Foster took a long sip of his tea, allowing himself the pleasure of watching the Indian's discomfort.

'I'll take that as an affirmative,' he said as he put the cup down. 'You used that key and overrode them, didn't you?' His voice was quiet but firm. 'That was the only way you could get the boiler to start. You were under great pressure from Sam Miller ...'

Mahajan suddenly spotted a way out of this awkward confrontation, if it only offered a temporary respite. 'Miller-ji is dead, sir,' he said. He was desperately clutching at straws, but the effect was to stop Foster in his tracks.

Foster reeled back in shock. 'What?' he exclaimed.

'Some bad people broke into his home,' Mahajan explained. 'They were robbers. Villains. Thugs. Police think he disturbed them ... but one of them had knife .... They were brutal thugs sir; police said Miller-ji was tortured before they killed him. He choked to death.' He paused to look at the door, to make sure his wife wasn't listening as he concluded, 'His ... his genitals were cut off, you see, and pushed down his throat. Police think the men wanted him to divulge hiding place of money.'

'Christ!' Foster doubted the police theory. He had little doubt that the attack had been much, much more than a simple burglary that had gone wrong. Burglars might kill if they are discovered; they might even resort to torture to lead them to hidden money and valuables; but this level of obscene punishment pointed to more complex motives. He was pretty sure that the D-Company had acted quickly and decisively, exacting brutal revenge on the man who had led two of their foot-soldiers to their deaths. Miller had paid the penalty for enlisting the help of extremely protective and violent forces, and his death closed another loophole: removed another threat to Global. It was yet more evidence of the close links between GCR and the D-Company.

The terrible manner of his death – whose gory details the D-Company would make sure were widely circulated around the community – would serve as a grim warning to others.

'So who's in charge now?' Foster asked.

Mahajan's reply was a bombshell. 'Mr McBride has taken on job,' he said.

'Peter McBride?' Foster barked incredulously. 'But surely he's resigned.'

'He had indeed resigned sir, but company requested him to return – until replacement can be found for unfortunate Miller-ji.'

Foster's mind went into overdrive. He could understand McBride being tempted to stay on for a while longer – especially as the hated Assassin was now safely out of the picture – and that fact could prove to be useful to him; but however honest and diligent the Scot may have been inclined to be, he would inevitably come under the same intense pressures that had driven Miller. Where would his loyalties fall? Would he – *could he* – help Foster? That question would be answered in due course, but for now he had to pump Mahajan for as much information as he could obtain.

He tried to control himself so that no hint of his inner turmoil could be detected in his tone or manner. He had to appear unaffected; relentlessly pressing the Indian for answers. And he had to return to his original course: he had been deflected for far too long.

'Be that as it may,' he continued, 'On the day of the accident I think you acted under extreme pressure to get over a persistent hurdle. You used the override key, didn't you?'

In the silence that followed, the room seemed very still. It was as if everything around the two men – the walls, the tables, the chairs – were waiting to hear the answer.

When it came, Mahajan's voice was subdued almost to the point of being inaudible: 'No sir ... I swear that I did not use key.' Then almost immediately in a torrent of words, the Indian began to blurt out his defence. 'There was great pressure that day sir. Miller-ji was insisting the unit should be starting, but every time we started boiler it tripped out. It was flame scanners, Dr Foster; they were never seeing flame; not even igniters. Now you are telling me that oil film was cause ... but we did not know that then sir. Miller-ji said if plant was not starting he would fire me, sir. It would be absolute disgrace ...'

As his voice spluttered to a tearful close, Foster could almost have felt sorry for him. Was he lying? If not, who else could have used the override? Whoever it was, that single act of turning the key had left the plant unprotected, its safety vulnerable to the vagaries of fickle luck.

And luck had run out that morning. Men had died as a result.

271

Foster was grim-faced as he returned to Hyderabad. Although he had wrung some admissions from Mahajan, he was still missing the last few pieces of the jig-saw. He felt that he was still short of evidence that would bring GCR to book. As his hired car drew up to the hotel he just felt tired, sweaty and grimy.

He went to his room and as he stripped off for a shower there was a gentle tap at his door. Cursing, he wrapped a towel round his waist and opened the door.

A smartly uniformed bell-hop offered him a tray bearing a single white envelope. 'For you, Dr Foster,' he said.

'Hang on,' Foster said as he took the envelope. He retrieved a 50-Rupee note and gave it to the hop and as he closed the door again he studied the envelope. It bore an Indian stamp but no markings except for his name, "Care of" the hotel.

He opened the envelope and extracted the single sheet of white paper that it enclosed. As he read what was written on it his eyes widened in surprise. Then he called Klein.

As they sat at the bar, Klein read and re-read the brief note. Then he looked up and said, 'Just who is this guy, Praveen Jampani?'

'I met him when I first visited the plant,' Foster explained. 'Mahajan introduced him to me. I was very impressed by him; he seemed to be particularly bright, well-trained and competent. Sometimes you get guys who know all the theory and they can work wonders with software, but I wouldn't trust them to wire up a three-pin plug.'

'Three-pin plug?' Klein asked, looking perplexed.

Foster smiled as he explained, 'A power plug: the thing you plug into an electrical outlet. Anyway, although I didn't get to spend much time with him I didn't feel he was one of those whizz-kids.'

Klein looked down at the letter again and said, 'Looks like he's worried.'

'Yes. He doesn't explain, but I'm happy to meet him.'

'He wants to come to Hyderabad.'

'Yes, I suspect he doesn't want to be seen talking to me and Varikhani's a small community: somebody'd be bound to see if we met up there.'

'OK. Will you set it up? He's given his cell there.'

'I'll call him right away,' Foster said as he reached for his mobile. 'I presume you'd be interested in being there when we meet?'

'Too damn right!' Klein said with a vigorous nod of his head.

Foster recognised Jampani as soon as he walked into the small café where they'd arranged to meet. He was of medium height and clean shaven and his luxuriant jet-black hair was neatly trimmed.

When the introductions were over they sat down over cups of hot black tea. Foster asked how things were progressing at the plant under McBride's leadership.

'They are very good now, sir,' Jampani said. 'Mr McBride is very good engineer and most thorough. He understands the importance of our C&I systems.'

Klein's brow furrowed, so Foster explained, 'Control and instrumentation. McBride's own specialization once.'

The frown cleared and Klein asked, 'So what's the problem, Mr Jampani?'

The Indian looked at him for a second or so before turning his large dark eyes on Foster. 'Mr McBride is trying to get plant commissioned – he is re-doing much work that Miller-ji has bypassed or cut totally.'

'That's good,' Foster said. 'About time it was done properly. It won't be easy though.'

'That is indeed correct Mr Foster. Progress has been slow because we have had to undertake some construction work ...'

'Like ducting cool clean air to the flame-scanner lenses?'

'Yes sir. That has been done already and the BMS system is now working very well.'

'Burner management systems,' Foster explained for Klein's benefit. 'They start up the burners and make sure they run safely. The flame scanners are their eyes.'

Klein nodded again and repeated his question.

'It is not Varikhani,' Jampani explained. 'Or it is only partly so.'

'What do you mean?' Foster asked.

Jampani emptied his cup before answering. 'About one year ago,' he started. 'Company sent me to attend training course at Global Consolidated Resources headquarters.'

'In Houston?' Klein interjected.

'Yes sir. It was great honour and privilege. I had never been outside of India before.'

'And what happened?' Klein asked, eager to press on.

'At first it was introduction to company, then information on company structure …'

'And?' Foster asked.

Jampani looked at him nervously. 'We were addressed by very … very vigorous and dynamic gentleman sir. He was high-ranking official in Global company. His name was Mr Hamer …'

'That bastard!' Klein interrupted. When Foster looked questioningly at him he said, 'Cameron Hamer. He's crossed my path before. Tell you about it later.'

'Carry on, Praveen,' Foster urged.

'Sir, his message disturbed me greatly. It disturbed everybody. We had many discussions afterwards. Nobody was happy about it.'

'Why?' Foster asked.

'Mr Hamer said we were to comply with all safety procedures … but if progress on any project was delayed, or production adversely affected by our actions … then "we would be held responsible" he said.'

'Meaning?' Klein asked.

'It was very clear sir. We would be fired. Mr Hamer told us there were many people who would be waiting to take our jobs if we did not want them. He said it was progressive thinking; too many important projects had been held up by over-complicated rules.'

'No doubt that's the same message Sam Miller'd been given,' Foster growled, 'the one that he passed down to all the staff here.'

'Yes sir, but it is much more.' When the two Westerners looked at him quizzically he continued, 'You see, sirs, there were other engineers there. They were all given the same message.'

'Where were these engineers from?' Foster asked.

'From throughout company business areas: mining, drilling, on-shore and off-shore operations, refineries, power plants, everything.'

'Christ!' Klein said. 'No wonder the rot ran through the whole of GCR's operations. I bet that's why Gamma blew up.'

'I don't suppose any of this was documented, was it?' Foster asked.

'No Dr Foster,' Jampani answered. 'There were no hand-outs and we were given very strict instructions that no notes were to be taken. It was top secret briefing, they said, for people who were destined to rise through company ranks. That made me very proud; but later I began to be fearful.'

'Why?' Foster asked.

'Because I felt we were being asked to act against ethical principles, sir. It was clear that we were being threatened as well as praised.'

'So you were given no hand-outs,' Foster said, but as Jampani shook his head Foster caught a flicker of a smile on his lips. His heart quickened.

Klein had missed the sign. 'Pity,' he said. 'We could have really made something of any printed stuff.'

Jampani's faint grin gave way to a shy smile before he said, 'But I have recording, sir.'

'What?' Klein and Foster chorused.

'I was nervous,' Jampani explained. 'It was my first journey outside India, my first visit to United States. I found it difficult to understand some of the speech …'

Klein laughed. 'I bet! 'Specially broad Texan!'

277

'So I took mobile with me and turned on voice recorder,' Jampani continued. 'It was against all rules. But I wanted to play back conversations in hotel room afterwards, to resolve mishearings. I should have deleted recording afterwards ... but I forgot.'

Foster shook his head in amazement. 'You kept the recordings?' he asked.

'Oh yes, sir. When I came back here I copied them to PC and then burned onto disk.' Jampani fished into his shirt pocket and brought out a mini-CD. 'The recording is not best quality sir; the telephone was in shirt pocket.'

But as Foster took the disk from him he knew that he was being handed a detonator to an enormous bomb – one that would totally devastate Global Consolidated Resources.

It worried him.

Chapter 13

Klein had gone to town, literally and metaphorically. He'd rented a small suite of offices in an air-conditioned building in Hyderabad's business district and hired a handful of temporary staff: a receptionist, two secretaries and a *chaprassi*.

It was important to make an impression; faced with undeniable evidence of widespread malpractice throughout their operations, Global Consolidated Resources had rushed in a team of fire-fighters to contain the damage. But the fire-fighters were facing a major conflagration: some of the news had leaked out already, and the national and international media were waiting like vultures. In the face of widespread criticism, the Indian judiciary had moved to sweep aside the familiar delays and 'pendencies' and threatened to summon all the protagonists to New Delhi.

Global had moved swiftly and requested a period of conciliation and arbitration. Their team was flying out from Houston, and it was headed by no lesser person than their Vice-President of Global Operations.

'Got the bastards!' Klein had exclaimed when he heard the news. 'No lesser luminary than Cameron Hamer II, hey?'

'The guy who spoke to those engineers in Houston?' Foster asked and when Klein nodded he asked, 'You said you knew him.'

'You bet I do! And his turning up here is good news; if he's appearing it means they've decided to keep this out of the courts. They'll do anything to avoid that. A small coroner's court in a small town, with no media attention focussed on it

279

is one thing; a major court action in the full glare of international publicity is the last thing they want. No, Hamer's objective will be to negotiate and, take it from me, he's a first-class negotiator.'

'That's a good thing?' Foster asked. 'I thought you wanted them in court.'

'I do, but their determination to keep it out of court means that they realise they're onto a loser. I'm gonna win this one, Dan.'

Klein had rushed to make sure that the odds were stacked as far as possible in his favour; hiring this suite and the temporary staff was the first step. He wanted to impress on Hamer that he was facing a formidable and well-entrenched opponent.

Over dinner on the night before the first meeting, he and Foster discussed the strategy that they would adopt. They examined each piece of evidence they'd collected and considered how GCR might explain it away or otherwise defend themselves.

'Look Dan,' Klein said as they sat in the bar afterwards. 'No offence, but from here on in this is my show. You've done what was needed on the technical side – and a great job you've done too – getting that recording was just amazin'. It's the silver bullet that'll finally finish them off. But now it's down to legal wheelin' and dealin'.'

'No problem, Scott,' Foster replied. 'I understand that.'

But for the first time in this saga, Foster began to sense that things had changed. Initially, as an engineer, he had been intrigued by the technical background to what had happened at Varikhani; then, as he made his discoveries he had developed a strong sympathy for the innocent people who had been caught up in the accident and had decided to track down what had happened; then he had become concerned at the appalling state of affairs at the power plant. But now the ground had shifted; he was becoming embroiled in a personal battle between Klein and his powerful adversary. It was heading towards a confrontation that could very well bring down the entire company.

And that was far beyond his intentions.

'Don't get me wrong,' Klein continued. 'There'll be times when I'll need your input again; but I'll say when that will be.'

Foster pushed his thoughts into the background and nodded his acceptance. 'That'll be fine.'

On the following day everything stalled. A nervous-looking Indian lawyer turned up at the offices alone.

'I am Raj Patak,' he announced as he handed business cards to Klein and Foster. 'My practice has been instructed to advise Global Consolidated Resources in these matters.'

'Where's Hamer?' Klein growled.

The Indian's embarrassment seemed to deepen and he bowed his head to his chest so that his words were barely audible. 'I regret that Mr Hamer and his entire team have been struck down, Mr Klein.'

DAVID LINDSLEY

'Struck down?'

Foster could not help laughing out loud. 'They've got Delhi-belly!' he said gleefully. 'The galloping ab-dabs!'

The Indian threw him a puzzled look. 'They have experienced severe diarrhoea and vomiting, Dr Foster,' he explained needlessly. 'They are recovering now, but they are all very weak, and hotel doctor has advised them against making undue exertion.'

'Christ!' Klein said after the lawyer had left. 'I was all fired up for the skirmishin' and now I've gotta wait while those bastards' bowels firm up.'

'I'm afraid that's how things go occasionally,' Foster said. 'Especially here. You're just lucky that you had me to advise you against drinking the water and eating salads.'

But whatever brave face they put on it, the delay was frustrating. They were like soldiers on the brink of a major battle which had suddenly been postponed by the onset of an unexpected storm.

It took three days – nervous, nail-biting, annoying days – before the Americans were fit enough to make an appearance at Klein's rented office, and even then they were ashen-faced as they took their places at the rectangular table. The two contending parties sat facing each other across the table: Klein and Foster on one side, Hamer and two acolytes with Raj Patak on the other.

282

Everybody handed out business cards, and Foster carefully laid the GCR team's in a row in front of him, matching their seating order; it would help him link faces to names.

Cameron Hamer II, the long-awaited leader of the company's delegation was short, florid, balding and going to seed. Foster decided that he must have sought advice from the Internet on the correct attire for the tropics, and had chosen the worst advice. He was wearing pale cream-coloured safari suit whose linen was already heavily creased, and a pale green shirt with a collar that looked two tight for his massive neck, buttoned down over a gaudy floral necktie. With the grey skin of his face he looked hot and uncomfortable, even in the air-conditioned office. Hamer introduced one of the acolytes as his technical adviser and the other as a paralegal executive who would be supported and advised on Indian legal procedures by Raj Patak.

Hamer opened the meeting. It was all sweetness and light. 'Gentlemen,' he said calmly, 'my company has sent us here to see if we can reach an agreement with you over the wild accusations that you are making – needless to say, totally unwarranted and unsubstantiated accusations, but accusations that nevertheless have the potential of doing some damage to our Company's fine reputation.'

'You say!' Klein said with a sardonic smile on his lips.

'I do,' Hamer barked sharply. 'I've dealt with you before, Klein, and I know that you're always out to make trouble for us. You're doing it again now.'

Wow! Foster thought, *that's hardly a conciliatory beginning.* He saw the paralegal at Hamer's right throw an anxious glance at his leader and noted that his fingers twitched as though he was about to put a restraining hand on Hamer's arm.

Hamer ignored him and continued, 'Let's get down to the basics.' He nodded to the paralegal before saying, 'I'll ask Frank Macdonald here to summarize the situation.'

Macdonald took a document out of a folder and started to read from it. 'According to court records,' he said, 'the explosion at Varikhani was the result of a failure of a minor component: a gas valve…'

'Garbage!' Klein interjected. 'Those findings were overturned on appeal.'

'But that decision was itself reversed on a subsequent appeal,' Maclean continued resolutely.

'And we contend that the decision was based on falsified evidence ...' Klein started.

'Falsified evidence!' the interruption burst from Hamer and he put both elbows on the table in front of him, rested his chin on his knuckles and glowered at Klein from a distance of a few inches. 'Your so-called "expert" here,' he tossed a nod and a dismissive look at Foster. 'He tabled a bunch of photographs that were fakes; they were taken somewhere else, and then he claimed they were taken at Varikhani.'

'And we can prove that they were *not* fakes,' Klein said.

Hamer looked astonished and faltered in his stride. 'That's impossible,' he said. 'How can you prove …'

Klein snorted. 'Don't worry, we'll prove it all right … and we'll be happy to do it in open court.'

Trying desperately to recover his composure, Hamer said, 'That's crazy! Our people took the legal team to the plant and showed them round. Everything was hunky-dory. Nothing like on those pictures.'

'Yeah!' Klein drawled. 'They were shown round all right; shown things they couldn't understand and had it all explained to them by a bunch of guys who'd been told to lie through their teeth.'

Hamer glowered at him, and there was an extended silence while he planned his next attack. Finally he said, 'You're bluffing, Klein. You know it. But anyway, let's move on.'

He nodded at Macdonald, who continued: 'Global Consolidated Resources is an internationally-respected company...'

'With a spotless record of safety no doubt,' Klein interjected with sarcasm sounding clearly in his tone.

'Absolutely!' Hamer said. 'I defy you to show otherwise.'

Klein tilted his head slightly and smiled. 'Challenge accepted. I do intend to show otherwise. I will provide undeniable evidence of widespread breaches of safety standards, all-pervasive corruption in obtainin' operation permits, widespread defiance of good-practice governance ... Do you want me to go on?'

Macdonald's jaw dropped and his mouth gaped open. Hamer took the opportunity to interject. 'You're bluffing,' he repeated. 'You don't have a shred of evidence. These are all old allegations Klein, and we've fought them before. You lost, remember?'

Klein's face was an impassive mask as he replied, 'I do remember. But I also remember winning. In fact, I remember winnin' more often than I remember losin'. And this time I've got rock-solid evidence. Believe me; I'm not gonna lose this time.'

Hamer glowered at him until Klein took a deep breath and said, 'All right, gentlemen. I agreed to this meeting because I thought that you'd be willing to negotiate. I was wrong: it seems you're not. So that's it – as they say, I'll see you in court.'

He started to gather his papers together and made as if to stand up. Hamer's already dark expression became thunderous, and Macdonald's eyes switched from his boss to Klein and back again. Unlike Hamer, he looked panic-stricken.

'What'll it take to stop this, Klein?' Hamer said, his voice quiet but full of menace. 'You know that nobody wants this to go to court; not Global, not you.'

Klein leaned back in his chair and gazed at him coolly. 'No, I don't know that. At least, not half of it. I don't care if this does go to court – not at all – but I'm damn sure you'd move heaven and earth to stop it gettin' there.'

For the first time since they'd sat down, Raj Patak spoke up. 'Sirs,' he said. 'This is highly unfortunate. This matter is now in the jurisdiction of Supreme Court. Judge has agreed to allow a temporary delay, to allow for a process of arbitration. Without agreement here, now, Court proceedings must take place.'

'Stall them!' Hamer barked.

'Sir, I cannot …' Patak started, but he was silenced by an angry gesture from Hamer.

'You can, and you will,' the American commanded icily. 'I'm calling the shots now, remember?'

The Indian attempted a protest. 'Sir, this is Supreme Court matter ...'

'The fuck it is!' Hamer shouted. 'This is the future of my company, and of the tens of thousands who depend on it. You just stall them for one more day while I get Klein here to back off.'

Klein sniffed loudly. Backing off was clearly not on his agenda.

Hamer glowered at the rest of the party. 'I want a face-to-face with you, Klein,' he said quietly. 'Just the two of us. Here and now.'

'OK,' Klein shrugged. 'But you're not gonna change anythin', no matter how hard you try.'

'Negotiation!' Hamer said sharply. 'Remember: I'm the king of negotiators.'

With that, the rest of the party filed out of the room. As Foster left, Klein said, 'I'll see you back at the hotel, Dan.'

Foster and Alexis met in the hotel's coffee shop, Le Café. She hurried towards him and kissed him lightly on the cheek.

'That's a bit formal,' he said as they sat down.

'Don't want my reputation being harmed,' she smiled. 'Not good to be seen kissing a man old enough to be my father.'

He smiled and ordered coffee for them both.

'What's happening?' she asked and he outlined the morning's proceedings.

'He won't deflect dad,' she said. 'He's going in for the kill.'

'Mmmm.' Foster looked thoughtful.

'What's the matter?'

'I don't know,' he replied. 'I've suddenly begun to see things from a different angle.'

'How?'

He told her his thoughts about his own involvement; then he concluded, 'So as I see it, your dad's aims and mine have diverged; in fact they're very different now.'

'Are they?'

'Yes. As you said, he's closing in for the kill. And …'

'And what?'

'Well, I'm not sure I *want* to see Global brought down. There're too many things at stake: lives, jobs, energy supplies even.'

'But right from the beginning,' she protested, 'you knew that dad was out to get them.'

'Yes …' he said. 'And no. I thought he was out to get compensation for the victims who survived … and for the families of those who didn't.'

The coffees arrived and she picked up her cup. 'Perhaps that's what he's trying to negotiate with Hamer right now.'

'Perhaps,' he agreed. 'But somehow I don't think so.'

'Why not?'

He looked at her thoughtfully as she sipped at her drink. 'It's much more than compensation, Alexis,' he said. 'I think he's hell bent on revenge. Nothing less.'

She stared at him, her cheeks colouring slightly. 'You don't know my dad. He's not the vindictive sort.'

'How much do we ever know about our parents, Alexis? I suspect there's always a firewall between the lives they lead at work and the faces they present to their families at home.'

'But are their essential characters so different? Can someone be kind and fatherly at home and … Oh! She stopped herself. 'I'm answering my own question, aren't I?'

Foster looked thoughtfully into his cup before saying, 'I don't know anymore.'

'What do you mean?'

'Do I want to go on with this?'

'You can't abandon him – not now, when he's so close to success. He still needs your advice.'

'I know that.'

It was over an hour later when Klein arrived at the hotel. By then they were stretched out on sun-loungers beside the pool. The savage heat of the day had passed and now they were able to enjoy the warmth of the setting sun.

Klein pulled another lounger over and ordered beers for them all. He draped his jacket over a nearby table and stretched out beside them.

'Well?' Alexis asked. 'What happened?'

Klein gave a broad grin. 'The big bastard's wriggling like a hooked marlin. He's desperate not to get into court.'

Foster clenched his jaw and asked, 'What did he offer?'

'He ended up at twenty-five million bucks.'

Alexis gave a low whistle of surprise, but Foster stayed calm as he asked, 'For whom?'

Klein tilted his head and gave him an arch look. 'Twenty million to the victims and their families, five mill to me – us. And I'm going to get Desai, that Indian lawyer, fully reinstated and compensated for what he's been through. I haven't forgotten that it's because of him that we've got where we are today.'

'Twenty million!' Alexis blurted out. 'That's life-changing; 'specially for people out here.'

Foster nodded his agreement.

'It is,' Klein agreed as their beers arrived. He waited while the hop poured them into tall glasses. After he left, Klein passed the glasses round and offered a toast. 'Here's to winning,' he said.

As they clinked glasses Alexis asked, 'To winning? Surely you've won already.'

'Not what I meant, kiddo. I meant winning in court.'

'In court?' she burst out. 'You're going on with this?'

Klein nodded and Foster stepped in. 'Why, Scott?' he asked. 'You've got compensation and you've made a nice fat fee. Why carry on?'

Klein looked hard at him. 'Because Hamer's the guy who created all this mess. He's the one who drives Global. His ruthless drive to make them the biggest corporation ever is what killed and injured all those folks here at Varikhani. And those on the Ocean Venture Gamma platform. And God knows how many else. It's all down to him and I want to see him in court – being forced to admit it all.'

'But it'll bring down the whole operation,' Foster pointed out. 'The world's press will be there …'

'Damn right!' Klein interrupted. 'I'll make very sure of that.'

'But think of the implications,' Foster protested. 'It'll destroy the companies. People will lose jobs …'

'Nah!' Klein said, grinning. 'It's too big for that. People need what Global produces. The sharks will be circling, ready to grab the pieces. OK, Global won't be there anymore, but the pieces of their empire will be; and they'll all carry on working

– well, eventually at least; there's bound to be some disruption in the short term.'

Foster stared at him. 'It's not what I signed up for, Scott,' he said quietly. 'I came on board to sort out the incident here.'

'Sure! But in the process you exposed a lot more.'

'Beside the point. I think you should settle. Give these poor buggers full compensation for what they've suffered. Then get the hell out. You've probably damaged Hamer critically anyway. If he doesn't quit Global they'll fire him.'

Klein shook his head. 'You're probably right. But remember, I know how this outfit operates. There'll be another Hamer somewhere along the line. Sure, they'll probably make some cosmetic changes but they'll carry on cutting corners, risking lives. They have to; the poor schmuck who steps into his shoes won't stand a snowball in Hell's chance of keeping things running unless he does pretty well everything Hamer did.'

Foster thought about it. Eventually he agreed: 'I guess you're right.'

'Good!' Klein smiled. 'Let's drink to the continuing partnership.'

Chapter 14

W hen the collapse came it was every bit as cataclysmic as Klein had forecast. When the case came up before the Supreme Court the world's media was recording every word of the hearing and when each day's proceedings ended the protagonists were confronted by batteries of TV cameras and reporters' voice recorders.

Within the court, Hamer had tried everything to wriggle out of the mess, from abject contrition to explosive bluster. But when the damning evidence of Praveen's clandestine recording was produced all his arguments collapsed.

Foster made only one brief appearance at the hearing, where he repeated his allegation that the legal team's visit to site had been stage-managed, and that the examples he had photographed were genuine. When GCR's advocate tried to throw doubt on the statement, the prosecution wheeled out McBride who confirmed the facts. In spite of clever cross-examination that desperately tried to shake him, McBride stuck to his story.

The judge's summing up was cruelly damning and GCR was found guilty of flagrantly violating safety rules, the concealment and fabrication of evidence, and perjury in the preceding case. Settlement was deferred, but was expected to be the equivalent of hundreds of millions of US dollars.

GCR's shares became virtually worthless, and the company collapsed.

As Klein had forecast, the circling predators closed in, snapping up fragments of the empire and re-opening their operations one by one.

The financial situation of each piece became very different from what it had been as part of GCR: even allowing for the loss of economies of scale that they had enjoyed previously, the need to implement higher safety standards and to re-engineer dangerous situations drove up costs enormously.

But they survived. People were quickly re-hired and in fact more skilled staff were taken on. Operational costs rose, of course, and these were inevitably passed on to the consumers, but the rises were ameliorated by the reduction in the massive stripping-off that Global's top brass had enjoyed previously: the lavish favour-currying entertainment of would-be clients and political supporters; the spectacular advertising budgets; the fat bribes paid to ministers and civil servants; the fleets of corporate helicopters and executive jets.

Compensation payments transformed the lives of those affected by the disasters and – to Foster's immense satisfaction – little Kalpak Desai found success as a lawyer.

The night before they were scheduled to finally leave India, Klein threw a party at the Novotel. He invited his legal team and his temporary employees to join him, his daughter and Foster at a pool-side reception, from which they would migrate to a private room for dinner. As a gesture of friendship he also invited a select group from Verikhani power station: Station Manager Sundip Singh and Ashok

Mahajan, with their wives, and Peter McBride. These invitations were gratefully accepted and the five of them arrived from the plant in a minibus bearing the Indian power corporations NTPC logo.

It was an excited crowd that stood beside the pool that evening, picking at *rotis*, *samosas* and *pakoras* while they drank and talked about the momentous events that had passed. Foster was treated as a hero and everybody wanted to ask him about his current and past exploits. He eventually broke free and found Alexis standing at the far end of the pool gazing at the trees silhouetted against the sky. Night was falling quickly as it did in the tropics and brilliant stars were emerging above the dwindling heat haze.

She took a deep breath and looked at him as he arrived. 'It's so lovely here,' she said. 'I'm going to come back, you know.'

Foster smiled. 'There's a lot to see.'

'Next time I hope it'll be less dangerous.'

He grinned. 'Nah! You'll miss the excitement.'

'I'll miss you, Dan,' she said softly.

It was all that needed to be said. As they had neared the end of this adventure, they had both begun to realize that their affair had to come to an end soon. Neither of them actually voiced the thought; it was quietly understood between them. But neither did they feel sad at the prospect.

'It's been fun,' she continued. 'And I'm sure going to miss having you around.'

'I'll miss you too. It's been fabulous.'

After a long silence she said, 'You ought to find somebody, you know.'

He shrugged. 'You mean someone nearer my own age; someone to iron my shirts and darn my socks?'

She punched him on the arm. 'Don't! I don't even know what "darning socks" means.'

'Doesn't matter,' he said. 'Anyway, we'll just have to see what happens.'

'What're you going to do?' she asked. 'About working?'

He paused before answering. Then he shrugged. 'Don't really know. With what I've made on this job I don't really need to work. I'll go back to the boat and socialize with all my pals but ... well, I don't think I'll be settling down into my dotage, not yet awhile. Things seem to come at me somehow.'

'Well, as long as you can help people, and as long as you're doing the job you so plainly love, I guess you ought to carry on. And you do help people; just look at what you did for all those poor guys here. You sorted it out for them, and I don't think anybody else would have or could have done that.'

'Mmmm!'

'What?' she said, looking back at him with a puzzled look on her face.

'There's one shadowy thought that still plagues me,' he said. 'Although everything seems to be settled, one question still nags at my mind.'

'What's that?'

'Remember what caused the explosion?' he asked.

'You said it was somebody turning a switch they shouldn't have,' she replied. 'What was it you said? Oh yes, you said it left them blind to danger.'

'That's right. But I never got down to putting my finger on who actually did it.'

'I thought it was him,' she said, pointing to Mahajan, who was deeply involved in conversation with McBride beside the pool..

'I thought it was him too,' he replied. 'But he denied it when I questioned him. Stuck to his guns. And in the end I believed him.'

'So who …?'

'I've been over all the names: Sam was behind the pressure but I doubt he had the knowledge to take such a big risk; Ashok Mahajan could have done it, but I think he was too terrified, he was happy with his textbooks and theories – but the plant frightened him, I could see it in his face whenever he was out there; none of the more junior engineers would have ever dared to touch that switch.'

'But who does that leave?' she asked. And then realization dawned on her. She put her knuckles to her mouth. 'Surely not?'

Foster nodded sadly. 'There's nobody else. It has to have been Peter McBride.'

'But he gave you that information,' she said, her eyes wide with doubt.

'Yes he did. And the data proved that it was the turning of that switch that led to the accident.'

'You're saying that he handed you the evidence that showed his own guilt? Surely not?'

'I think it was a sort of expiation of his own sin,' Foster said. 'Remember, when he gave me that stick he'd just resigned. He thought he was on his way out of the country. And he said he'd deny that he gave it to me. I could use the evidence in court – to show that the switch had been turned, leading to the accident – but I couldn't prove who operated it.'

'Mahajan must have known ..' she started.

'I'm sure he did, but he'd never speak up about it.'

'Not even if the blame fell on him himself?'

'Not even then. Remember, nobody could ever prove who had operated that switch.'

She switched her gaze from Mahajan to McBride and then back to Foster.

As if he had sensed her interest in him by some sort of telepathy, McBride looked across at her. Then he said something inaudible to Mahajan and strolled over to Foster and Alexis.

'You've been talking about me,' he said pleasantly. 'I can tell.'

Alexis fell silent, and even in the dim glow of the pale poolside lights the colour that came to her cheeks was clearly visible.

'And I bet I know what you were saying,' McBride said.

Foster nodded. 'The last piece just fitted into the puzzle,' he said.

McBride pursed his lips. 'It's not easy, Dan,' he said. 'I have to live with the knowledge. I've got blood on my hands and I can't ever get rid of it, or forget it.'

Foster held out his hand and McBride took it. As they shook hands, Foster said, 'I'll be leaving here in a few hours, Peter. And I want you to know that I understand. I understand what happened on that day and I understand the circumstances and pressures that led up to you doing what you did. You've done your best to put it right: you gave me the evidence I needed to prove our case and you've done what you can to improve safety out here.'

'Thanks Dan,' the Scotsman replied. 'You don't know what it means to me to hear you say that.'

Foster held out his hand to Alexis. He no longer cared what people thought and from the way she took his hand and came with him it was clear that she didn't mind either.

McBride smiled as he watched them walk over to her father. Some of the burden had been lifted from him and he squared his shoulders with relief.

'Thank you, Dan Foster,' he whispered. 'Thank you very much.'

THE END

Made in the USA
Charleston, SC
26 January 2012